CW00691096

THE
SHE DEVILS

THE SHE DEVILS
Pierre Louÿs
ISBN 1 84068 013 X
Published 2000AD
Copyright © Creation Books 2000AD
The Erotic Adventures Of Toinon
Translated by
John Phillips 1998
The She Devils
Originally published in 1995
by Velvet Publications
All rights reserved
Published by
CREATION BOOKS
A Butcherbest Production
♦
Design:
Bradley Davis
Cover illustration:
Franz von Bayros

CONTENTS

FOREWORD

Pierre Louÿs' *The She Devils* is described by Susan Sontag, in her essay "The Pornographic Imagination", as being one of the very few works of erotica to deserve true literary status; and indeed this remarkable book was once cited by William Burroughs, in a letter to Jack Kerouac, as being amongst his ten all-time favourite novels. *The She Devils* is, surely, the apotheosis of the erotic novel, an archangelic hymn to sodomy and polymorphic excess which absolutely refuses to baulk at any perversion imaginable, and tries to imagine them all.

Pierre Louÿs pursued his cherished themes of lust and lesbianism amongst young girls throughout his writings, which also include *The Songs Of Bilitis, Aphrodite*, and *Le Roi Gonzalve*, a tale of a king's incestuous love for his young daughters. The brief but potent fragment *Toinon*, here translated into English for the first time ever, was amongst Louÿs' final papers. It is included in this new Creation Classics edition as a complementary coda to *The She Devils*, luxuriating as it does in the same themes of sexual mania, leavened with coital *tristesse*, in adolescent girls.

—*James Havoc*
Series Editor

THE
SHE DEVILS

Chapter One

'I must say,' she exclaimed, shaking her head, 'you certainly work fast! We just finished moving in yesterday – mother, my three sisters, and I – and today when we met on the stairs you already kissed me, pushed me into your apartment, shut the door... And here we are.'

'And that's only the beginning,' I remarked rather brazenly.

'Oh? I suppose you don't know that our two apartments adjoin each other? That there's even a blocked-off door between them? I don't even have to fight back if you decide to act a little unwisely, my good man. It would be much easier to shout, "Help mother! Rape! Satyr! Attack!"'

The threat was no doubt intended to intimidate me – and successfully, I might add. However, she soon reassured me, and my scruples began once more to fall away. My desire, unfettered, once more flamed high in a new atmosphere of freedom.

This young girl, scarcely sixteen years old, whom I had so easily made captive, wore her jet black hair knotted in the back, a plain, slightly crumpled blouse, a short full skirt, and a wide leather belt.

As slim, brown, and trembling as a kid in something by Leconte de Lisle, she pressed her legs together and lowered her head without lowering her eyes, as if to charge towards me with her horns.

The willingness in her words and manner had already prompted me to attempt to take her, however I didn't think things would go as quickly as they did.

'What's your name?' she asked me.

'X—. I'm twenty years old. And you?'

'Mauricette. I'm fifteen and a half. What time is it?'

'Three o'clock.'

'Three o'clock,' she repeated, lost in thought for a second. 'Do you want to go to bed with me?'

Dumbfounded by words I was far from speaking yet myself, much less expecting to hear, I recoiled a step – stupefied and unable to answer.

'Listen,' she said, placing a finger to her lips. 'Promise me to speak in a low voice, to let me go at four o'clock... Above all, promise to – No. I was going to say to do exactly as I wish, but perhaps you don't like that sort of thing. In any case, promise not to do what I *don't* want.'

'I'll promise anything you want me to.'

'Good. I believe you. I'll stay.'

'Yes? You mean you'll stay? I mean...'

'Oh, come now!' she said laughing. 'Cut out the kid stuff!'

As provocative and gay as a child, she touched, then grabbed the front of my trousers together with what she knew hung therein before flitting across the room to a corner, where she took off her dress, her stockings, her slippers... Then, taking her slip in her two hands and pursing her lips in a little mocking pout she asked, 'Can I... Completely naked?'

'If you want me to, I'll promise again... With all my heart and soul I...'

'And you won't blame me for it afterwards?' she said, mocking my over-dramatic tone.

'Never!'

'Then... Here is Mauricette!'

We fell together onto my double bed, clasped in each other's arms, she forcing her mouth against mine, crushing our lips together, her tongue probing feverishly. Then her eyes, which had been closed until they were only slits, opened suddenly. Everything about her at that moment was the girl of fourteen, the look, the kiss, the flare of nostril... Finally a tiny smothered cry, as from a small impatient animal, escaped from beneath me. Our mouths parted, ground together again, parted once more.

And, not knowing exactly what mysterious virtues she had

Pierre Louÿs

bound me not to violate, I ventured a little idiotic nonsense to try to pry her secret from her without asking point-blank.

'Ah! And what are these pretty little flowers you've stuck to your chest? What would a florist call these little buds?'

'Knockers.'

'And this little *Karakul* here just beneath your stomach? Is it the fashion now to wear fur muffins in July or do you get cold down there?'

'No! No! Not often!'

'And this? I can't possibly understand what in the world this little thing could be.'

'So you don't know what that is, eh?' she said with a sly little smile. 'Well, you're going to tell *me* what it is.'

With the impudence of youth, she spread her legs wide, put her two hands between them, and parted her flesh. My surprise was all the more complete, as the boldness of the gesture hardly prepared me for what I saw.

'A cherry!' I cried.

'And a pretty one!'

'Is it for me?'

I thought she would say no, and I must confess I hoped so. It was one of those absolutely impenetrable membranes such as I had already encountered twice. God, what I had had to put up with. Nevertheless, I was slightly annoyed to see Mauricette reply to my question by passing a finger under her nose and wrinkling up her mouth as if to say, 'Like hell!' or worse. And since all this time she flaunted the forbidden fruit in front of me, I said maliciously, 'I see that you've fallen into some nasty habits when you're alone, young lady.'

'Oh! How did you know?' she cried, closing her legs.

This remark did more than anything else I had said to put her completely at her ease. I had understood her correctly and now nothing could shut her up: she even began bragging. With a malicious child-like air, she repeated in a low little voice, rubbing her lips each time against mine:

'Yes. I finger myself. I finger myself. I finger myself. I finger myself. I finger myself. I finger myself.'

The more she said it, the gayer she became, and these

first words unleashed a whole string of others, all tumbling out as if they had just been awaiting the signal:

'You'll see how I can come.'

'I hope so.'

'Give me your rod.'

'Where?'

'Find a place.'

'Which one is forbidden?'

'My virginity and my mouth.'

Since there are only three paths to the heart of a woman, and since I have an intelligence used to the exercise presented by difficult enigmas, I understood.

However, this new surprise caught me speechless. I could say nothing. What was worse, I not only remained silent, but I remained silent in such an imbecilic way that Mauricette finally decided that she would have to explain the mystery herself. She sighed deeply, smiling, and shot me a distressed glance that could only be translated, 'God, but men can be stupid!' Then she began to look a little worried and started to ask me questions.

'And what do you like to do? What do you like best?'

'Making love, my sweet.'

'But that's forbidden... And what don't you like at all? What do you really hate?'

'That little hand there. Pretty though it may be, there is nothing I want less.'

'It's too bad that I...' she began, obviously troubled, 'that I can't suck you... Did you want my mouth?'

'You've already given it to me,' I said, taking it again to mine.

But it wasn't the same mouth. Mauricette had lost her composure, could no longer speak, thought that all was lost. It was time that I brought a smile back to that stricken little face, so I slid one of my hands, now pressing her so tightly to me, down her back and pressed it lightly against the spot that she had given up trying to make me accept or even to understand.

The timid child looked up quickly into my face, saw that I had not been serious, and with a sudden change of countenance that thrilled me, squealed, 'Oh! You louse! You rat! You brute!

You swine!'

'Hey! Shut up there!'

'For fifteen minutes he pretends he doesn't know what I'm talking about, he strings me along because I don't know how to say it.'

She quickly recovered her good-humoured brat attitude and, without ever raising her voice, but nose to mine, growled, 'I don't feel like it any more. I ought to get dressed. You deserve it.'

'You don't feel like what?'

'Having you buttfuck me!' she said laughing. 'There, I said it. And you haven't heard the last of it, either. I don't know how to do much, but I do know how to talk.'

'The only thing is... I'm still not exactly sure I heard you right.'

'I want you to screw me through my ass and I want you to bite me! I don't like men who tease. I like 'em vicious.'

'Tch. Tch. I think you're getting a little hot under the collar, Mauricette.'

'And you call me Ricette when you screw me.'

'So as not to say any "Mau"? All right, fine. Let's go, but try to calm down a little.'

'There's only one way to do it. Fast! You want to or not?'

Not in the least angry with me, perhaps even more ardent, she returned the kiss I had given her full on my mouth and, undoubtedly to encourage me, said, 'Ah! Your prick gets as hard as iron, but I'm no softy either. I've got a good solid asshole myself.'

'No vaseline? All the better.'

'Sticking it in me is like sticking it in a vice.'

With a quick flip of her body she turned her back to me, lying on her right side, and with a single wet finger began to play with herself. Apparently she demanded nothing to satisfy whatever modesty she may have had. Then, with a movement that amused me, she closed the lips of her membrane, and just in time, for I had begun to think that I might penetrate there despite my promises. However, although the wet finger might have been enough for her, it certainly wasn't enough for me, and I began to discover that she had been telling the truth when she said that she was 'no softy'.

I was on the point of asking her if I wasn't hurting her when, turning her mouth towards mine, she whispered to me the contrary.

'You've already taken virgins through the ass before this.'

'How do you know?'

'I'll tell you that when you tell me how you knew that I play with myself.'

'Little bitch! You've got the biggest, reddest snatch I've ever seen on a virgin.'

'It expands,' she murmured, her eyes growing soft. 'It's not always this big. But don't touch it. Leave that to me. And now do you want to know how I know you've taken virgins through the behind before?'

'No, later.'

'Well, I'll tell you anyway! I've got positive proof! You know enough never to try to talk to a virgin who's fingering herself with you in her ass. Because she's fucked if she'll answer!'

Her first loud laugh subsided quickly into a low moan, became almost abstracted from herself. Her eyes began to narrow. She ground her teeth together and parted her lips.

After a silence she said, 'Bite me... I want you to bite me... There, in the neck, under my hair, like cats do to each other.'

And then she said, 'I'm holding myself in... I can hardly do it, but... Oh! I can't any longer! I'm going to come, my – what's your name again? – my... darling. Do it like you want! With all your might! As if you were screwing me! Oh, I like that! Again! Again! Again!'

The spasm stiffened her, held her trembling... Then her head fell and I held her little body, completely limp, against mine.

♦

Love? No. The flame of an hour, but within myself I couldn't help saying, '*Bigre!*' (a word we often use to explain the mixture of wonder, allure, and restlessness which the precocity of a young girl inspires in us), and I greeted her awakening with less irony than admiration.

　　　　　　　　　　　　　　　　　Pierre Louÿs

'You do very well for a virgin.'

'Huh!' she grunted, shooting me a long seductive look.

'Naïve child! Sacred innocence!'

'Did you feel how hard my asshole is?'

'Like a rhinoceros.'

'And we're all like that in my family.'

'What?'

'Ha! Ha! Ha!'

'What did you just say?'

'I said that that was how we give our behinds. And this is how we come from the front.'

With all the natural vivacity of her character, she suddenly threw open her thighs to expose the dripping centre. I hardly recognized the terrain, so heavy had been the downpour.

'*Les Jardins dans la Pluie!* I cried.

'And with the fingering!' she replied, laughing.

'Wait! I'm going to give you something. First, do you want it? Yes? Good! Do you have some scissors?'

She pulled a silken thread from one of the blankets and lay it on her stomach.

'A lock from my virginity. Will you keep it?'

'All my life. But choose the hair carefully. If you don't want it to look like what it is take a long one.'

'Oh! You know that too?' she asked disappointedly. 'What have you got, a collection?'

However, she cut the lock, a single incurably rounded curl. M. de La Fontaine, of the French Academy, once wrote a poem called *The Impossible Task* in order to teach youth that the hair of certain women could never be uncurled. He obviously tried it... What libidinous old bastards these academicians can be!

Mauricette linked the hairs of her black lock to a green silk thread, then sliced them at the base. 'A kiss-curl... wet by the come of a virgin!' she said, and with a burst of laughter jumped from the bed and closed herself into the toilet. However she reappeared as quickly as she had entered.

'I would like to know...' I began.

'Why we're all like that in my family?'

'Yes.'

'From my earliest childhood...'

'Good beginning.'

'I was boarded out to school while my mother and sisters earned their living together with men, women, kids, whores, girls, old farts, monkeys, negroes, dogs, dildos, eggplants...'

'Is that all?'

'And everything else you can think of. They did everything. Would you like to take my mother? Her name is Teresa. She's Italian, thirty-nine years old. I'll give her to you. I'm very kind. Maybe you'd like my sisters too? None of us are jealous, but keep the lock I gave you and you'll come back to me.'

'Ricette! Do you think I want to...'

'Ta! Ta! Ta! Everyone takes all four of us, but they always come back to me. I know what I'm saying when I'm not fingering myself.'

After another youthful laugh she seized my hand and rolled close to me, trying to be serious.

'Until I was thirteen years old I lived in this boarding school with a bunch of girls from families in society. Since you know so much, tell me what the directrices and mistresses are like who spend their dirty little lives working in a bordello of boarding students.'

'Lesbians?'

'You should see them,' said Mauricette with a charming irony. 'And since they knew all about my mother you can guess how they treated me.'

'The beasts! They abused your innocence? They forced you to drink the poison of vice?'

'Forced me? They perverted me!' Mauricette was getting warmed up. 'Four times they surprised me fingering my little friends!'

'Ah! So it was...'

'They hid in the garden, in the dormitory, in the corridors, outside the windows of the rooms, always trying to spy! There's nothing as vicious as a boarding school mistress!'

'Did they pay for it?'

'A bad point. And yet... The things we showed them

without wanting to! Some really wonderful combinations, things they would never have seen alone! But finally I became a close friend of one of the older girls. She gave me ten lessons in Sapphism the likes of which you only hear about.'

'Which means?'

'The art of using the tongue delicately, at exactly the right spot, without skinning the end of it just anywhere. That was what I learned best by the time I left the boarding school; much better than I ever learned biblical history or geography. But my great friend and I sought out all the corners of the school, and on the one hundred and twenty-fifth time we were surprised by Mademoiselle Paule.'

'Who in turn perverted you fifteen minutes later?'

'Yes. In her room, under her skirt. With pants that had buttons everywhere. And a pretty little pussy she had, the bitch! The hairs, the skin, the snatch, the lips, everything was wonderful. I liked to do it with her much more than with my friend. Can you top a mistress for viciousness?'

'Terrible. And you haven't told me all...'

'No. I forgot something. Do you know, she didn't even know how to use her tongue? I had to show her.'

Here, Mauricette was overcome with such hilarious laughter that she fell over backwards almost to the foot of the bed, and so gracefully did she do it that I began to be in a hurry to end the interval. I was regrettably more interested in her present than her past.

Finally, it was my turn to leave the room and go to the toilet. I must have stayed there longer than was prudent, for when I re-entered the room, Mauricette, already dressed, was putting on her slippers.

'You're leaving?' I said, slightly annoyed.

'Not entirely. There's a little lock of me that's staying. And besides, I'm not going far; just there, behind the door. I suppose you don't remember promising to let me go at four o'clock?'

'In the morning!'

'In the evening, unfortunately!' she said in my arms.

Instead of fleeing, she had come to be kissed with a confidence that restored mine. Finally, however, she disengaged herself with a start and I could no longer keep her in my room, nor even join her on the landing. She had found her own door partly open, slipped in, and disappeared.

Chapter Two

A half hour later, her mother came in, and at first glance I could see that my little farce was already getting complicated: mother was much more beautiful than daughter. Now what was her name again? Oh yes; Teresa.

In any case, she had a wrap thrown around her lithe and supple figure that scarcely covered it. I offered her a chair but she refused, sat down on the edge of my bed, and said point-blank, 'Was it you that buttfucked my daughter this afternoon?'

This is the sort of question I always find rather distasteful; I never have liked interviews of this kind. I made some sort of vague depreciating gesture intended to signify absolutely nothing, but she said, 'No, no. Don't protest. She told me all about it. I would have scratched your eyes out if you'd broken her cherry, but you only went as far as I let her go... What are you blushing for?'

'Because you're beautiful.'

'What do you know about that?'

'Enough.'

I too was getting to the point as quickly as possible. The premature departure of Mauricette had left me even more ardent than had her arrival, and, besides, with women I would rather, much rather, spend my time in demonstration than conversation.

I didn't give Teresa time to say whatever it was she had prepared, feeling that to change the direction of a touchy scene is the only way to improve it. And I'd managed to turn my corner without even slowing down. Even though she was still in a stronger position than I, she had lost her breath for a moment and she closed her thighs with a smile. She knew where we were heading before I made a move, but I could see that my sudden change of tack had not hurt my chances any. In fact, our little exchange of gestures placed us on a new level of familiarity.

'So what do you want me to show you? What I have between my legs?'

'Your heart!' I replied.

'And you think it's down there?'

'Yes.'

'Try to find it.'

She gave a low laugh. She knew that the research would not be easy. My hand wandered blindly in an impenetrable forest of hair, and I lost my way several times. The wool grew everywhere, from the top of her thighs to the base of her stomach. I began to get even hotter when Teresa, too adroit to make me look maladroit, lifted her wrap and her slip, either to console me or to distract me or perhaps to give me a second prize as encouragement.

A magnificent body, long and full, lean and brown, fell into my arms, and two ripe, full, but scarcely maternal and never pendulous breasts pressed against my chest. Two burning thighs clasped me and when I tried to...

'No. Not that. You can screw me later.'

'Why later?'

'So we can finish up there.'

She was revenging herself. It was her turn to change the direction we were taking, but she did it so skilfully that in refusing what I wanted she seemed to be according me an even greater favour.

In my silence she sensed that it was her body now that was master of the situation, and in a new tone that simultaneously questioned and offered me nothing at all, she said, 'Do you want my mouth or my ass?'

'I want all of you.'

'You're not going to get my come. I don't have a drop left. They've given me too much to do since this morning.'

'Who?'

'My daughters.'

She noticed me pale. I saw Mauricette again completely

nude and saying, 'I'll give you mother.' I no longer knew exactly what I felt. An hour before, I had thought that Mauricette was to be the heroine of my adventure, but now her mother inflamed my senses ten times more. And she knew it even better than I. She lay on my desire, sure of her power over me and, caressing my distracted flesh with her hair and her stomach, had the audacity to say, 'Would you like Mauricette again? I know she's got a crush on you. She fingers herself thinking about you, and I know that you like her. Do you want me to go get her? I'll hold her behind open for you.'

'No.'

'But then you don't even know Lili, her little sister. She's even more depraved! Ricette is a virgin and she doesn't even like to suck. She's only got one talent. Lili knows how to do everything: she likes everything; and she's only fourteen years old. Would you like to screw her? Buttfuck her? Come in her mouth? In front of me?'

'No.'

'Don't you like little girls? Then you should take Charlotte, my oldest daughter. She's the best looking of the three. Her hair is so long it falls all the way down to her heels. And she's got breasts and buttocks like a statue. She's got the most beautiful cunt in the family. I get hot for her myself when she takes off her clothes, and I'm no kid anymore; I'm a woman who likes a good prick. Charlotte... Imagine a beautiful young girl, dark, warm, soft, without the slightest prudishness of vice, a perfect mistress accepting everything, playing any way you want, and who loves her trade. The more you ask of her the happier she is. How about her? All I have to do is call through the partition here.'

That woman was the devil in female form, and I would have given anything to have been able to take her at her word and cry out, 'Yes!' in her face. But as I was gathering my shattered will for the effort, opening my mouth and drawing breath, Teresa said with an expression of sincere interest, 'Did I give you a hard-on?'

This time the fury came. With a 'You're making fun of me!' followed by a few other choice expressions of rapidly increasing strength, I began to beat her. She laughed at the top of her voice while trying to ward me off with arms and legs. Helpless with laughter she could only defend herself blindly, and I covered her with blows and squeezes that didn't seem to have the least effect; then that laugh exasperated me so that, not knowing what to do next to get at her, I grabbed a handful of hair from the most sensitive place I could find and pulled... She cried out.

Thinking I'd really done her some serious harm, I fell into her arms covered in confusion. I waited for a thousand reproaches to rain on my head, but she would never have dreamed of saying anything that might have cooled my ardour. Even through her squeals of pain she never stopped laughing except to berate herself.

'That's what happens when you have so many hairs on your ass! When you sleep with Lili I defy you to try that.'

The incident ended my violence and hastened the denouement of our little piece. Teresa didn't waste a minute in offering me her favours as a pardon for what I had done and she offered them without a word, with a facility of movement and coordination of body that smacked almost of the art of juggling.

Lying on her side next to me and taking my buttocks between her spread thighs, she put one of her hands beneath herself and did something that I couldn't see... Then directed my body as she wanted it.

The magic that some courtesans effect can often work some really incredible wonders... Like a young stage hero that awakens in the garden of a sorceress I could have sighed, 'Where am I?' for my enchantress was lying absolutely still and I wasn't at all sure where I had entered. I kept silent to preserve a doubt that left me a little hope. But both vanished with her first words.

'Don't bother with me,' she said. 'Don't move. Don't try to prove that you know how to take me there. Ricette just told me all about it. I don't give a damn this evening. When you buttfuck me I can come without touching myself, but now I'm going to buttfuck myself. You'll see in a minute! I don't feel like coming tonight.'

'And if I'd rather you came than I did myself? If I decide to give you the works?'

'The works, eh? Be careful, young one, or I'll empty your balls with a twist of my asshole... There! There! There!'

She was maddening. The violence and agility with which she could use her ass surpassed anything I had ever experienced before. Her motion didn't last more than a moment, but it was enough to put me in serious trouble. Then she stopped and lay still again.

Despite the fact that she had me on the very brink of coming, I still did not want to separate our bodies: I wanted her to know that I did not like to be hurried.

I told her that I thought she was beautiful and desirable, but that since I was twenty years old I was no longer a child; that I was not the type that liked to be run by a woman. I don't know how I ever managed to get all that out, for she had worked me up to a point where I could hardly hold myself in. She could have easily told me that she was just finishing something I had already started, but she said nothing, merely remained silent with a secret little smile that seemed to reflect some inner thought.

Then finally she said tenderly, 'Don't worry, I won't break your tail. I'm sucking you. Can you feel it? I'm sucking you with my ass.'

I didn't know what she was doing, but it was true that her mouth couldn't have excited me more than her ass was doing. It was becoming difficult for me to speak at all.

She watched the reflection in my face of the sensations that were pouring through my body and, without ever needing to ask a question to find out how close I was, began to increase bit by bit the excitement of her loins to a slow crescendo. I think that I must have said, 'Faster!' but that she refused. I have only a very vague memory of those last few seconds, for the spasm that she wrung out of my flesh was a sort of unconscious convulsion that I do not know how to describe.

♦

The first question I could regain composure enough to ask her came after several full minutes of silence.

'What did you do to me?'.

'A pretty little trick with my asshole,' she said, laughing. 'But you've already buttfucked so many women...'

'Yes, an hour ago. A pretty little girl that didn't do too badly either, but...'.

'Not badly at all. She's got a muscle there, hasn't she? And she can really move.'

'But you...'

'But I'm the first one who ever sucked you with her asshole, eh? You want to know how I did it? I'll tell you tomorrow, but let me get up now. You want to know the reason for that too, I suppose? To put the little child to bed that you just gave me: the little sister of my three daughters.'

When she returned, arranging the hair at the nape of her neck, but still nude, my mouth failed to realize that she was less interested in repairing her coiffure than in showing off the breasts of which she was very proud.

I'm not one of those children who pine away for older women, but a thirty-nine year-old seductress, when she's beautiful from head to foot and at all points between is what a sculptor would call a real 'woman,' and what a lover would call a real 'piece'.

'And which one was *not* this woman?' Put the question to a contest and she would have had the vote of every man in existence going both ways.

Nude, Teresa resembled an operatic mezzo. To a whore, in other words, you will say. But I answer, not at all. You murmur that it is much the same thing? No. Not unless night and day are the same. If the only way you know actresses is through smoking-room conversations, don't say any more.

The type of beautiful singer that practically lives in her bed, and the often even more beautiful women that sing out their inner souls on the primrose path have scarcely any more in common than their habits of walking around nearly nude and treating themselves like whores.

However, the woman of the theatre always aspires with all her heart to greater and yet greater freedom, while the woman of the bordello needs more than anything else to enslave herself. Of the two, the profession that seems the most servile is the first, but in most cases the woman who follows it does so out of a spirit of independence: in order to free herself from a family or a lover. The whore throws herself into her career out of a need to obey the caprices of others rather than in order to carve for herself the path of her daily life.

From her first year at the conservatory, the daughter of the theatre also makes herself a student of every crudity of the language. She considers it great sport to group fifteen words around an idea that doesn't merit one, and it is one of her talents to detach each from the other according to the strictest rules of articulation. The whore, on the other hand, has neither the taste nor the talent to make a science of cynical language. Freedom of language tempts her as little as does freedom of life. Thus there is no mistaking your woman when you don't know where she comes from. It suffices simply to listen to her cries in the act of love to determine whether a woman comes from a bordello or a theatre. Many men are fooled solely because they fail to realize this.

I had more proof than I needed in order to guess in Teresa's case what no one had told me. Her body, the unrestraint of her character and the crudity of her expression all pointed in the same direction.

'Are you an actress?' I asked her.

'No more. I used to be, but how did you know? Did Mauricette tell you?'

'No. It's easy to see. Or hear. Where have you been on the stage?'

Without answering, she lay down next to me on her stomach. I replied a little maliciously:

'You'll tell me tomorrow.'

'Yes.'

'Stay here until then.'

'Until tomorrow morning? You want me to?'

She smiled and I thought she was going to accept. I was still a little weak, but she inspired me so that I was almost as ready to go as if I had not just finished. She lay stretched out next to me and said, 'What do you want with me from now until tomorrow morning?'

'First to make love.'

'That's not hard.'

'Don't say that. You exasperate me. Why are you staying now, then?'

'Because my little work in the toilet would be ruined if I got up now. And then what would you want?'

'Everything.'

'How many times?'

'Oh, I don't know. With you I don't think I'd be keeping count. However, that shouldn't be "hard" either.'

Teresa gave me one of those long, silent looks of hers that I had so much difficulty in reading and understanding. And I suddenly felt that this woman who refused to answer any of my questions had suddenly inspired in me the most unexplainable and unexpected confidence, as if the certainty that she now had of being able to attract me could assure her also of my discretion. Or guard any secret if I happened to hear it from lips other than her own.

'Ricette told me that you kept your word to her. Can I tell you a secret? Yes? All right then; I used to live in Marseilles with my three daughters in an apartment. I had to leave because they changed their chief of police. There it is. You understand? Here I can probably stay quite a while without moving; but since I have a daughter with fire in her behind who was come to be buttfucked by you the very first day... and her mother after her.'

Upon this, she began to laugh again, first to convince me that her secret really was quite unimportant, and secondly because she wanted to see me in a good humour before she told me the rest of her plans.

From the laugh she passed to caresses, and when she was sure of my state of mind as well as body she posed me a question in such a way that it was also the extraction of a confession.

'You're not enough of a virgin not to know what it's like with a young girl, are you? A real one, without much hair, small teats: ever screw one like that?'

'Yes, but not often. Two, maybe four in all. Two real ones; the other two not quite as authentic.'

'Two, that's enough. You know that you don't run it into

Pierre Louÿs

a virgin like you do with a woman; you can only stick it in as far as the head. They can't take any more. You know that?'

'Sure. Why do you ask?'

'Because I'm going to send you my little Lili, since you seem to have this mania for fucking. I don't want you knocking me up.'

The patient persons of both sexes that assumed the charge of my education taught me that when at a party, if one should invite a woman to dance and she should reply, 'Dance with my daughter,' I should show neither regret, nor pleasure, nor indifference. The situation is very complex.

I knew it, but, completely nude, my polite education was less at my fingertips than usual. And then again I am much like Alexander. I destroy complexities rather than circumventing them.

'I don't think I'd exactly know how to handle myself with her. You'd better give me a lesson,' I said.

She suddenly became a little nervous and, turning her head, gave a little laugh.

'You've never even seen what you're asking me for.'

'Show it to me.'

'Not from the front. You buttfucked me from the front before, now you can see my pussy from the rear. But you know what I said?'

'And that will be the end?'

'Poor thing! If I stuff your cock into my mouth you'll be something to be pitied. And if I make your balls dance at the end of my tongue... You don't know my tongue, do you? Hold it... There, look!'

Still looking, I tried to take Teresa in a simpler, though not less agreeable manner, but she shut her thighs and held my arm.

'Don't you understand that you can't keep three daughters on a chain like three monkeys on a string? You think if they make love in Marseilles they're not going to do it in Paris? That if I take a lover they won't take six? Listen. You want me? You can have me. But you're going to have all four of us.'

I almost asked, horrified, 'Every day?' but held myself in and tried to mask my anxiety with a thankful expression.

'I'm going to send you Lili,' she continued, 'because she has to go to bed early and because kids like that are like society women: they get itchy asses in the afternoon. This evening I'll send you Charlotte for the night and tomorrow evening I'll come again. And if that doesn't satisfy you, you can go to the exchange department and get your money back.'

'I'm overwhelmed... Unfortunately, you seem to be getting ready to leave...'

'Not yet. In five minutes when I've kept my promise. But on two conditions. First, no coming. I won't either. Second, I'm not going to show you my beauties because I don't want you sucking them.'

That was all right with me. I would much rather prove my virility than try to compete with lesbians. And this preference becomes an unbreakable rule when the woman has other lovers.

Always supple and agile, Teresa flipped around quickly to face the other way on my prone body. She was keeping her promise, all right. And the parts that I now had before my eyes I can only call extraordinary. Each was abnormal in one way or another: a protruding clitoris, great thin delicate lips, as black and red as the petals of an orchid. Within them, the throat of her vagina narrowed suddenly making the lips seem monstrous by comparison, while her anus formed a strange rosette of blackish brown on purple. But all around each one of these objects was the strangest of all her singularities – namely, her hair. Never before had I had a so thoroughly furred woman in my bed. The hair was everywhere: on her stomach, thighs, groin, crossing between her buttocks, mounting all the way up her rump, even climbing to...

Suddenly I could see nothing more. Teresa's tongue had touched my skin. My stung muscles tightened and knotted, and her tongue wandered everywhere, turning, probing, going under... I shuddered... Teresa raised her head and jumped from the bed.

'Enough for now,' she said.

'You promised to leave me up in the air like this? You'd leave me in such a state?'

'For Lili. I'm going to get her now. Make her think that you're hot for her. And tomorrow, you and I... all night. Okay?'

There's nothing I hate more than changing partners in mid-fuck. To desire one woman and have to possess another is really odious. So when Teresa had gone I decided that little Miss Lili would have to make me want her on her own, or else do without.

That resolved, I took from my library a heady novel by Henri Bordeaux that I had purchased expressly for the purpose of beating down rebellious erections.

By the seventh line it had achieved its purpose.

Chapter Three

At the fifteenth line I was just dropping off to sleep when the doorbell gave a tiny metallic tinkle.

'Who's there?'

A small voice, weak but distinct through the wood, answered, 'The child of a whore.'

I hadn't felt like laughing, but that manner of announcing oneself slid easily into my list of short phrases which stand out like peaks in the monotony of existence. I opened the door. A droll young girl, cute, cunning, frank, and delicate, arms swinging, nose in air, strolled in.

'It's me, Lili,' she said.

'l don't doubt it,' I replied, laughing. 'And Lili is very nice.'

'You're nice too. I feel like staying.'

I wonder why I've never acquired the vice of wanting young girls. They're spiteful among themselves, but so tender with us, and I must say I was flattered by this perky specimen. With a woman, every word of love is veiled by the mist of uncertainty with which our prudence screens our credulity. An adolescent girl *makes* you believe. I kissed Lili on the left ear.

She wrapped one tiny arm around my neck and whispered very quickly in my ear, as if trying to excuse herself, 'I'm fourteen years old and I don't have much pubic hair. Is that all right?'

'You won't tell your mother?'

'No... But wait. Look. I don't have any pants on. Mama took them off me so I wouldn't stain them with come.'

'But that's very pretty! You're very good down there!'

'Should I take off my dress? Or should I just pull up my

Pierre Louÿs

skirts?'

'Oh, but that's immoral! The only way I like to take teenage girls is completely nude.'

'That,' said she with a charming frankness, 'is the only thing about me that's pretty. That and my little ass. Everything else is ugly!'

'I'm sure that the rest is very pretty.'

'You'll see. But you've just been in bed with my mother. When you see my thin little body I'll have to work for a quarter of an hour to give you another hard-on.'

'Oh no you won't. I'll bet you a sack of candy.'

'And what do I give you if I lose?'

'A discretion.'

'Done,' cried she. 'I don't give a damn about that. I know how to do everything you can think of.'

It took Lili twenty seconds and six movements to shed her clothes – her dress, her slip, her socks, and her slippers... And when she had done it there seemed to be nothing left of little Miss Lili, so slight was her figure.

Her arms and legs were as thin as broomsticks and her hair hung down in black folds to her waist. Her body itself was thin, delicate, with a great mound and a sex already dripping and flowing. If it is true that a well-ordered menu ought to bring together the most dissimilar possible dishes, then the serving of Lili after Teresa would have been the work of a master.

♦

Lili's first movement gave me a good impression of her. Instead of throwing her arms around my neck, she immediately began searching between my legs with her tiny hands. Do I need to tell you the delight I found in this simple innocence?

The poor girl had announced herself earlier at the door (like others of her age call themselves Children of Mary) as the daughter of a whore. A kid who calls herself that isn't like the others; it takes guts to come out with it like that. And this whore's baby, as nude as the day she was born, came to me like an artless young girl, the type that lowers her eyes and tries to find out what it is that boys have and girls haven't. Little prostitutes often have a strange and unalterable candour.

As I felt myself still under the effects of my recent refreshing reading, I took Lili in my arms and we began to chat and exchange the sort of caress that is called breach of modesty committed without violence.

'Lili, you're a very pretty kid,' I said.

'That's not true. When I finger myself in front of the mirror I can't even excite myself.'

These words sent me off into gales of laughter.

Lili's face remained sober and, since it is easy to seduce adolescents, she affirmed to me with a solemn little air, but without either preamble or reason, 'I like you very much.'

'Oh, my little Lili, you've only got two ideas in your pretty head.'

'Why two? But yes, it's true. I've two. How did you know? Your finger tell you?'

'Exactly. The ideas that young girls have in their heads...'

'Come from their cunts?' said Lili.

It is difficult for me to hide, at this point, where the finger was resting that was sending me so much information.

'You certainly know a lot, my pretty,' I replied. 'Wise before your time. But I'll bet you don't know why you have two ideas. It's because when you love someone you want with all your heart to give him a great pleasure and at the same time to procure one from him.'

For that she had to reflect a moment, the time it takes for a school girl to understand a maxim. Then she smiled and buried her face under mine before replying, 'You don't think my little sou-sized pussy is too small for you? Do you still want to fuck me?'

'You get nicer and nicer, Lili. The first thing you think of is my pleasure instead of your own.'

'Yes,' she stammered, a little confused.

'And for you. What would you like the best?'

'To suck you.'

She'd said it. And she followed by throwing her arms around my neck and repeating it ten times, in a sing-song, wheedling tone, like a child asking for candy at the circus.

'I want to suck your prick, your cock, your pole, your rod, your dick. I want to make your peter hard in my mouth and then make it shoot. I want to nurse myself on your penis, your log, your bone, your dong.'

'What? Still nursing at your age?'

'Yes, but not for milk, only for come.'

'Is it good?'

'It is when you like it.'

'Then how much do you want, my little lady? A sou's worth? Two sous? Three sous?'

'All you've got in the shop! And I'll pay you in advance, sir, with my holes.'

'What?'

'It's a joke.'

'No. I'll give you credit, little miss. You can owe me. Sit down at the table.'

But Lili still had a few things to say to me. With her arms still around my neck, she sighed:

'The only thing is... Listen. I had to promise mama not to make you come more than once. I have to leave some for Charlotte tonight. So we'll have to do everything the first time.'

'Just once?'

'Yes. I'm the youngest in our family. but I always do the most. The only thing I can't do is let you make love between my teats because I don't have any. So will you fuck me, then buttfuck me, and then stick it in my mouth? I'll tell you why afterwards.'

And quickly, vivaciously, turning her head, she cried, 'Oh, look! It's getting hard without me even touching it! I've lost my sack of candy!'

'You'll get it just the same.'

'Really? And for the discretion I have to give you. What do you want?'

'You to give me your mouth and your two holes. What else can I ask?'

'My tongue!' she cried gaily.

And she was quick to pay her debt... How can I tell you the way in which she offered me her tiny tongue? I stopped her too late.

'Lili! What did you do?'

'A tongue in the rear!' she said joyously. 'That ought to merit a cock in the front.'

She threw herself onto her back, her feet in the air, her sex spread. She rinsed it in enough saliva to violate a cat and I soon saw that I had been very naïve indeed not to have known how to take her, for most young girls are easier to take than a good many women I know. I entered without much difficulty...

'That's all,' she said smiling. 'When you get just the end of it in you've taken up all the room. There's no more... It's hardly worth the trouble.'

'Nonsense!'

'No. I'm only good from one side, and it isn't this one.'

'For what you've just said, I ought to give you a child.'

She laughed, but quickly added, 'Will you give it to me in the mouth?'

Since my temperament is about equally foreign to the spirits of sadism and presbyterian morality, the two that seem to share the greater part of society about equally, what I am going to say is only the expression of a personal feeling and will probably offend everyone: I took as much pleasure in screwing Lili, who wished it with all her heart, as I would have felt displeasure and guilt in taking a young girl against her will. I might add that I have never yet been guilty of rape.

She played at fucking like most other young girls play at dolls, taking a certain instinctive satisfaction from it. And even though she had long done this, even though it was certainly no new thing for her, she was very proud to be able to tempt a man, to be able to do all at her age that her mother could do... but after a minute or so she said softly to me, 'Change holes. You'll be able to go further.'

Quickly she jumped from the bed, ran to the toilet, lathered up some soap in order to open the passage and, returning to me, squatted down on top of my rod, her eyes always on mine. A couple of seconds prodding and squirming was all that she needed, and she entirely swallowed from the rear the pole she had barely been able to insert the head of from the front. And she took it all, right to the root! With her lithe buttocks on my testicles, she drew up her knees, and spread her thighs, so that she was squatting there like a little devil on a Saint Anthony. Then she spread the lips of her smooth red sex and began to beat herself off with her finger like a young girl in the privacy of a toilet.

I took her into my arms, but she was so slender that even by lowering my head I could only reach her hair.

'You know, I'm really happy! When I think that you just slept with mama and that you can get a hard-on for me all by yourself... Even when my mother is so beautiful and I'm so ugly. I never get a chance to go with young men. Mother takes them all. I have to take the old ones. And you can drive it so far into my ass! So far! All the way to my heart!'

I don't think I have ever heard more tender or nicer words than those. But again, very few will understand my feeling. The moralist will blame me for having abetted a young girl in an act of sodomy, and the madmen will not be able to understand taking pleasure in a young girl without striking or whipping her so that she's crying and screaming like a pig having its throat cut.

Lili was motionless for a few moments and then turned softly on the pivot in her behind and laid on me on her back, her head down by my feet. And when I put one hand between her legs, her face took on an expression as if she were praying silently, until I suddenly took the initiative and said, 'Your mouth now.'

'Ah!' she cried.

And then, as soon as I had said that... But should I tell this too? I really feel quite embarrassed, but I swore to tell everything, just as I lived it...

Lili withdrew the member from her behind, the same that had been working it for fifteen minutes, and put it in her mouth exactly as it was.

'Oh, you dirty little devil!' I cried, pulling it out.

'It's too late. I did it already.'

'How can you...'

'I like it like that.'

The sentence, 'I like it like that,' didn't admit to a reply, and Lili took my penis again, pretending to want to bite it rather than have to give it up, and began to suck it, greedily, hungrily, in an orgy of delight.

Knowing well the reproaches and compliments that had been hers on other beds before, she had warned me that this last exercise was not what she did the best. However, I was becoming a little tired from the long state of excitement she had held me in and, holding the great opening of her little ass, which she had turned over to my care with my right hand, I warned her to be ready.

If the comparison is not irreverent, I would like to say that a young girl who likes to suck men is like a child on her knees in front of the holy altar at her first communion. She seems to be awaiting some sacred nourishment from the bosom of an incomprehensible mystery, something the God of Love is going to give her.

But Lili had so touching an expression on her face that it would have been cruel to have laughed. She raised her eyes to the heavens and stretched her smooth mound as well as she could over the cock that seemed so enormous and out of proportion by comparison. And when she felt me suddenly ejaculate, she breathed little clucks and gurgles through her nose. I don't know why, that struck me as irresistibly comic. I finally had to hide my eyes behind my hand.

The whole thing lasted no more than a second. Lili wasn't one of those girls who throw up everything they take in and leave more regret than remorse in the men who have perverted them.

She sucked badly, but she swallowed well.

Chapter Four

Four hours slid by, and I was dining in a little restaurant by myself, alone without women, trying to recover first of all my strength and most of all my spirits.

The first was easy, the latter not so.

And when I returned to my apartment around eleven o'clock I was still having a little difficulty understanding exactly what had happened.

I had just acquired for a neighbour a beautiful Italian woman who sold her daughters. That I should have taken one of them was nothing extraordinary. Students and girls of fifteen have been sleeping together since antiquity. That the mother, a woman used to sharing lovers with her daughters, should have rung at my door soon after was also perfectly normal. But why had she sent Lili to me? And why had she promised that the other would...

There was a knock. It was repeated... I went to open the door and a voice at once both soft and mild said, 'It seems that it's my turn now.'

I was stunned. Teresa had warned me that Charlotte was the most beautiful of her three daughters, but I had never hoped or thought that she was *that* good. And I said it to her face.

'My God, but you're beautiful!'

'Please don't say that,' she said sadly. 'It's worthy of any woman.'

'Are you Charlotte?'

'Yes. Do you like me?'

'Do I like you!'

She interrupted me to say, with a sort of relief and lassitude, 'That's good because I can only give myself like I am...

I'm not going to play the coquette, and... and...'

'And we kiss?'

'As often as you want.'

I took her mouth passionately. The kiss that she gave was soft rather than tender, but there was a welcome in it. Only when I put my hand beneath her skirts did she say, 'Let me undress.'

'I don't know if I have enough time.'

'You've got all night.'

And unhurriedly, with all the simplicity of a model taking off her clothes before a painter, she removed her black dress, her stockings, her slip, and, nude before me, sighed, 'You can see that I'm just like all the rest.'

The only word to describe her is delicious. A little less dark-skinned than her mother, but with the same black hair, she had a wonderfully soft figure, and, in fact, everything about her was of a quiet softness: her look, her voice, her skin, her caress.

When she was on my bed and in my arms she murmured almost humbly into my ear, 'I want to make you happy... Just ask me to do whatever you want, however you want it.'

This time, an overwhelming desire seized me to possess this girl in the most natural and normal of all ways, and I told her, in such a way, I thought, as not to leave any doubt as to my wishes, that I loved her and that I only wanted her pleasure first.

But Charlotte lifted her eyebrows and with supreme innocence asked, 'Fuck? Oh, if you wish. But if it's really for my pleasure, I... But no! I'm not a very complicated girl, you know, and there's only one thing I really like.'

'What?'

'When I'm fucking, the fear I have of becoming pregnant destroys all my pleasure. I don't like fucking. I don't like people to eat me either because it tires me out. Mother loves it and I do it for her, but I won't let her return it to me.'

'Then what do you do when you feel like sex?'

'I do the same as any other young girl. I finger myself,' said Charlotte with a sad smile.

I was dumbfounded. I asked her to repeat what she'd said.

'What? You're no longer a virgin, you make love in every

possible way, everyday you have both men and women, and... and you finger yourself? I can understand a kid like Ricette, but you're over twenty years old!'

'You're nothing but an overgrown kid yourself,' she said. 'Don't you know that almost all whores do it?'

'Charlotte, you shouldn't treat yourself like a whore.'

'Excuse me,' she said drolly. 'Didn't you know that all virgins do it?'

I scarcely smiled. I was annoyed. Charlotte paid no attention and continued:

'I don't ever try to hide anything. I don't care who I'm in front of, I finger myself whenever I feel like it.'

'Do you feel like it often?'

'Certainly... I don't like to get excited. It tires me out. This morning I didn't do it before getting up, but the water in my bidet was hot, my snatch began to expand... I fingered myself.'

'Sitting on your bidet?'

'It was hardly worth going back to bed for. Then later, after lunch, because... But you'll laugh at me.'

'Tell me everything.'

'Lili stuck a cookie into my crotch and I had to finger myself on it before she would eat it.'

'Because you're a good girl, I suppose?'

'Oh, I do everything I'm asked to. Then after dinner they were talking about you, and since I haven't slept with a young man for eight days, I began to think of certain things... and because of that... because I felt like...'

Without finishing her sentence, she slid a finger between her legs and, giving me her lips, began slowly and peacefully to masturbate.

'Oh no you don't!' I cried. 'Not in my bed! When I'm lucky enough to have as beautiful a girl as you in my bed, you don't think that I don't want to play with her myself, do you?'

'And don't you understand that you *will* be doing the playing if you have your prick in my behind and your mouth on my mouth while I finger myself?'

'I'll be damned,' I said loudly, 'I can't buttfuck all four of you!'

There was so much ill-humour in my voice that poor Charlotte began to cry.

'There go my chances,' she said through the tears. 'Everyone always says that I'm so nice, but it's always me nevertheless that gets trapped into these things. You've been charming for my mother and sisters, but when I come to stay all night I have a scene on my hands right from the start.'

She cried simply, without a single sob, and only seemed all the more pitiful to me for it. I took her in my arms and stammered, 'Charlotte, don't cry any more. I beg you!'

'And naturally now you're losing your hard-on,' she said with an absolute desolation that made me smile despite myself.

'Charlotte, my love!'

'I'm not your love, because you're losing your hard-on. You got erections for mama, for Ricette, for Lili, but for me... *that!*'

The tears flooded on, and I was despaired. I was wondering how and if I should ever stop that unreasonable tide of sadness when Charlotte did it herself and, with the logic and clarity that is the property of simple souls, said in her slow, musical voice:

'I told you that you could do whatever you wished. You can play in my pussy if you want, in my ass, in my mouth, between my breasts, under my arms, in my hair, on my face, in my nose if that will amuse you. I can't do any better than that, can I? Could I be any kinder to you?'

'Charlotte, my Charlotte...'

'But my dear, you asked me what my greatest pleasure would be and I told you that it would be to finger myself while you buttfuck me. All four of us are like that; it's in our blood and I can't help myself. And we're not the only ones, God knows. When I was a kid, the things I saw... School girls and shop girls who have told me in strictest confidence, "I like being buttfucked too."'

'But...'

'But do what you want to me if it's your pleasure you're after. Only if it's mine, buttfuck me and let me beat myself off in my own way. Understand?'

Pierre Louÿs

Our mouths met again passionately, and the first effect of our reconciliation was to put me once more in a state worthy of her. I gave in to her wishes, but she never said a word to me en route. Then after reminding me that she didn't like to have her cunt eaten, she turned to sixty-nine me for a few minutes first.

Charlotte had one of the prettiest cunts I have ever seen, possibly because it was so seldom used... But no, because her other hole, the one that was so much more exercised, was absolutely faultless also, like Teresa's.

Soft and calm as she was, Charlotte had a really moist cunt. She was one of those girls who could say, 'I flow for you,' like others say, 'I'm on fire.' Her pubic hair was long and well planted, not so long as her mother's, but more lustrous, And, like Teresa's, it crossed and tangled at the top of her thighs and filled her ass.

After everything that she had just told me, I didn't want to leave Charlotte in any doubt as to my intentions. I opened her buttocks with my hands and touched the spot she offered me with my finger. I remember doing that once to a girl who immediately began crying, 'Oh! Your cock! Your cock! Your cock!' Charlotte, however, emitted a considerable flow but scarcely shuddered and didn't cry at all. She was much more accustomed to giving caresses than to receiving them, and by a mistake that was easily explained considering her profession, took my touch for a signal and, since she had only been licking my testicles, immediately gave me her tongue lower yet.

But there was nothing nasty about Charlotte.

Most men are so ignorant of the psychology of the adolescent female that they would find it impossible to understand how a girl could admit her taste for fingering herself while being buttfucked without, at the same time, having the least sense of the vice of it. You women will understand what I am trying to say much better, and that's a good deal of consolation, for this book will obviously be more read by free women than by husbands.

Charlotte, therefore, had absolutely no sense of vice whatsoever, happily for both herself and me. But she was certainly sensitive. And without either cries or sighs or little flutterings of her ass, her fountains flowed so abundantly that Lili (there was one with a real sense of vice) had been able to dip three cookies into the foaming stream. It overflowed her vulva and passed through the forest of hairs... I got out of the way just in time. I was a little consoled by what I saw for not having been able to take her through this flooded passage.

When we were again side by side, face to face, a new incident stopped us momentarily. Charlotte would neither propose nor suggest a position. She had neither taste, nor caprice, inventiveness, nor the imagination for the task. To decide or imagine was tiring for her.

'As long as you buttfuck me and I finger myself, I don't care,' she said.

'Then put your head over the edge of the bed onto the floor and leave your ass up here,' I replied.

'If you wish,' she said simply.

When she suddenly saw that I wasn't really serious, she took my face between her hands and said with a smile, but without bitterness, 'You like to make fun of me, don't you? All right. Do it all night if you want, and any time we sleep together. That's the simplest of all games. I believe anything anyone tells me, and nothing makes me mad.'

'You're completely disarming,' I told her.

'I'm the one who's disarmed,' she said, 'because I know that I'm nothing more than an animal.'

♦

What an unfortunate, tragic word! I will never forget the tone of Charlotte's voice when she said that word to me. And women are crazy to think that they can seduce us through the art of beautifying themselves. Charlotte, in all of her simplicity, missed taking my heart completely only by the margin of that avowal she made.

She lay nude before me, her head on the pillow, her hands crossed on her stomach where the hair began, and it seemed to me that I was really seeing her for the first time. I saw that her beauty, like her character, was absolutely true and unpretentious. She wore neither rouge nor paint, nothing on her eyelids nor on her eyebrows, and I found her so simple, so beautiful, and so good that I took her by the elbows and hips and said, 'Yes, you're nothing but a poor animal, Charlotte, if you don't believe what I am now going to tell you. Listen, Charlotte, to every word. You're lovely from head to foot. There isn't an expression on your face, a hair on your stomach, a nail on your toes that isn't pretty. And you're as good as you are beautiful. I know you now and it's up to me to say this: do what you will on my bed. There is only one thing I forbid you to do and that is to injure the woman I love and against whom I am now pressing my rod. If you ever again treat her like a whore or an idiot...'

'No,' she said gaily. 'I'm going to make a little love to her. I'm going to finger her because I know that she wants it now. And I'll open her buttocks for you myself so that you can buttfuck her.'

'Show me how.'

She was lying next to me and she turned over without the least intention of proposing a position. Nevertheless, I quickly followed her example.

All of this was done with an extraordinary facility that I was able to confirm many other times. Charlotte's anus resembled one of those rigid, but perfectly adjusted scabbards where the blade literally enters by itself. To put it crudely but clearly, as soon as I pressed my cock between Charlotte's buttocks I entered. And this despite the fact that her entry was as firm as it was supple. I might also add that through a series of qualities that it would be indecent to go into too much detail over, it was much easier to get into her than get out.

Charlotte buttfucked was even more Charlotte than before: softer, sweeter, moister, more tenderly abandoned. I had turned over, almost to the point where she was lying on her back on me in order to allow her to open her thighs as far as she could spread them. I placed my hand in front of her and found a lake. Thinking that she had not yet started to finger herself, I began to wonder what sort of phenomenon I would witness when she got going in earnest.

Her moans began at the first moment she put her fingers

into her hole and lasted eight or ten minutes without crescendo, without effect. It didn't seem necessary to her to either hide her pleasure or to cry it out like an actress. She rubbed herself so slowly that her hand seemed scarcely to move, and I, knowing that she preferred a calm voluptuousness to a violent one, contented myself with slow imperceptible movements in her warm entrails. Towards the end, with a sudden odd scruple that was entirely typical of her, she turned a languid eye towards me and asked feebly, 'Do you want me to talk to you? You see how happy I am when you buttfuck me? Do you want me to tell you each time how it feels to have your prick in my asshole?'

'No. Only tell me when...'

'When I come?'

'Yes.'

'When you want me to. As many times as you want. I did it once when I was kissing you before and I'm ready to do it again now.'

'Soon?'

'Yes, of course. Haven't you noticed that I've been rubbing myself around instead of in? When you tell me to do it, I'll do it.'

There are some things you just don't signal like that. I told her that I would wait for her to come again, and when she did, sure enough, I came just a few seconds after. It probably increased her pleasure because women take longer to finish their orgasms than we do.

♦

In the moments that followed, we did not separate. Charlotte remained in my arms looking at me with that expression of gratitude that all lovers know.

'I love your breasts,' I said, caressing them.

I hadn't said anything else and was hoping to find something a little better when she interrupted me with an exclamation of surprise.

'Oh! You're very kind! – You love my breasts *now*, my dear? You've just finished coming and you love my breasts?

You've just buttfucked poor Charlotte and you're not disgusted with her?'

'Disgusted? You're crazy.'

'If you knew what the life a whore leads is like...'

'Now listen, I thought I forbade you to talk about yourself like that.'

'Then what am I if I've lived the last twelve years with four or five men taking me through the behind every day and any idiot that comes along rubbing his asshole against my mouth? If I tell you that almost every whore who exists fingers herself, then there must be a good reason. When you're working you have to do it, otherwise you'd never get anything out of it; otherwise the girls would hardly ever do it. In any case, you always know one thing: as soon as you've finished pleasing the man, you're back to being nothing for him but a wretched, dirty whore and the daughter of a wretched dirty whore.'

'My "poor Charlotte", as you call yourself, I assure you that...'

'I'm just not used to people making compliments about my teats when they've just buttfucked me, that's all.'

She had tears in her eyes again. I didn't know what to say. Did I love her enough to make her love me?

In order to give myself a little time to order my thoughts and reflect on what was in my bed and in my mind, I asked her one or two questions which she answered by telling me a whole story: that of her life.

Chapter Five

Charlotte lay on the bed leaning on her elbows, her breasts hanging into the hands I had cupped to receive them. She began her story in her customarily soft voice.

'As far back as I can remember I've been seeing my mother buttfucked. She was like me; she did everything. From time to time she would bring home a man who would rather be sucked, or occasionally she would come back with a lesbian, and, since even in those days she had more chest than I have now, every Sunday she had a friend that came and made love to her between her breasts. That always amused me because he shot his wad into her face. And once in a while, on a few rare occasions, my mother even did a little fucking, but that was exceptional! Mother was renowned for taking it through the ass. You buttfucked her and that was all there was to it.

'In that way, Mama is like me, she never played any other way. Ricette is like that too and Lili will be. Only, believe me, there are days when a young whore can be buttfucked by seven or eight men without ever finding one that can excite her. And even if she does find one, there's usually no reason for wetting her nightdress or getting bags under her eyes for him.

'When I was a baby, my mother beat herself off every day on the bed, and not just once, but twice at least and always in the same way; it was always when a man had just left and she was lying completely nude on the bed. She would go to a dresser drawer and take out a candle she'd melted a little bit on the end, or a roller she'd warmed up in the oven, or, later on, a dildo that she'd bought to screw lesbians with, and she would jam that into her rear. I never once saw her beating herself off without

Pierre Louÿs

something in her behind. Then she would lie down in the middle of the bed and with her finger... But what more need I say. That's how whores manage to come afterwards.

'Mama always told me that when I was really small she made me suck her come at the same time as her milk. The only thing I can remember is that all through my childhood I used to watch her beat herself off and then afterwards I would go and lick her cunt. And the more come there was, the happier I used to be. She also told me that I was five years old the first time I sucked her well enough to make her come. I can't remember that time, but I know I was very small.

'But you shouldn't accuse my mother of always forcing me to do that sort of thing. I'm over twenty years old now, I'm free, and I still do it to her everyday. I still get as much pleasure from it as ever. I quite enjoy sucking her.

'Naturally, I was also very small the first time she made me taste the come of a man. It seems now that I've always drunk it. I used to lick her when she had it in her hairs, or elsewhere, and I remember an old man who beat himself off in my mouth, but that was a long time ago and I already knew how to suck a dick anyway. It was the first thing I learned. I remember I had a little friend on the same street who was like Ricette. She couldn't suck a cock without spitting out the come. I was very proud because that never happened to me. When I was five or six years old they gave me men who hadn't relieved themselves for fifteen days. I used to swim in it. I let my mouth get too full and I swallowed all the wrong way, but I always liked it.

'When I was eight I lost my virginity in the rear. Mother has always said that I was too old, that it should have happened much sooner. But to prepare me for the occasion she fingered me in the ass for a good week before, and then we had two amusing little ceremonies. The first was in front of a little circle of lesbians who had made a special dildo for my mother to buttfuck me with. They were crazy to see a mother break the cherry in her daughter's rear and when she had finished they were in such a state that they all started buttfucking each other with huge black dildos. I'll never forget that scene as long as I live! There was one young girl there who had never been buttfucked by either a man or a woman. She was horribly wounded by their huge instruments and there was blood everywhere. The poor thing's behind was nearly torn out. Oh, I can assure you that you see some terrible things when your trade is a whore's. Even when I was only eight I'd lost my *naïveté*.

'Several days later the second ceremony took place. I was again presented as a virgin before another audience and they had a little boy my age to buttfuck me. The poor thing worked with all his might to get a big hard-on. Thus my mother graduated my experiences so that I got used to larger and larger pricks without too much trouble and with never an accident. Never in all my life have I ever bled from behind. I have an asshole made for buttfucking.

'And another thing... It's really elemental. Every young girl wants to do the same things as her mother. The little daughters of actresses are wild with joy when they get a part at the age of eight. And the daughters of whores... when they first take a man they think... My dear, I don't really know how to speak well, but I wouldn't want you to think badly of mother because she sold me. You see me like I am. I don't roll around all over you like a monster, and I'm really not vicious, but I can assure you that when I was eight I was the happiest of little girls because I could be like my mother. And the times when she called me into her room and I saw her lying on a bed with a nude man, when I saw that all I had to do to give him a hard-on was to raise my little skirts, I was really happy. I was proud! I would let them stick it into me from my hole to my mouth. You know, a prick is the nicest present you can give a little girl.'

She sighed, turning her eyes away, and saw something she had completely forgotten.

'Oh,' she said. 'You've got a hard-on!'

'But you're more than twenty years old, my little girl.'

'And do you think that that makes me less happy to have made you hard?' she said, throwing herself around my neck. 'Why don't you say something? Do you want me to suck you?'

'Yes and no.'

'What do you mean? Lili told us at dinner what she did with you. If you want me to, I'll do the same thing. I'll be overjoyed, in fact, and I hope that you'll like it too.'

She said it so kindly and I had so little imagination myself at that time (what can you do with a girl who doesn't like to fuck?) that I let her do whatever she wanted.

She climbed down into exactly the same position as the first time. If I ever write a novel I'm going to make sure that I vary the positions that the people take in it, but I'm writing this exactly as it happened and there is nothing to be done.

In the same sort of situation (and that is certainly rare enough) women ordinarily can't help becoming passionate no matter what their natural nature. And Charlotte was no exception. She was more ardent and above all more loquacious even than before. She talked unceasingly with a soft, obscene tenderness that it would be impossible for me to try to copy here.

Since she was lying with her back against me, I embraced her and said, 'Your buttocks are as pretty as your breasts.'

And that simple little sentence was worth a fleet of words.

'My buttocks? They should be rosy! They certainly want you to stick your cock between them! But don't move! Don't move! We have plenty of time. Let me caress your cock with them since you like them so much... You know, you're very kind to have said that. I think I like my buttocks better than any other part of my poor body.'

'But you're beautiful, Charlotte!'

'No. No. I'm just like the others, only... when I see other good-looking girls, and when I finger myself in front of the mirror, I think... I like to think... that I have beautiful buttocks. But when you asked me first of all for my pussy I thought that maybe you didn't like my ass.'

'But why shouldn't I like it?'

'Because I've got as much hair there as in front. I even have a fine black down that covers half of each buttock,' she said laughing. 'But you like it and so everything is all right. And you're getting a hard-on! You're getting a wonderful hard-on, you angel...'

'If you can really say that an angel can get...'

'I have a crazy desire to beat myself off when I feel your cock under my ass like that. But a desire! A real desire! I've already come four or five times today, but that isn't anything. I don't even count any more. The more I beat myself off the better I feel, and when I'm hot, like now, when my snatch is throbbing and my ass is twitching...'

'Yes, I know you now,' I interrupted. 'Because if I say to you, "Charlotte, don't get your snatch or your asshole all excited now. I want to go to sleep," you will say, "If you wish."'

'Oh, if you wish,' she said unhappily.

'And if I say the opposite: something like, "Charlotte, it's only twenty minutes after twelve, I've come four times already today, once I went eight and I want to beat my record with you. I have every vice, every passion, and all the strangest manias; but we only need to go five more times and you can leave?"'

'Oh! That! Well, as much as you want!' she said with her calm smile. 'Do you want to try? I'm not sleepy.'

All the time I was talking – I've already told you how easy it is to slip into Charlotte's ass – we were united in the position she liked best, and she used all her ability to what, in the last resort, I found very agreeable.

A long deep kiss cut off our conversation, but then, looking at me from over her shoulder with a long smile that, despite the exact similarity of our ages, I can only call maternal, she said in a voice full of the sadness, patience, and tenderness with which a professional is permitted to treat an apprentice:

'You have every vice, my dear? You're the victim of strange manias? Tell me all about it! You know that you can ask me anything you wish. Why don't you say something? Are you ashamed? Do I have to be the one who...'

I hadn't said anything because my only vice was fucking and I saw no hope of making her understand.

Charlotte, who was the best girl in the world, misunderstood my silence. With her eyes fastened on mine and an expression on her face that seemed to pardon in advance my most infamous and tyrannical vices, she said easily and without lowering her voice, 'Shit in my mouth.'

Even today, I can't understand how I managed to keep myself from leaping up from the bed at those words. I suppose the beginning of our conversation had pretty well prepared me for

Pierre Louÿs

anything, even that. And besides, the poor girl was so pretty, so kind... She had said that to me simply by chance, one of the most natural things in the world... And despite my stupefaction she insisted.

'Oh, don't think that just because I said that that I'm begging you to. Don't think that I like to do it like Lili does...'

'Lili likes *that?*'

'Certainly! Lili! What doesn't she like! For me, I only like one thing, that's...'

'Well then?'

'But I'm used to everything. Don't get angry. Later on in the night shit in my mouth. You'll get another hard-on.'

'Charlotte!'

'And besides, I don't know what's come over me. Your cock sets me on fire. I want your shit as well as your come.'

She said these last words in such a strange way that it no longer seemed like Charlotte talking. So soft before, she had suddenly become hard and crude. With her head beneath a pillow, she suddenly came without warning me, spreading her legs so wide that they reached each side of the bed.

The silence hardly lasted a minute; she remembered more quickly than I what we had been talking about. She removed her now red face from beneath the pillow and said, 'In the meantime, it's your come that I want in my mouth.'

Already bewildered by what I had just heard, it didn't occur to me to be surprised that Charlotte would suck the cock that just came out of her ass without first washing it. I was becoming used to everything and if I did jump that time it was for another reason.

'Oh, no! You're not going to suck me like that!'

'What's wrong? You afraid I'll catch something?'

'You don't like people to eat you because it tires you out, and then that's how you suck your friends? Do you want to kill me?'

'Oh! I hate to think what you'd say if my mother sucked you! But how do you want me to do it?'

'Open your teeth, close your lips, don't use your tongue, and I'll guide you.'

Saying that, I entwined one of my hands into her hair, and, with all her natural docility, she moved as I pushed her and remained still when I told her to.

When she was again lying next to me, more beautiful than ever (for a young woman who has just offered her mouth takes on a certain radiance that she gets no other way), I said to her, 'My pretty Charlotte, tell me again a little about yourself.'

'I'm a poor whore who is very happy tonight.'

'Then why do you suck like a young society girl?'

'Are you saying that because I drank it?' she said laughing. 'You be quiet. I'm happier to have drunk your come than you are to have been sucked.'

'Again the girlish expressions. You not only suck, you speak like a young girl ready to marry.'

'That's because I've eaten so many women,' she said with a sigh, 'I've wet myself with the come of so many virgins that I've begun to look like one myself.'

'Then what you've just said is awfully funny. You claim that you're a slut and a whore, but you certainly don't look like it.'

'Ha!'

And she continued her story.

♦

'So at the age of eight, I was a whore with mama, who was twenty- four. Ricette had just been given out to a nurse and was later sent to a boarding school, so we were alone, mother and I.

'She didn't try to tire me out, only kept me exercised just enough to stay in form: usually about an average of one customer a day. If I did it more often we said that I was "going out". If I went two or three days without one, she buttfucked me herself with the dildo so that I shouldn't tighten up. I practically never ate her. She used to say, "you're kind to want to, my child, but I'd rather finger myself." I licked her, of course, but only when she'd just finished coming and that was all.

'In those days I had only four costumes that I wore according to the occasion. First there was a little girl's dress, a very elegant thing with a great silken belt. Then a little dressing gown with insertions like those that the whores wear. Then I had a black, schoolgirl's apron. I plaited my hair when I wore that. Finally there was a little boy's costume that I wore with a wig. Those costumes amused me more than the screwing.

'Mother never left me alone with a man. Every time that someone buttfucked me she was there to hold my buttocks and to put the cock into my hole herself so that no one would hurt me. And I really took some pricks in those days! It's funny, but the men with the biggest rods seem to be the ones that like to buttfuck little girls. But even so, thanks to mama, I never bled once.

'At the same time, I learned to help my mother. When someone was buttfucking her I would lick his balls or, what Lili does now... It's a little hard to explain... I put my whole hand into my mother's cunt and took the cock that was in her ass by grabbing the skin that separates the cunt and the asshole. Do you see what I mean? That way I could beat off both mother and the man at the same time. Lili will do it for you tomorrow if you want.

'I had lived this sort of life for about a year when I had the strangest experience of my entire life. And I've had some strange ones, believe me! When I tell you about it you'll see what I mean. But you probably won't believe me unless I swear that...'

Charlotte raised her arm.

'I swear to you on my mother's head that what I'm going to tell you is true.

'I was nine years old, and it was in July. We had dinner with a man whose name I know well even now, and at four o'clock in the morning we all three went to bed together naked. Mama was drunk, even though it very rarely happens to her, and I remember that when we got into bed she said, "Give me your tongue. I'm too plastered to beat myself off." While I was doing this the man was buttfucking me (he was probably as drunk himself as my mother) and he said to me before coming, "Give your mother a child with your ass. Shit my come into her cunt."

'Of course I would never have done such a thing myself, but mama had drunk too much champagne, she was in heat, and she was ready to come at any second. The combination was too much; she wasn't responsible for herself at that moment and you can guess what she said: "Yes"!

'She put her behind up on one of the pillows with her cunt spread wide. You can believe how full my little ass was with come. So I squatted, did what she told me, and since she didn't really think that she could become pregnant like that she didn't go to the bidet until two hours later.

'Well, she was supposed to have her period about two days later and it didn't come. She became pregnant – and pregnant from our little affair all right, because she hadn't fucked for six weeks. And do you know who was born from that little episode? Lili.'

'Does she know it?'

'I'll say she does! There's a kid that I carried in my behind before my mother carried her in her stomach. Today there are plenty of sons who screw their mothers and give them children that are both their sisters and daughters at the same time. But they've pissed them from the end of their cocks like their fathers did before them. Whereas I, Charlotte, I who don't know how to do anything, even after twelve years of experience, who can only do well what I'm told because I have neither a sou's worth of vice nor a centime's worth of imagination, who couldn't even suck you properly because I don't know how to measure the progress I'm making on a man's dick, I, the poor Charlotte who makes all kinds of mistakes and is now telling you her life story, I gave my mother a daughter when I was only nine years old, and with my ass! Do you ever think such a thing will happen to me again? And I swear to you on my mother's head that it's true!'

♦

After a short silence, she took up her story again.

'My mother's size in the nine months after that didn't hinder her a bit. In fact, it allowed her to fuck all she wanted without even keeping her from being buttfucked as she was used to.

'Above all, during the last two months she had a steady stream of regular customers. I guess certain men will always be attracted by the abnormal. Her stomach had grown enormous and was a tremendous contrast with my tiny body. This enabled a man to come and take his choice between buttfucking a little girl without a hair on her body or, in the same bed, her mother who had a tremendous number and was nine months pregnant to boot. I never thought there were so many men avid to screw a woman as large as that.

'Finally Lili showed up. My mother was out of her bed as soon as possible and we once again took up our work.

'I was ten years old then, and at that age there are certain things that little girls adapt themselves to much more easily than women. Small girls are all a little dirty, and they keep their little rendezvous with each other like a bunch of puppies. They would rather piss on each other's stomachs and stick their fingers in each other's asses then suck them. You know all that as well as I do.

'Thinking that it would come in handy later on, mama had me play with a little girlfriend of mine that taught me a whole stack of filthy practices. It's kind of funny when I think about it; I had been a whore since I was two years old and that kid, I swear, invented a series of grubby games that I had never seen a man even think of. She wised me up as to the possibilities between two women, and the things I learned with her I later practised with lesbians.

'It bothers me to tell you all this, but yet it doesn't bother me any more to do the things I've described. You don't know what it's like to be a whore. I was ten years old when mama had a banker sleeping with us who... Can you guess what? Who liked to buttfuck mama right up to the root and then withdraw his prick and put it in my mouth to be sucked. And the dirtier it was the more enjoyment he got from it.

'I'm used to that sort of thing, though. And then I did the same things that I did with mama to another woman, and... But a child gets used to these things so quickly... The other woman was a very pretty prostitute named Lucette whom I used to like and who slept with us all the time. She never used to go with men except through the behind like the rest of us. And when mother saw that I liked her, the two of them got together and told me that at my age it was time I was learning to eat shit, that it wasn't hard, and that Lucette would teach me how.

'Oh! I can see what you're thinking... that it was easier for Lucette than for me... But that isn't true. Think about it a minute and you'll see what I mean. I know you now. Suppose you have a poor little girl about ten years old who has never done that. Do you think that you'd have the courage? I think that Lucette was very kind with me. And she pitied me, the poor thing. I remember that each time she did it she kissed me on the mouth afterwards so as not to seem to be trying to humiliate me. Poor Lucette!

'What do you want? I do everything that I'm told. I learned that like I learned the rest. Besides, you don't need to think that I had to do it every day. Actually, it's a very useful thing to know, because you always have to do things that resemble it very much. A man that takes two whores, that buttfucks the first and makes her shit the come into the other's mouth – that sort of thing happens all the time... The other evening at dinner Lili was laughing because you were shocked when she put your prick into her mouth just after it had been in her ass. That's nothing! You see some really bad things when you're a whore, let me tell you!'

She uttered a deep sigh, not thinking of her past, as one might have thought, but because of her lack of eloquence. On her knees in the middle of the bed, sitting on her heels and holding her hands in the hair between her thighs, she said in a despairing voice:

'I don't know how to explain myself. I'm as dumb as a dodo.'

'Again!'

'And also... I don't think you know what a whore is.'

'What don't I know? Tell me. Take your time, get your ideas ordered before you speak.'

'You think that things like that disgust us. No. It's the men rather than the acts.'

'See? You can explain yourself very well.'

'You, for example, I don't have any crush on you, at least I don't think I have. We'll have to see tomorrow. But at least I'm content in your bed. I'm not making a declaration, it's just that, well... put it this way: shit in my mouth if you want. I'd rather you did that ten times than have to suck the prick of some men I can think of. Do you know what happened to Ricette?'

'To Ricette?'

'Didn't she tell you? There's a kid that got out of a boarding school when she was thirteen and a half. She left there with all her virginity and she didn't know nothing from nothing. Oh, she could finger herself and eat another girl out, but that's all she'd learned. Mama fixed it to have her buttfucked right away and after that we thought that she was going to beat us all. Eight days afterwards she could take it better than I. She could stick her feet into the air in a hundred and thirty-two positions, did nutcrackers better than mama even, and without a drop of vaseline – without anything in her ass except a little saliva on the end of her finger. Then, of course, they tried her on sucking. But unfortunately the first man that she had in her mouth was an old one who hadn't had a piece in three months. You don't know what that means. You have to be a whore to know. The poor kid threw up everything she had in her stomach and, since that day, we've never been able to teach her how to suck. Every time a man comes in her mouth she pukes! It's too bad. She's such a pretty little thing and so warm, so gay, fingering herself everywhere, a girl who only thinks about cocks all day long and who takes it in the ass much better than I.'

'No.'

'Why do you say no? You know it very well.'

'I'm going to reply as simply and frankly as you've spoken. I say no because after being here half an hour you've done everything you could and more to completely disgust me and yet I'm not disgusted. You have nothing but eulogies for everyone but yourself and nothing but injury for your own head. You excuse and adore the mother that prostituted you. And after twelve years of work and sadness you still place yourself under a little sister who is just starting and who refuses everything that you accept. You even retain a tender memory of your "poor Lucette" who was so "kind" to you...'

'Shut up!' she cried, tears streaming down her face.

'But if I believed *you* I'd think you a beast, a bitch, a whore-arch-whore, an unspeakably filthy girl not even fit to be kissed on the lips because...'

'No! I'm *not* fit to be kissed on the lips!' she wailed, hiding her face and crying even harder.

'And everything that I've seen as proof of all this points in the opposite direction. First of all you're one of the prettiest girls I could ever hope to hold and becoming nicer the more I know you. Secondly, you are a woman who, from the time you were eight years old, has always made love for the pleasure of others only, who has sacrificed everything to the interest of her mother and the caprices of men, and who offers herself completely every night, with all her heart, even to me whom she doesn't love.'

'To you whom I don't love?' she said. 'Whom I don't love?'

And with her arms around my neck and crying on my shoulder, she sobbed out, 'You see! I'm nothing but a beast after all! You haven't understood anything I've been trying to say!'

Chapter Six

When she once again took up her narrative after a long interval, she said:

'And now I'll tell you whatever you want to know, just as if I were confessing. If you want to know names, I'll give you names. If you want frank language you can have that too. If I forget a detail, ask me and you can have it.'

'What are we going to call this history of yours?'

'The story of all the hairs in my ass!' said she, laughing.

'We'll never get finished. There's enough material there to fill a hundred volumes.'

'This will only be a condensation for use in elementary schools!' she cried, laughing even more.

Charlotte had changed completely. She was gay now and it showed all over her face. If I had been her most intimate girlfriend, she couldn't have told me the story of her life with more frankness and abandon.

'While we're on the subject of elementary education, I began mine at the age of ten. Ricette is the only one of us who was properly educated in a girl's boarding school with a bunch of young society girls who say their prayers every night before going to their room and beating off.

'I went to the public school in my quarter and was one of those who conducted themselves with the most propriety. You can guess why. On leaving the school, there were those who played ball in the fields nearby or engaged in their little bitcheries with the daughter of the man who ran the creamery, a girl who liked to show her hairs to those who were willing to run their tongues around her asshole. And of course there were the others who played with any boys who would let them jerk off their pricks.

'You can easily realize why I wasn't curious about the pricks and the hairs. And besides, mama was always waiting for me. Classes ended at four o'clock and there were days when I was being buttfucked at a quarter after. I barely had time to get back.

'The next year I made a first communion the like of which there are certainly very few. A friend of mine who mounted me an average of three times a week amused himself by making me learn a catechism of his own composition which I had to recite. There were sixteen pages of it and nothing but filth on any of them. The morning of the ceremony he came at seven o'clock and wanted me to suck him so that I should have some come in my stomach... Mother said that under those conditions it was hardly worth bothering to have a first communion, but he had given a hundred francs and... And that was only the beginning. What a day! I can really look back and call that day my first one as a real whore. All my lovers came and wanted to take me under my communion dress, and they all wanted to buttfuck me! There were twelve of them. Can you imagine that? We didn't eat until nine in the evening on that day, and I was buttfucked five times! Five times! And I sucked four men! I don't know how the other three came, but my pretty white dress was as full of come as if it had been dipped in it. I'll never forget that first communion!'

Charlotte shook her head with a smile that seemed somehow consoled. Her sadness had completely gone, and she narrated her story vivaciously. She ruined the effect several times in trying to prepare it, like all young girls who are inexperienced at telling tales, but her errors only served to underline the ingenuousness of the rest of her story.

'I know you're not expecting what I'm going to tell you now, but really I've seen everything in my life. A year after that first communion five dirty little urchins made fun of me because I was still a virgin!'

I've got to admit that at this point in Charlotte's narrative if I was expecting a *coup de théâtre* she hadn't come up with it.

'I promised you,' she said, 'the story of all the hairs in my

Pierre Louÿs

ass, and we've only begun. I was twelve years old and I'd been a whore for four of them when my pubic hair first began to sprout. But they didn't take long once they got started. By the end of six months I was as hairy as a woman of thirty.

'You're beginning to know me now. I never was one of those passionate girls who take you by the hand and say, "I'm burning up inside..." No. I don't burn, but I overflow often and for no reason at all. And when my cunt is flowing I want to finger myself. And when I want to finger myself, I do it.'

She turned over laughing. Her good humour had transformed her completely.

'So it was when I was twelve that I learned how to beat myself off and began to do it as much as I pissed. And now I can't even say that truthfully because, today for example, I haven't pissed as often as I've come.

'Mama always advised me to finger myself when there was someone buttfucking me, obviously, but she was also happy to see that I would do it alone in front of her too. And since I was very clumsy at first, she had the patience to teach me herself, first doing it with her own finger and then taking mine in her hand to help me. God, how stupid I was! When I think that my mother had to take my hand in here to teach me how to finger myself!

'At that time I was still going to school and we were living in a part of Marseilles where there were hardly any whores and even fewer virgins. I think that all the girls at school fucked more or less often: some with their brothers, others with their fathers, their cousins, their neighbours... I knew one little wretch who used to brag that she would give herself at least six good ones every evening against a paling at a construction site near her home. There was another one I knew named Clara who was as skinny as a little skeleton. You could even see the bones in her buttocks, and she didn't have a hair on her body. Once, in front of me, she sobbed to a woman of forty that she had to sleep every night between her two brothers and that they did it to her both at once, one from the front and the other from behind, they were so hard up. And the woman replied, "Ah! How I'd like to take your place!" I've got some real memories of my childhood.

'One time I was in a corner of the schoolyard with five of

my girlfriends and each was telling how she beat herself off. When I said (without mentioning mama) that I stuck a candle in my rear while I rubbed at my snatch they thought it was terrific and invited me to come with them into a little garden at the home of one of them, a girl named Regine. There we were going to show each other everything and amuse ourselves like little queens. That was a day when mama had to go out in the evening, so I followed my little friends and then...

'Ah! The things that happened to me that day! But first I have to tell you that I had one of those virgin cunts that you hardly ever see; a mere pencil mark on my body. The other five lifted their skirts first: none of them were virgins; the three youngest had no hair whatsoever, and the other two had only a little light down. When they lifted my skirt and saw my virgin slit surrounded by a great tuft of black hair they screamed with laughter. They'd never seen such a thing. Then, you know, the little beasts made a ring around me and danced around repeating their same filthy little joke over and over: "Look at the bearded virgin, the bearded virgin, the bearded virgin! Look at the bearded virgin, the bearded virgin, the bearded virgin!"

'I was crying with rage when I told mama about it that evening; and very few things have ever been more important to me in my life, for mama decided that my girlfriends had been right about two things.

'First of all, she said that I had too much pubic hair for my age. And you'll never be able to guess what mama did for me! Do you know, she found the time and patience to shave me herself for three years after that! And it wasn't easy to do, because I had hair everywhere, under my arms, on my stomach, in my pussy, on my thighs, and even between my buttocks. When I was fifteen I still had a shaved cunt like a harem girl, and everyone liked it like that, from lesbians to men. I don't know why they've never done that to Ricette.

'Next, when mama saw how ashamed I was to still be a virgin, and that all my friends made fun of me because of it, she promised to find someone to break it, knowing very well that I'd never do it myself.

'But first... Have you ever broken a girl's cherry?'

Pierre Louÿs

'Yes and it isn't funny. You're a very good girl not to have yours now, especially since it was only a pencil mark.'

'Good! Then suppose that someone said to you: "Here's a kid named Charlotte. She's twelve years old; you can buttfuck her in any position you want; you can come in her mouth; she'll lick your stomach, suck your balls, kiss your ass, and do anything you want. She will eat out her mother in front of you or buttfuck herself with a dildo, etc., etc. And all that will cost you only twenty francs. But if you want to take her virginity it'll cost you ten thousand." What would you say?'

'I'd say it was one hell of a lousy joke.'

'Then it wouldn't surprise you if I had to wait a long time before I lost my virginity and that Ricette still has hers.

'Besides, mother was really in no hurry. I had learned to take it from the rear and she was happy. And all the more since the older I got the better I liked it. What good would learning to fuck do me?

'But I was really happy when the time came for me to learn something new. Guess what. Look at me and if you like what I'm talking about you'll be able to guess... You can't guess? Then it's because you don't like it... Flagellation!'

'You're right. I don't like it at all. But why are you so good at that?'

'Because I cry like a fountain and that makes the people who like it happy.'

'My poor Charlotte!'

'For the twentieth time: you don't know what being a whore is like. Imagine this scene: here am I, age thirteen, dressed in a black schoolgirl's apron with pigtails down my back, on my knees next to the bed, my dress pulled up... I hold up my buttocks. My little ass, which will naturally be buttfucked at the end of the session, is in the air with the shaven cunt beneath it. And a man stands there whipping me with all his might, only getting a hard-on when I burst out sobbing. Of course, mama was always there to make sure they didn't kill me, but all the same... What a time! And it was always on those days that the things happened that I told you about earlier. The man who did those things to me used to bring his mistress with him, a great horse of

---

a woman who looked even more ferocious than he. He would buttfuck her on top of me then take his prick out of her ass and make me lick it so hard that I would always wind up crying. He liked that so much one time that he began to play with his cock in my mouth until he finally came, and then he blamed me for having made him discharge too soon, because he had also wanted to stick it into my whipped behind. He gave me such a slap in the face that, although my lips were shut tightly, the come squirted out of my mouth like the juice out of an orange.'

'Your mother permitted all this?'

'Now don't speak badly of mother. I've seen her whipped harder than me and it hurt me more than it did her.'

'That's typical of you. And was the gentleman happy?'

'Probably. I never cried so hard in my life as the night he gave my mother such a slash with the whip that she was bleeding from the lip of her cunt to the middle of her ass. I thought I was going to have a fit. After that, mama never tried that sort of thing again for almost two years!'

Charlotte sat dreaming for a second and then smiled vaguely.

'That was the year I was most successful with lesbians. There are girls who never come until they're eighteen or twenty years old, but I had started early and with mama's idea to shave me I was considered a prodigy.

'Take a lesbian who's lying on a bed sixty-nining with a little shaven virgin licking her and getting as much come (and what come) as a wet-nurse can give milk... you think she gets excited? I said, "And what come." You know that there are two kinds of lesbians, those who lick their maids' asses because there is more taste there than in those of their friends, and those at the other extreme who are always seeking the most delicate of sensations. For these latter, a virgin cunt without hair that flows like a gypsy is something they can't keep their tongue out of.

'I had a lot of lesbians when I was thirteen and, would you believe it, I suffered almost as much as when I was being beaten. A tongue down there irritates me. It's ten times more than I need to come. You saw how I beat myself off a few minutes ago – hardly even touching it? I can even do it without touching it at

Pierre Louÿs

all. Would you like me to do it for you?'

'How?'

'However you want. You can buttfuck me without me beating myself off and you'll make me come with your prick as if you were really fucking me.'

'Then why do you finger yourself?'

'Oh, it's still better that way. I can come when I want to.'

'Charlotte,' I said. 'You say the most horrible things.'

'I'm not surprised. I'm so stupid!' she said hiding her head.

And when I took her affectionately into my arms and she felt secure, she said with a laugh that changed her whole manner, 'If the "Story of the Hairs in My Ass" is going to be a hundred volumes, how many would it take for the "Story of my Stupidities"?'

'Why do you have this mania for self-injury?'

'Tell me what I said that was so awful..'

'You pretend that I don't know anything about your life as a whore? And I reply to you that you don't know anything about your life as a lover.'

The sentence was put so clearly that even Charlotte understood.

'A lover?' she said, throwing herself on me. 'Haven't you been listening to what I just told you? Who am I supposed to be in love with? The pig who buttfucked me three times a week and then made me swallow his come before my first communion? Or the cow who was fifty years old and a grandmother six times and who rubbed her ass across my face? Or the madman who shit on my body while my mother was sucking him? Or the maniac who forced me to watch him whip my mother's cunt, the cunt from which I was born, and who whipped it until it bled? I don't know what other way I can say it so that you'll finally understand. Whores, like virgins, have only one love that can really console them: their fingers.'

After a quick shudder, she got control of herself again.

'You've made me say more than I've even thought. I don't have the right to treat those people like pigs, cows, and madmen. They never raped me... But what I'd like you to understand... is that the more whore you are the more virgin you are also.'

This time I took her face in my hands and with my eyes close to hers said, 'That's the nicest thing you could say.'

Who would have thought it? And yet that sentence expressed Charlotte herself body and soul. She looked up at me out of her pretty eyes without in the least penetrating into my thoughts.

'Why do you compliment everything about me? My hair, my eyes, my breasts, my pubic hair... None of it is worth a hundred sous, my sweet. Go to any whorehouse and you'll find better. As for my buttocks, you made my night when you told me that you thought they were beautiful; obviously, they're the best thing about me. But don't mock me by admiring the words I speak...'

'The words that you speak come from the sentiments that you feel.'

'That's another point. Whores speak with their hearts like other young women speak with their cunts.'

The sentence had been spoken without any effect intended, as if it were the most obvious verity in the world. But I did not reply. I felt humiliated. Charlotte thought herself to be without any thought, any spirit, and yet every one of her replies had been more interesting than any of mine. I found (as my reader undoubtedly has) much more pleasure in listening than in interrupting, and I was awaiting the rest of her narration when she cried, stupefied:

'What? You getting a hard-on again?'

'It's your fault.'

'What have I done to cause that?'

'You've shown me your hair, your eyes, your breasts, which aren't worth a hundred sous, as you claim, and I should probably find much better in any whorehouse. Right?'

'Am I giving you this hard-on without even touching you?'

'I'm afraid so. I'm going to complain to your mother.'

'And what do you want us to...'

'I don't want anything.'

'You're joking now! But *that* makes *me* feel like doing something!'

Pierre Louÿs

'Be patient. Be like me. I'm in no hurry.'

'All right then, I'll do it myself. Let me alone.'

'No you don't, dearie. I forbid you to deliver yourself to the vices of onanism on my bed. Moralists and doctors are agreed that...'

'Shit on them. My cunt is getting wet and I feel like beating myself off, and when I...'

'And when you feel like beating yourself off you do it. I know it by heart. All right, but you're not going to beat yourself off until three in the morning.'

'With me next to a young man who has a hard-on between my legs that goes halfway up to my ass? You don't want that to excite me?'

'On the contrary, that's exactly what I want. It will liven up your story.'

♦

'Don't defy me,' she said. 'I'm always tired and lifeless because I play with myself as much as I want, whenever I want. You won't be able to recognize me if you make me wait. You'll have me spouting all kinds of idiotic filth that I'll regret. Are you vicious enough to do that to me?'

With one hand over her eyes and the other on my shoulder, she whispered and repeated:

'Oh, God yes! All kinds of filth! That's all I can say astride a prick like this with you holding me in your arms.

'And besides... Oh, fuck it! You know that I'm a whore, the lowest of the low, a whore that everyone can buttfuck, that will suck anybody's prick and even the prick of a dog; it's the same price.'

'Charlotte!'

'I don't give a fuck! You know that I've done everything with men and women and boys, and little girls; I've drunk the come of donkeys and horses; I've done everything! I've eaten the turds that whores have shit! You know that I've lived my whole life in come and shit.'

'You're crazy!'

'In come and shit!' she cried. 'Even with you. Your prick had just come out of my behind when I...'

'But you yourself...'

'And now I disgust you so that you get a hard-on against my ass and you still don't want me. Even when I'm getting myself wet from my cunt to my knees!'

'But...'

'Do I have to disgust you so that you won't even shit in my mouth when I tell you three times that... that...'

She burst out sobbing. In a case like this there is only one solution: namely, to fuck as soon as possible, or rather to buttfuck, should the female prefer it that way. Making women come in order to shut them up is a principle known and used throughout antiquity.

Unfortunately, if desire had pushed her to spout so much filth, as she had warned me, this same filth had destroyed the desire which I had had. There are some things in love which are not reciprocal. Besides, Charlotte seemed to be in too much of a frenzy to know what I was doing and what I wasn't. She was crying and fingering herself. Being unable to stop her tears, I decided not to stop her hand either. When she finally realized that I was letting her do as she wished, she stopped crying, raised her eyes to mine, and said in a low voice but without changing her tone, 'Tell me with your own lips that I'm a slut.'

'No.'

'Yes. It would make me happy.'

I finally understood. She was speaking to me in a very low voice and trembling from head to foot.

'Call me a whore while I beat off for you. Whore and slut and trollop! Say that you'll buttfuck me for four sous, will you? You'll stick it into my asshole right to the bottom, to the bottom! You'll buttfuck me for a half an hour, scraping me with all your force, and then you'll give me four sous afterwards. If you don't want to come in my ass then I'll suck you besides. I always want to have my mouth full of your come. Not only my mouth, but all my body. I'll beat you off into my face. But what do I have to say to get you to call me slut? I'm pulling out my finger; I'm hardly touching myself. Now call me whore and slut and bitch. Tell me that you'll piss on my knockers and you'll shit in my mouth! Tell me while I'm coming that you'll make me eat your shit! Say it! Say it! Say it!'

♦

She half swooned and was silent a long time before she again opened her eyes. Her first words were, 'I must be cracked!'

Then seeing that I had said nothing to contradict her, she said, 'You must have a fine opinion of me! And it's all your fault... no, it's mine. You had no way of knowing.'

'What did I do?'

'Mama always says, "When Charlotte feels like beating herself off, it's better not to try to stop her. Hold her up for five minutes and she goes nutty." You held me up...'

'Are you sure? That's funny for a man, isn't it. To see a girl that can't help shouting all kinds of dirt when she's in heat.'

I took her in my arms and, speaking in a low voice, holding her head so that she wouldn't have to look into my face, said, 'Now you're going to make me a little confession. Or rather I'll make it for you and you can answer yes or no. Ready?'

'Yes.'

'The men that you have are hardly ever attractive to you; but... be frank... you like being a whore.'

'Yes.'

'Not only do you like to make men come, but you like to be at their feet, at their command, something like a slave.'

'Their whore.'

'That's less than a slave?'

'Yes. You rape a slave, but with me...'

'And something that always excites you in the arms of a man is...'

'Is for him to tell me that I'm the lowest of all sluts; that there isn't anything a girl can do that's lower than offering her asshole and her mouth to every man that comes along for him to do as he wants. Yes, I said it despite myself a few minutes ago. But, I beg you on my knees, tell me that I'm right! Try to understand that I would kill myself if that didn't excite me a little!

And instead of consoling me, hurt me. Well... Go on...'

She smiled without insisting on the tragedy of her last words. She smiled more and more. It was as if she were playing.

'Be kind to me for once. Do what I want you to do. You see? I'm not fingering myself any more; I finished coming. But now that you know what I like, do what I want. Treat me like a slut and a bitch and a whore. Tell me that I buttfuck myself like a girl in a whorehouse or a gypsy behind her wagon. Are you going to call me whore? Call me whore, whore, whore. What a numbskull! He doesn't say a damn thing!'

Always smiling and trying to defy me with her impatient teasing, she insisted:

'And in my mouth? Tell me what you're going to do in my garbage pit of a mouth. You can do it... I want you to... I want to be treated like that by the man I love... And for you to fill up my mouth... Say it. Say what I'm asking you. You will...? You will...? You're as stubborn as a mule!'

I replied simply, 'Are you going to finish your story?'

'Ah! Now that you know all about my character!' she said, laughing. 'And then – poof! Too bad! I don't give a damn! I'm completely naked, I'm not hiding anything.'

Pierre Louÿs

Chapter Seven

'Where were we?' she asked. 'I can't remember. I don't feel the same as usual. What did you make me drink?'

'Nothing.'

'Nothing? When I drank your come with my mouth and my ass? I'm blotto. Tell me where we were in my story.'

'You said that when you were thirteen you came like a woman and that with your shaven cunt you...'

'The lesbians! The lesbians! Yes, and it used to hurt me because I didn't know how to hold myself in. I remember one woman that wasn't much to look at, but what a tongue! The old cow! She used to make me sit on her face so that she wouldn't lose a drop. She once made me come three times in a row and every time she drained out more come than I thought I had in my whole body. The third time my legs were trembling as if she were sucking my blood.

'And I used to take on lesbians in all kinds of ways: there was a young English girl who never took off her clothes and who beat herself off while she was kissing my cunt! And a huge woman who always did it lying on her back and who tried to hide it the first time she came so that she could come twice for the price of once! And a kid of about fourteen who couldn't come yet and whose friend had mama and I work on her for about an hour. Then when her pussy was covered with saliva we made her think that she had come! And a hermaphrodite that dressed like a man and buttfucked me with a dildo while mama did the same to it with another.

'And all this time I was a virgin! It didn't seem to bother anyone. Mama used to say that it didn't make any difference whether or not a prostitute had a cunt.'

Charlotte laughed at her own words. And her laugh was so frank that I smiled despite the absurdity of the saying. But she took my smile for approbation and, sprawled on the bed, her arms stretched over her head, her knees in the air, seemed to be enjoying herself hugely.

'Ah! You don't know how happy it makes me to be able to show myself as I really am to you, to tell everything all night long! With every word of filth that leaves my mouth, I feel cleaner, as if I were washing myself.'

'Whoever invented the confession knew what he was doing.'

'But then again...' (and she laughed once more) '...with every word of filth I utter I feel like saying another yet.'

'Those who oppose the confession claim that you're right.'

'I once had a girlfriend whose mother made her confess every Saturday. The poor kid could never confess without fingering herself, so she had to hurry and beat herself off before going to receive absolution. Otherwise, she got so excited by what she'd just said that she'd have to go and get fucked as soon as she left the church.'

'Charlotte! Hands on the table, as they say at school!'

'But I too feel like...'

'You're completely crazy. Try to hold off for a quarter of an hour.'

'Oh well, it's your funeral. You know what you're risking.'

And, hands behind her head, legs crossed, she continued:

'While we're on the subject of churches... But first, I haven't said anything yet but you can guess: I had four times as many buttfucks when I was thirteen as when I was ten. It was then that I first got my "solid" asshole, as Ricette calls it, and mama no longer rationed the number of men that could take me, as she had before.

'I owe everything to my mother, even the character I have now – the one you see before you. She gave that to me when I was thirteen. It seems that I used to cry too much. It made my eyes red and it worried mama, because she was always afraid I was going to chuck myself out of a window somewhere. So she taught me...'

She interrupted herself to change the position she was in.

'She's a wonderful woman, mama. In only eight days she made me a completely new character, the same as she would have made me a new dress.

'For a full week she slept alone with me, only taking on customers in the afternoons. She told me that I was old enough to know everything since I could now come like a woman, and that at my age it was ridiculous not to have any vices. So she wanted to give me a vice that would stand me in good stead the rest of my life.

'How did she go about it? She played with me (you're still such a kid when you're thirteen) and she beat me off while calling me all the names she could possibly think of. And since I got more of a kick out of being fingered by mama than anything else, the words that at first disgusted me ended up by exciting me. Both the words and the things. I won't say any more about that now, but I'll continue later on.

'So, in connection with the church (we certainly got a long way away from that!) one of my friends got a strange idea that same year. He wanted to buttfuck me in a country church. Guess why.'

'Because you were so pious?'

'Exactly. He knew that I prayed every day to the Holy Virgin and that I often went to church for nothing except to say a little prayer. So he proposed... And, so pious was I, I immediately agreed. It was because...'

She paused, thinking a moment.

'It was because my prayers, you know... I always told everything to the Holy Virgin just like I'm telling you.'

I couldn't help smiling at that.

'Therefore,' she continued, 'the Holy Virgin knew that I had been buttfucked since I was eight because I always asked her to protect me there as well as in the mouth and to choose my lovers and my lesbians and to make me come as much and as often as possible. So I thought it wouldn't surprise her, the Holy Virgin, if she saw me doing it... A little vicar to whom I told that one evening in my bed said that when I did that I committed a terrible sacrilege. I hardly doubt it.

'It was even one of the gayest days of my life. We left together, alone in his auto. My friend was rather young. When we arrived in the village, where he was well known, he got the keys of the church from the beadle under the pretext of showing me the monument. In those days, I had the innocent attitude of a school girl, and I've hardly changed since then, have I? Look at me. Do I look like a whore?'

'Not in the least!'

'Mama is always saying, "Charlotte would find a husband in a desert before she would a customer on a streetcar!" And within an hour after I asked you to treat me like a slut you couldn't.'

'No, my dear. However, continue the story of your devotions in the country church. Your hair is the longest and most beautiful in the world and you look like a Magdalene.'

'That's the first time you've ever called me whore!' she said, laughing.

But I finally got her back to her story.

'So you two entered the church with the keys. And naturally you locked up again from the inside?'

'Oh, yes. And then we were feeling so gay that we really made a scene. I went and kneeled in the Virgin's chapel and he came and said, "Are you praying, miss?" "No sir. I'm fingering myself." "Oh, but whatever for?" "Because my snatch is itching and other things are bothering me that I hardly dare tell you of." "Why does all that itch so?" "Because I can never kneel down without wanting someone to buttfuck me." I was a brat! You could have had me coming from morning to night. So then he got down behind me, but the kneelers in a church are very poorly constructed for buttfucking little girls.'

'You say the damnedest things, Charlotte.'

'My asshole was too low. So I went and knelt on one of the altar steps and it was just right.'

'Altar steps are better planned for buttfucking young girls?'

'You would have thought they were made for it! Our position there was so good that as soon as he was in me I felt like coming, and I really discharged a wad! I thanked the Holy Virgin because I thought that I owed it all to her.

'After that, I didn't know what to do with the come that I had in my ass. They don't have any bidets in churches and the Holy Water basins are all too high. Those basins are really very badly placed. But, lifting by chance one of the kneeler-covers, I found a new handkerchief that some old woman had put there for crying her sins out into the next Sunday. Instead of tears, however, it received my come, and I wiped my ass properly with it. Would you like to do it sometime? Buttfuck me in a church? I'll do it again if you want.'

♦

Charlotte was excited. She fidgeted her legs about and became very red in the face.

The brutality of her last two sentences whispered to me that a new crisis was approaching, for the tone of her voice had changed along with the expression on her face. Harsh, pained, a little breathless, she continued:

'That happens to me all the time, to come when someone sticks a rod into my rear. Every day it happens, even with old men. And all the thanks go to mama for it.

'She used to fake it in front of me so that I would get carried away until I let myself go like men do, and I would do the same things as she only with all my heart. When I was thirteen and fourteen I could already come without touching myself just from being excited in the ass. And the more the one working me over scraped me the better I liked it.

'I was still a virgin by the time I was fifteen, and mama kept on shaving my mound and my cunt, but she let the hair grow back into my ass. Nothing excited men that came to see me as much as seeing a bare scrap of a kid from the front and a hairy asshole in the back that they could buttfuck or put their fingers into or rub with their tongue.

'For *Mardi Gras* they made me a clown's costume with a little panel of cloth over the asshole that could be removed so I wouldn't have to undress completely. I supped with seven men and a woman named Fernande who was naked. Mother was naked too but, because of my last remaining virginity, she kept me partly dressed and wouldn't let me dine alone with anyone. The seven men bet that they could buttfuck me three times each and that I would have enough come in my ass when they finished to fill a champagne glass; and Fernande said that if they succeeded then she would drink the glass.

'Mother replied that she had done as well as that when she was my age and that I was old enough to do the same. And she said that she would take it upon herself to give anyone a hard-on who needed one if they couldn't get it themselves.

'I had never been buttfucked more than thirteen times in a day before, but I was ready and excited and I cried, "Done!" and raised the panel over my ass.

'It probably doesn't seem like anything to you, but twenty-one buttfuckings lasted from one to four in the morning.'

Charlotte, more and more excited, got astride of me, lay on me and cried with a sort of triumph in her voice:

'So! You won't treat me like the slut I am, and...'

'No! Shut up!'

She was in such a state of excitement that I had to satisfy her at all costs. And I didn't want to wait for a new outburst of frenzied filth.

For the few seconds that it took her to get into position so that I could penetrate I managed to keep my hand over her mouth; but after that, when she felt me solidly inside her, she freed herself from the gag and couldn't stop trembling.

At first she only touched me with her thighs, then began rubbing the hairs of her ass against my cock, and finally began to twist the lower part of her body down and away from me while raising the top half, as if she wanted to get her face as far away as possible from where I was screwing her. And she never stopped trembling.

From her head to her stomach to the tips of her toes she never stopped trembling.

Slowly she became more and more beautiful.

◆

Pierre Louÿs

'The first series of seven went quickly; the second slowly; the third seemed as if it would never end. The thing that hurt me the most was the fact that we were doing all this in a private room at a restaurant and they didn't even have a sofa. I was three hours, prick in ass, on the floor or on a table. You can see why I began to get a little tired.

'But finally I won the bet, and Fernande won it too... I filled it right to the brim and... oh! I'll say it until you cry out! That's what I did when I was fifteen! I got myself buttfucked twenty-one times in a row and after that I filled a champagne glass with come and I gave it to a woman to drink... What else do I have to tell you for you to admit that I'm a slut?'

She fell back on the bed weak and exhausted, as if she had just relived her story. I thought that she had finished talking and was going to quiet down at last, so I replied in a low voice, 'Nothing. Be quiet now and go to sleep. I'm going to stretch out myself...'

She suddenly arose, leaning on one elbow, and began talking again, but so calmly that I let her go on. I never suspected what I was to hear.

'Do you know Mr. W— who is [she gave me his title] at Aix? The year before last, when I was eighteen, he took me for the first time one June evening. I could see that he was the vicious type, and he had a huge dog with him, so I proposed to him to suck the dog.'

'Charlotte!'

'Dogs' come tastes terrible and it's very tiring to suck them because they never finish coming, the poor beasts. But I was used to it. And when you're a whore a mutt is less disgusting than a magistrate. Unfortunately though, this guy had never seen his dog sucked by a woman and it excited him so much that for fifteen Sundays in a row, until the end of September...'

She interrupted herself with a sigh, turning her head as if she had just lost her breath.

'Excuse me... listen... You'll never guess... He had a house in the country with a barnyard... He used to give all his servants the Sunday off... even the gardener, and he brought me... I was there alone with him... always naked with my hair loose down my back, it was in the summer... To do what? Make love? Oh, no! Not with a whore! It amused him tremendously every Sunday to see an eighteen year old girl drinking the come of all his animals.

'He had a carpenter make him a kind of small wooden stable or corral like those they use to hold cows and mares when they're breeding them. But instead of putting the female in it, he would put the males into it, aud when the stallion or bull was tied up, I would get underneath them... I didn't have a big enough mouth for the horses, but with my hands and my tongue...'

She saw me grow pale and, obeying that quirk of her character that made her rise around the word 'whore' and its connotations from the plaintive to the exalted, she began to grow more excited from sentence to sentence.

'You know, I drank the come of horses, donkeys, bulls, dogs, even pigs. The fourth Sunday he gave me a bowl with the come of a donkey in it and asked me what it was. I knew easily, I know the different kinds of come better than the different kinds of wine. I've emptied more balls than bottles in my life.

'And it's nothing at all to do that sort of thing. Even the horse is easy as long as you swallow right. All you do is stick your head underneath, do you follow me? Put it between his chest and his parts so that you get his milk on your palate and not down your throat. That way you don't strangle on it. I swallowed everything like that. Believe me, I wasn't thirsty afterwards.'

'For God's sake, shut up! This is worse than anything you've said!'

'Oh, no. The worst of all is the goat! I'm brave when I'm fingering myself, but what stuff...! I had to get rid of it, spit it out! When my lover, I mean my customer, saw that I couldn't stand it like that, he still wanted his goat to do something, so he had me sucking his donkey, his bull, his dog, and his pigs for four or five Sundays and then he had the goat mount me... He put me on all fours in the garden, completely nude... You still don't want to call me a slut? But I came, you hear? I came all the time the goat was fucking me.

'And after that I drank the goat's come the last few Sundays. Listen to me... Look at me... I drank the goat's come five times! So to pay me for it he bought me a monkey, and the monkey buttfucked me too and I drank its come just like I would a man's. You wouldn't believe the things I did between the twentieth of August and the end of September!

'That's when he got tired of making me suck the male animals and decided to have me eat out the females. He had three: another goat, a heifer, and a female ass, and I ate them out on my knees. Then he screwed them himself, saying that he would rather come in an animal than to give his wad to a whore like me, but that I could look for it in their cunts... or in their asses when he buttfucked them.'

'You're delirious! You're mad! You're making all this up!'

'On my mother's head. I swear to you that it's true! You want proof? Do it in front of me and I'll tell you in advance how it is. You don't know anything, you. How would I know how it all goes if I hadn't done it myself five Sundays in a row? In an animal's cunt, the come goes in deeply, you have to fish it out with your finger. But in their asses, it comes out by itself and you can just lick it off!'

'Charlotte, I can't take any more! That's enough! Don't say any more, for God's sake! Go to sleep! Lie down! Calm yourself! I don't know what to say to you... You're crazy, you're pretty, you love me, you don't ever fuck... You love me and yet you'd do more to disgust me than you'd ever do to attract someone...'

'You'll never put your mouth against mine again?'

'No.'

'Tell me that I'm a slut.'

'No. You're too beautiful. Go ahead and roll your beauty in filth, it will still be your beauty.'

'Tell me that I'm a slut just the same.'

'You're a poor unfortunate girl! I don't believe all this stuff you've been saying, and I've scarcely even heard it! You can only make me feel two things towards you: desire, despite what you say, and pity, a great deal of pity.'

Two things? I felt rather three. The weakest was desire; the strongest what I hadn't mentioned. Don't think it was disgust. I pitied Charlotte so much that I could cover the rest of her life, her unknown life, with this cloak. My strongest feeling and instinct was to go to sleep.

The tremendous upsetting emotions that are left in residue when our most tragic moments wash away exact a heavy toll from our minds, our hearts, our memories. I think that Shakespeare was the only man who ever used the word 'sleepy' after a terrible scene. It was the supreme, the only apt word. And I felt like sleeping. To sleep without ever dreaming, to roll even my most intimate and subconscious thought away in sleep. To sleep like a dead man.

◆

'I'll do anything. I defy you to find something I won't do with you, for you, under you. Order me; you'll see how I'll obey you.'

She was trembling from head to foot, but her craze was none the less frightening to me because she was no longer mysterious. And what struck me the most was that Charlotte became more and more beautiful the wilder became her delirium.

Very seriously, with an expression I might even call tragic, and holding her face away from mine to show that she wasn't even worthy of a kiss, she ceased for the moment to imagine all the things that I wouldn't ask her to do or to tell me everything that she would do and (I've already mentioned the logical instinct of those persons with essentially simple souls) she recovered her spirit on a basis of reality.

'You buttfuck me,' she said, 'and you've been doing it for my pleasure, but it's also my trade. I'm nothing but a girl who earns her living with her asshole. What is a slut if I'm not one? I'm in my twenties, I come to your rooms without ever knowing you, strip myself, finger myself, spread my thighs, and say, "Buttfuck me!" And you buttfuck me three times like the whore that I am! And the more you do it the more I love you!'

She fell against me with her mouth open against my shoulder and said in a plaintive voice:

'I beg you... You see, I'm not touching myself and yet I'm going to come... But while you're getting a hard-on in my ass, tell me... tell me... what you're going to do later in my mouth. Please! Tell me when you discharge... Call me slut! I... I... And I'll say... Yes, oh, yes!'

Pierre Louÿs

Then, as if even that idea wouldn't do in her present state, she shouted, almost crying:

'No, I love you too much now... That wouldn't be enough... You'll have to do it to me first! You'll do it to me now, tonight! I want you to do it to me so I can forget the others. But then... tomorrow... you can show me that I'm the lowest of all whores... You'll bring one of your girlfriends here and fuck her in front of me without even looking to see if I'm fingering myself or crying...'

'You think I'd do that?'

'And then when you've buttfucked her she can be the one to...'

'You're not going to say another word!' I cried, putting my hand over her mouth.

'I'm coming! I'm coming!' she shouted between my fingers.

♦

This time, Charlotte, in coming, cried like she was being stabbed, then fell into a sudden deep torpor and immediately went to sleep.

As pale as the young man in *The Crimson Curtain*, I was trying to wake her from her swoon when I heard three small knocks on my door.

I opened the door to Teresa dressed only in a slip.

'What are you doing? Cutting her up in pieces?' said she with an expression like a good-humoured procuress that simultaneously shocked me, reassured me, and left me speechless.

I brought her into the room and showed her the body of her daughter. She caught at first glance the tiny tremblings of her hips, like the nervous twitch of a horse's flank, aud without the least anxiety drew me into the adjoining room and closed the door.

'What's wrong with her?' I asked.

'Virgin!' she replied.

'That's a little stiff! I know that I'm twenty years old, an age at which you let yourself be intimidated by every strange woman that comes along, but nevertheless I've had one woman, two girls, and one kid in the last twelve hours and I don't think that I missed...'

'No, but do you think that we let anyone miss any of us?' Teresa said merrily.

'Even so, I got six shots in and...'

'So... That makes three with Charlotte. And you're asking what's wrong with her! Don't look at me with that stupid expression, as if you were getting ready to say, "I think maybe she needs a couple more."'

'Thanks for prompting me.'

I sent you Charlotte last because she's the ideal companion for tired men.'

'Thanks again.'

'You had just had three odalisques, so I said to myself, "Charlotte is a good girl and she'll suck him. They'll talk for an hour or so and then they'll go to sleep." Charlotte is gentleness itself; she was born for sleeping at a man's side.'

'Oh yeah? You're as crazy as she is. She's nuts, your daughter, for screwing. She's a nymphomaniac, that girl, with her innocent, lazy attitude. She's an onanist and a masochist extraordinary. She's everything you can think of that ends in "ist" and "maniac"!'

'Like you say, she's everything that one could want,' said Teresa, her temper rising. 'You can mould her to your wishes like a lump of dough, and if she went crazy tonight it's because you made her like that. Did I come in your bed? How was I supposed to know that in saving my daughter for you that you would fuck her into heat without doing anything for her?'

With a smile she softened the harshness of her words and went into the bedroom. Taking off her slip, she laid down on the bed next to Charlotte, took her into her arms, awakened her, and from her first words, I understand that she knew a lot better than I what the girl needed.

With her first words, Charlotte opened her eyes. Her mother drew her close and said with a loving brusqueness, 'What's wrong, my poor little chippie?'

'Mama!' cried Charlotte in a tiny voice, throwing her arms

around her neck.

'Do you think I'd let you kiss me with that whore's mouth of yours? What have you been doing? I can smell come on your tongue.'

'I drank some,' said Charlotte, half closing her eyes.

'Little slut! Why don't you ever sleep with your mother? How come I find you naked in a young man's bed at three in the morning? What do you deserve?'

Bewildered, I sat on the end of the bed listening to this dialogue.

Do I have to remind you that I was twenty years old at the time and that Charlotte was not too much older? And that a girl of that age can dominate a boy her equal just about as she pleases? And beneath my very eyes I saw her accepting a scolding like a little child...! And this Charlotte that fought me in my arms when I treated her like a woman found it completely natural for her mother to speak to her as if she were a seven year old.

Teresa shot me a glance that said, 'Please be quiet!' or perhaps, 'Keep your damned trap shut!' I couldn't tell which. The vocabulary of glances is at best a little uncertain. Then she began again with Charlotte:

'What have you just been doing here? Answer me!'

'I've just been buttfucked,' sighed Charlotte.

'You mean he wanted to buttfuck a whore like *you*?'

'He didn't want me to be a whore,' she said quickly, her eyes closed. 'The first time he buttfucked me while I fingered myself and he came in my ass. Then the second time I came before he did, so I took his dick out of my ass and put it my mouth...'

'What a little slut!'

'Oh, that's not all!' said Charlotte, with a twist of her body that startled me. 'I asked him to–' (and she spoke so low that I couldn't hear what she said.) '–And when he buttfucked me the third time, I didn't even touch myself, I was so excited. I wanted to come just from him being in my ass and I wanted him to say it when I came...'

'Don't you have any shame at all?'

'Yes, I'm ashamed. But I wanted him to do it, only he's

even stupider than me. He didn't want either to do it or to say it or anything! anything! anything!'

Then, like a nurse or a nun speaking from the bedside of a patient who can't hear anything, Teresa said to me in a loud voice, 'She needs someone to beat her off once more.'

Completely nude, Charlotte's mother got up from the bed, left the room, and came back in a few minutes later carrying something wrapped in paper. With all the authority of a mother-in-law caring for her daughter in her son-in-law's presence, she said, 'Let me alone for a while. You don't have to do anything now. You've had your six shots, now take it easy. Sit down at the foot of the bed and relax.'

◆

Teresa hadn't warned me for nothing, because from the very first words the dialogue took on a strangely urgent tone. Pulling at her own flesh and in a trembling and plaintive voice, Charlotte groaned:

'Look, mama. Look what's coming out of my asshole. The crack in my behind is full of come, and he still doesn't want to say that I'm a whore.'

'The trouble is you haven't done enough yet.'

'But it's him! I'd do everything, but he won't!'

'He doesn't know that you're the lowest of all the sluts.'

'Oh! You'll say it to me while you finger me! You're the only one that understands me, mama!'

All of this was intended to make me think that Teresa was going to beat her daughter off in order to relax her; but I wasn't as much of a novice as the Italian woman thought and, without ever letting the slightest trace of surprise cross my face, I saw that beyond the shadow of a doubt she was masturbating poor Charlotte only in order to drive her even wilder. My young female readers will have understood by this time what I'm getting at, but for the others I will explain that Teresa, instead of hastening Charlotte's spasm, was indefinitely retarding it, making the girl wait and hope for it from one moment to the next.

I think that this little trick amazed me more than the entire

Pierre Louÿs

preceding scene, and I must confess that I began to wonder exactly what Teresa was trying to do and what she was expecting it all to lead to.

'Let's show him,' said Charlotte, breathing hard. 'Let's show him that I'm really the lowest of all whores. You told me that I've got the mouth of a whore and that my tongue smells like come. Now tell me to stick it into his ass! But the whole thing! All of my tongue right into the hole!'

'And you'll be happy?'

'Oh, yes! Yes! And another thing... I want him to make love to you in front of me and then I want him to make me get underneath you two. You'll be his mistress and I'll be his whore. And then you'll see how much I want his prick! But even so I'll put it into your body myself, and I'll lick his balls while he's buttfucking you, and then I'll... I'll do the two things...'

'Tell us what you'll do in a loud voice.'

'I'll suck his dick afterwards without cleaning it, and then you can shit his come out into my mouth! Oh, mama! Mama! Why can't I come?'

I knew why all right aud the whole purpose behind the scene became suddenly clear when, with a quick spontaneous movement, Charlotte threw herself around and jammed her head between Teresa's thighs as if she were looking there for her own pleasure. It was obvious that Teresa had known what was coming.

'Me first?'

'Yes, right away!'

'What about the thing I brought in for you?'

She unfolded the paper and took out the object that she had gone into her room looking for such a short time ago: a dildo, large, well-worn, and stained.

Charlotte laughed, and the laugh halted her crisis for a moment. She turned towards me and said, but in the gayest and most natural voice, as if it were the simplest thing in the world to do: 'Buttfuck mama.'

Teresa didn't protest.

'Buttfuck mama,' she repeated. 'I'll eat her out at the same time, and then afterwards I'll suck your dick. I want your come and hers and if I get them both I'll be the happiest of the three of us.'

Since she was silent for a moment awaiting my reply, Teresa said, 'Look at this big booby crossing his legs because he's shot six wads and can't get another hard-on.

'Try not to get an erection for my cunt, so try not to get one for my ass either.'

Even in the face of her mocking voice, I hesitated to say that the little scene which she and Charlotte had just performed had cooled me off much more than it had tempted me. I kept my mouth shut because my temptress was deliberately defying me. Teresa had done practically nothing to awaken my loins, but she attracted them with her cunt, as she had said, and with a science that I can only call remarkable.

In fact she soon had me back into a state of excitement, which, when she became aware of it, in turn had Charlotte trembling with passion. It would have given her less than half as much pleasure if I had taken her instead of taking her mother in front of her.

'My tongue first,' she cried. 'Look! Look how I can buttfuck mama with my tongue! Now give me your prick, I'll open her buttocks... Ha! Ha! I told you that I earned my living with my asshole, but no! I'm even lower than that! I'm the kind that is only good for licking asses and opening the cheeks of a woman when you're getting set to buttfuck her! That's the kind of woman I am!'

Then, since Teresa turned towards me while she was opening her thighs for her daughter's mouth, Charlotte, getting more and more excited, said, 'You want to say something mama? You want to say something? I know him. He won't say anything... and I, I can't. So say something, keep talking all the time or I'll quit and beat myself off.'

Teresa must have been used to this caprice of her daughter's because she began to speak and never stopped for an instant.

'Quick, your tongue! And I absolutely forbid you to beat yourself off while you're sucking me. What are you doing attacking my snatch like that? You want me to start coming in fifteen seconds? What's wrong, you have another customer waiting behind the door that you haven't finished sucking yet, whore? Don't press so hard. Lick my lips, you can return to the snatch when I tell you.'

She shot me a glance that said, 'That's how you have to talk to her!' and continued without stopping:

'What rottenness this girl is! There are children you nurse at the breast with milk, but I nursed her at my ass with come. And now that she's over twenty years old she still sticks her tongue into my behind. How could such a slut ever have come from my pussy?

'Who could you do the things to that I've done to you? I come into your lover's room, I take him away from you right under your eyes, and in the same bed while he's making me wet myself you come and lick my ass. You're lower than any whore I've ever seen! Even a procuress wouldn't do the things you do!

'You're mad, too! You spend your days beating yourself off in front of your sisters and crying that it's too bad to have so many lesbians in one family and even then you wind up coming all by yourself. And tonight you finally found a prick that could make you come! Now look where it is! It's in my ass right up to the root, and the only thing you have left is the balls to lick.

'Your tongue on my snatch now, dirty little lecher. But not so fast! Slow down! Your lover is buttfucking me very nicely and I don't want to come before he does... What's wrong now? You thinking of the come that I'm going to piss into your mouth, sow? And it makes you tremble? If I were on you you'd see how I'd scrape your hair. I'd show you how to lick an ass! Go now! Go ahead! You can have my damned come if you want it! But it isn't for you that it's flowing, it's because of your lover's prick! Oh, it's his cock that's driving me crazy! Faster your tongue...! Faster! Ah! Again! There where you are! Ah! Slut! Slut! Ah! He's fingering my teats while he buttfucks me...! And what a whore this Charlotte is when she's thirsty! Are you kissing his balls? Is that what's making him so hard way up inside me? Ah, you little... Oh, you're making me come too! Go ahead then, take it! There it is! There's my come for you! Wash your face in it you dirty little bitch! whore! slut! fairy! cocksucker!'

And Charlotte, already drunk with what she had

swallowed, 'washed her face in it', as her mother put it, and what followed I was too worked up to prevent. I would have liked to have missed the whole thing after that, and even as it was it all seemed like a dream or a hallucination.

I lost and regained consciousness before it happened, and as I re- opened my eyes I saw Charlotte kneeling, holding out her cupped hand... I can't finish the sentence. She was triumphant; she was crazed; she cried out to her mother: 'You see! You see!'

And then she licked her hand clean with her tongue before returning once again to Teresa.

She shook her head and cried again, 'Your come, mama! The come that you have left in your ass! Shit it into my mouth in front of him so he can call me a slut! Shit it into my mouth while I finger myself so he can call me a slut when I come!'

'In front of him?' teased Teresa.

'Yes! Yes! In front of him! Fill my mouth,' cried Charlotte, looking at me with haggard eyes.

◆

A person crazed by love is the most tragic sight of which the mind can conceive. Where is the man so gross that he doesn't shudder at the obscene songs of Ophelia? And what other man or woman could fail to understand why, in the middle of the following scene, I suddenly saw my face as white as a shroud in one of the room's mirrors?

I am trying to re-order my memories...

Teresa was more worried about me than about her daughter, and without listening to my feelings, said in a low voice, 'Well? You saw that? Eh? Well go ahead and tell her that you saw... No? Why not? *You* came didn't you? Can't you see what this means to her? If she disgusts you, say so; it'll excite her.'

Excite her! The girl was already half crazed with excitement!

Standing, Charlotte stuck the dildo into her behind and began working it with her left hand while she beat herself off in front with her right. She had her legs spread and her stomach working like a young madwoman masturbating herself in front of an unknown visitor to her cell; that is to say that she was using her finger, facing me directly, with an expression combining impudence and unhappiness on her face.

When I was fifteen I saw... I'm telling this to try to put off the end of this horrible narrative a little... I saw a girl fingering herself in a garden once, and she was facing me in the same position, but gaily, mockingly. I didn't know at the time that it was a gesture of the mad. I know it now.

Charlotte, still standing, still with her finger in her cunt, was spouting obscenities in a jerky, staccato voice. I'll let them pass. She finished like that.

'For two hours I've felt like... He doesn't want... My mouth disgusts him... Show him mama... How I could have taken it under him... The way I learned... without staining anything.'

When I heard those miserable words 'The way I learned... without staining anything'... But why emphasize a scene such as that one. The words she had just spoken seemed to me among the saddest I had ever heard, and yet Charlotte had spoken them with a real fervour.

She finally went into the bathroom, lay down on the ceramic-tiled floor, the top part of her body supported by a single elbow, her head thrown back, her mouth open, and began to masturbate frenziedly. She didn't seem to feel the cold of the tile floor.

The more she fingered the more avid she became to vilify herself. I used to have the words she uttered at this time written down, but I've just ripped up the page. I don't even have the courage to re-read it to the end. There are two things my reader will never know: the words that Charlotte spoke on this occasion and the haste with which I am finishing this chapter.

Scenes taken from life are much more difficult to relate than those invented by the author because the logic inherent in life is less clear and less easily seen than the logic of a tale. Do you think that the culminating point of this narration ought to be the act which I just witnessed?

I don't. And I don't know if I will be able to properly explain why.

First of all I was there for a quarter of an hour and the

things I imagine are generally more interesting than reality. Besides that, I can justly say that the most infamous role of the performance, Teresa's, was played with a prodigious feminine address. I consider it undescribable, probably only because my faculties for expression are limited.

Teresa had a remarkable body, as I've already said several times. She was the daughter of two acrobats, as you will learn, and she handled herself exactly like a gymnast rehearsing an exercise with her partner. And all this time she looked at me with the calm expression of one performing a classic among exercises; a classic that seemed to her much more natural than to my troubled mind...

Five minutes later I was alone.

Chapter Eight

I slept soundly for nine hours and awoke with irresistible desire to... Finish the sentence if you are young or if you ever have been.

Excesses of love lend more to the sexual drive than do long periods of inactivity and are much easier to take up once more on the next day than several weeks after. Everyone knows that. You can see, therefore, why I was in top form that morning. As the patriarch who was loved by Ruth said, it was a 'triumphant' morning; but triumphant though it was, I scarcely found it agreeable, for I still had this irresistible desire to... Do you understand? I think that if you have been following this story page by page through the seven preceding chapters you can guess what I did at the time during which the eighth opens.

Bathed, shaved, combed, and dressed in little more time than it takes to tell, I hurried towards the rooms of one of my closest girlfriends in the Latin Quarter. Fortunately, she was alone, and since she was dressed only in a slip, it took her less time to undress than it took me to slip off my tie. The more beautiful breasts a girl has, the more her slip weighs her down.

However, she was alarmed at my nervous state.

'What's wrong? What do you want? What's the matter with you?'

'My pretty little Margot, I want to make love.'

'Me too... and maybe if we know the right people in the government we might sleep together a while.'

'And... listen! I want to make love from the front, my little Margot! From the front!'

'From the front? For God's sake, I hope so!'

'Through here, you see? Through here. You get me? Not from back there.'

'You're nutty as a squirrel cage,' said Margot with a bewildered expression.

She was reassured little by little as her embrace calmed me, gave me the relief I sought like the glass of cool, fresh water that slakes the thirst alcohol has left. Still haunted by my recent adventure, I felt my head. I couldn't believe that this time at last... but simple little Margot wasn't mistaken. I doubt that she has ever known since a pleasure equal to the one that was ours that morning.

♦

That evening I returned to my apartment alone. I had a few things to write.

However, just when I had gotten undressed, there was a loud knock on the door. I opened it: it was, to my surprise, Teresa, dressed in a pink dressing gown with a flower in her hair.

I was still in a bad mood from what I had seen the previous night, and I took her by the arm and drew her into my room.

'So, it's you!' I cried. 'Good! Now you can listen to the words I wouldn't speak to Charlotte. You're the one who's lowest of all sluts! The worst of whores! The...'

She burst out laughing and, taking the tone that a woman of thirty-nine can take when speaking to a young man of twenty, she said, 'I might as well have saved myself the trouble of providing you with all those adventures last night for all the thanks I get, eh? You've buttfucked my three daughters and their mother; we gave ourselves in relays so that you could shoot your wad seven times in an evening, and the next day when you see me what do I get? You start calling me whore and...'

'That's because...'

'I'm not as nutty as Charlotte. I don't finger myself in front of your dick and I don't have to be called whore to make me come.'

'And besides, I know that I'm a whore, by the cunt, the

Pierre Louÿs

ass, and the mouth! And besides, I don't give a damn! And besides...'

There was not the slightest doubt in my mind that the words that Teresa caught on the end of her tongue were, 'And besides, as far as I'm concerned, I shit on you!' There was no question about it. Therefore, the only thing that her silence could mean was that she didn't want me to put her out. I took the offensive again.

'What's this passion you four have for being buttfucked? Was it you who trained those girls to act like that? Did you give them the taste for that sort of thing?'

'What about me? Who gave it to me? Why didn't you ask that? You forget that I didn't invent women with two holes in their bodies. And I didn't give them the power to make love through both, either. You forget that before I was a mother, my child, I was a daughter.'

She laughed. She was standing all this time, one hand on her hip, and with her robe and the flower in her dark hair she looked like a woman playing Carmen on the stage.

'Whose daughter.' I asked, seated near her.

No reply. She smiled and looked at me for a few moments, chewing a lock of her hair that had drifted down out of place. I couldn't tell what she was thinking about, but young men are all too disposed to think that every woman that comes along wants to sleep with them. Even when the woman happens to knock on their door at midnight, however, their plans are not always so simple. I repeated, 'Daughter of whom?'

'Prick! If I say daughter of a whore will you be happy?'

'Yes.' I thought that that might make her talk.

However she continued to stare at me fixedly with the same slightly troubled smile. Then she decided.

♦

'I was born into a family of Italian acrobats in which there were already four women: my mother and three younger sisters.

'Don't worry. They were all partially whores and very pretty. Even so, they were more lesbian than anything else. I never saw four little bitches so avid to lick each other's asses than my mother and my three aunts. Whenever they had an hour free they were always lying around naked giving it to each other, this one eating another's pussy, that one drinking it up like a polecat, the other letting it gush out so strongly that they always had a swamp in their sheets somewhere.

'As for men... I suppose you want to know why they didn't fuck? I never saw either my mother or her sisters fucking and I still don't know how I came into the world. They weren't whores like I am, but still there would be a man around from time to time. No fucking, though. Since the circus was their living, they could scarcely afford to become pregnant. The man would have, therefore, plenty to choose from for buttfucking, and all asses that took pricks like ducks to water. But the front was strictly forbidden. They called that the women's side.

'Would you believe that by the time I was seven I never saw a woman make love other than by the rear and that I didn't even know what fucking was? Still I saw some real scenes! Mother and her sisters were all acrobats and double-jointed to boot, and each one of them could suck her own pussy if she wanted. But what they did most often was to bend themselves double and suck the balls of a man who was buttfucking them. That was always worth a good fifty francs.'

With this she halted her story, though she had hardly begun it, took off her dressing gown and threw it on the bed.

'I'm hot,' she said.

This time she wasn't wearing any slip and, so suddenly nude, she sat down defiantly on the end of the bed.

'You disgust me,' I said turning my eyes away.

'Ha! Ha! Ha! But look! You're getting an erection like a horse!'

'Very clever. When you sit down completely nude on my bed, does that prove I like you?'

'There are some,' she said gaily, 'who say, "I love you" with a limp prick. But you, you hate me with a hard-on. That's much better for a woman.'

I reddened. Teresa's nudity was, in fact, irresistible to me, but I was ashamed that my physical state had made the speech

---

that I had been mentally preparing for the last ten minutes at most impossible and at least ridiculous. And my annoyance was such that if she had decided to mock me an instant longer, I would have been unable to retain what I had to say.

But instead of making fun of my desire, she decided to exasperate it.

She locked her hands behind her head, leaving bare two black armpits, as much to show me that she wasn't going to attack me as to display her breasts to best advantage.

Then, with eyes half shut and in a low, sultry voice, she had an inspiration: she decided to mock herself.

'My knockers aren't any good. My nipples don't harden half as well as your cock,' she said.

'You don't know what you're saying! They're one of your best features.'

Seeing that I was already contradicting myself, she no longer needed to bother flattering herself, and she insisted knowing well enough the attractiveness of her breasts to be sure that she was fighting on safe ground.

'They disgust you the least of anything about me then?' She was smiling broadly. 'Their odd shape, no doubt. Look how long and large they are. Neither apple nor pear, eh? And the ends! Do you think I could dye my hair blonde some time, and just leave these little black rosettes? These little licorice drops? These little negro boy pick heads? Ha! Ha! Ha! Do you know why my knockers don't look like anyone else's? Because I had three kids. Even so, though, they're big and full and they're full because I didn't let the kids suck them. They got their milk from my ass...'

'Whore! Don't re—'

'Yes,' she said, interrupting me volubly, 'they're whore's teats all right. And you've been sitting in front of them for fifteen minutes wanting to shoot your wad and you can't! You haven't gotten your prick between them yet, but you've been thinking about it. And the last time you came, when you had your prick in my behind, you were rubbing them with both hands, right? Did you feel them? Answer! Did you feel my whore's teats expanding?'

'Shut up! Get out of here! I don't want to see you any more! I can't forget what you did after that!'

I put my hand over my eyes so I couldn't see her any more and turned away from her on the bed. She leaped on me.

I expected it? No, it was exactly what I wasn't expecting. However, I never fooled myself either as to her desire or as to her vigour, and in a second I experienced both.

The surprise with which her leap caught me, my disadvantageous position, and above all the fear that I might hurt her all combined to put me out of the fight so quickly that I scarcely had time to discover what had happened.

'See how easy it is to violate a man?' smiled Teresa.

'Whore!'

'Thanks.'

The 'thanks' was another inspiration. The woman that I had seen (but I don't want to repeat here what I had so much trouble describing in the previous chapter)... This woman had the effrontery to sigh her 'thanks' in a tone that also said, 'You're not what I'd exactly call a gallant gentleman.' And I was naïve enough to blush, to cut short the injuries I was ready to hurl at her without realizing that she had suddenly reversed our roles.

In addition, after the sad little word that accused the slur made on her honour, Teresa continued in the same audacious voice. She seemed nervous, but she was smiling.

'You don't have to complain any more. You can fuck me. You can deflower me. You know what you call the cunt of a whore who is always buttfucked and who hasn't had a prick from the front in three months? No? You call it a cherry, and you're in it now. Now don't tell me that I never fuck. Just remember that the night I raped you I did it with my pussy. Are you happy?'

She remained solidly joined to me, but immobile and refusing to allow me to move. A minute sufficed for her to see that she'd tamed me and that I wouldn't try to leave her flesh.

'What I did to Charlotte...'

'No! Don't speak of that now!'

'On the contrary! I'll speak of it now when you've got an erection. I was wrong to do all that just after you'd come for the seventh time and when you no longer felt like erecting.'

'You mean you think that if you propose that sort of thing now... But that's absurd! The more desirable you are to me the

Pierre Louÿs

more revolting I'll find it that....'

'Take it easy. The best thing I ever did for my daughters was to make them like the whore's trade. Charlotte is as innocent as a saint. I had a whole nun's costume made for her once, wimple, rosary, and all, and everyone thought she was the real thing. I'll bet fifty men thought that they were buttfucking a Carmelite when they took her. So! You don't think it's something praiseworthy to have a daughter like that, to train her like a dog to make love with her rear and never to come unless her lover calls her slut? You think that I, the daughter of an acrobat, wouldn't have gotten along in the circus?'

'You're a monster of cleverness, but you've driven your daughter mad.'

'Mad because she wants to beat herself of from morning to night without hiding it? If she were reasonable she would be hiding it in some shithouse and wiping the come off her hairs with an old newspaper, eh? Shut up about that crap! She was excited last night and it was your fault. And as for what happened afterwards... What about it? She certainly said what she wanted often enough for someone to have done something about it. I didn't make her do it, did I?'

'No, but...'

'And even if I'd raped her into doing it, it wouldn't have killed her would it? I'm raping you right now. I'm making you fuck me by force, and I don't hear you complaining.'

All during this scene, which seemed interminable to me, Teresa stayed on top of me and me in her. I was thinking of everything but answering her questions and, since I didn't say no to the last one, she suddenly leapt away from me with as quick a movement as the one to which I had succumbed. Then she retreated to the end of the room and laughed at my desire which she had changed into real heat without even beginning to satisfy it.

'Excuse me. I won't rape you any more!' she said.

This time I too jumped. Certain that I wasn't dealing with a weak woman, I twisted one arm behind her back and, feeling little scruple as she laughed, gave her a good dozen smacks with my fist on her left shoulder.

Afterwards, she looked at me and, in a voice joyous and youthful as well as breathless, said, 'You're much nicer when you get vicious.'

And in the same gay voice she added: 'Does the gentleman like to beat his women? If the gentleman would like to slash my behind with a whip in order to get an erection, it's twenty francs more.'

I had let her see a great deal too much of my exasperated desire and she was speaking with the most cutting irony.

We fell again onto the bed; but Teresa, more agile than I, refused to let herself be covered and defended herself much better against my virility than she had against my fist. She continued to play and was bubbling over with an extraordinary youth and vitality.

'Aha!' she said mockingly. 'First you treat me like a whore and then you want to fuck me. No! No! My fine fellow! Whores don't screw, they only piss hot. Better be careful, my pretty blond, or I'll get bitchy with you.'

'Fine! Go ahead!' I said through my teeth.

'Look!' she said, still playing her role. 'Look how much hair I have under my arms: I know women who don't have as much on their pussies. You want to make love to me in there? You'll come very nicely. No? Then you must want my old whore's teats?'

'Not that old saw again.'

'Look, here are my whore's teats. Stick your dick between them. I'll press them together... You like that? Do they do their job well, my whore's teats? Listen, sonny, you give me a hundred sous in advance and you can come on my face. Okay?'

'Watch out! I'll do it without warning you!'

'Or would you rather come in my mouth? It's the same price. And I'll give you a pretty little working over with my tongue all around. You like that? I'll lick your balls and your ass and suck your dick afterwards. No? Not that either? You must have religion. You must be afraid to go confess that you've come in the mouth of a woman. Well, we can always do something else. How would you like me to beat myself off, my little whoremonger?'

That did it. That was the straw on the camel's back for

Pierre Louÿs

me, though the height of fun for Teresa.

'How would you like me to kill you?'

'Oh! That's even more expensive than beating me!' she howled in a burst of laughter.

Deciding to finish this action on the field of battle, I grabbed Teresa and started to force her thighs apart. Seriously, this time, she cried, 'No! Don't fuck me!'

'Because?'

A sudden anger rose in her eyes, she seized my arms and began to shout:

'Because, here, tonight, I'm not a whore, you understand? When a woman who wants to come rubs her body against a man with a hard-on, she gives herself through the hole that *she* wants! And if I get more pleasure from being buttfucked, and if I want to be buttfucked, then you'll buttfuck me!'

The violence of her words should have made me so angry that I would never have left her any liberty of either wish or action after hearing them. However, the sorceress didn't leave me any time to think about what I might do. Her agility in movement and position were a wonder, and I soon found that, for the second time since I had met her, I was in her body I knew not where.

Immediately, she said in her most tender voice and with her softest expression, 'Please don't do me the disservice of coming now.'

'It's all that you deserve.'

'So! A pretty woman gives a man her asshole and what does she get? After a minute he says, "I'm getting out, you can finish the best way you know how."'

'Wait a minute! About an hour ago you did exactly the same thing to me...! I waited, but...'

'You're a love.'

Then, in the same voice, she continued:

'You disgust me.'

'Same to you.'

'Now I'll tell you why Charlotte and I...'

'No!'

'Yes! I want to tell you while I've got your prick in my

ass. The truth is that... we were both hot last night. I wasn't in quite the state that she was, but... You saw didn't you?'

'Maybe.'

'And now?'

I remained silent. Then suddenly, with one of those unexpected crescendos that always announced another brutal verbal assault she cried:

'And now can't you see that I'm as hot as a two-dollar pistol? Can't you see that I came here to rape you, that I threw off all my clothes, that I let you treat me like a whore, that I let you fuck me, that I let you beat me, and that finally I put your prick in where I wanted it and that now I'm beating off in your arms even more than Charlotte? Can't you see that? And the come that I give you... When you have more on the outside of your balls than within, will I have to *tell* you that I've shot my wad?'

Chapter Nine

Trying to mount a wild-woman like that is as dangerous as trying to ride a horse to the hunt that has suddenly gone crazy. The only difference is that when you are riding a horse, about the only thing you risk breaking is a leg or an arm, while riding Teresa was ten times more dangerous, since she was bucking so hard or, to speak more exactly, had such a fire in her behind that on at least twenty occasions she came within a hair of breaking something far more valuable to me than an arm.

In fact, I was so afraid of an accident, that my life began to flash before my eyes exactly as if I were about to drown. And I began to think of everything at once, even the least little details that I would have had plenty of time to consider the next day.

I will list here a brief resumé of the high points of my mental excursion for those who are as yet uninitiated to this phenomenon:

1) I never suffered so much, even when I was taking the cherry of Miss X – from the front.

2) She's going to cripple me. What to do? Hold her in? Impossible. Gentle her? Even more difficult.

3) My God, but she's beautiful!

4) I never knew I was so young and clumsy! Imagine never catching on to her game all that time. Last night I thought she was faking passion in order to excite Charlotte and her game was real. This evening she came to me, stripped herself on my bed, and until the very last minute I didn't know what she wanted. She had to shout at me at the top of her voice, 'Can't you see that I'm hot to go?' And I blushed, I was ashamed.

5) She can do whatever she wants with me and she knows

it. Yesterday I was revolted by her. She came back this evening. I was determined to give her the gate and now look what has happened! How is this night going to finish?

Teresa regained her senses quickly; soon enough to hold me where I was in her, anyway. Most women share this instinct but are ignorant of the fact that in those moments when they hold their lovers immediately after the act of love their love is the most reciprocated. Teresa, as usual, knew what she was doing.

She neither asked for a word nor a kiss. She saw that I was careful to leave a distance between our lips, and she sensed that I was not caressing her body, rather only touching it. And that was treating her more as a whore than was calling her the name. Too adroit to whisper an imprudent 'Tell me you love me!' that would ring hollow and false, she seemed rather to accept my touches with pleasure. She opened her thighs wide to the hand that wandered distractedly there, her stomach shuddered, she closed her eyes and finally said in a voice at once both confused and ashamed, 'I drenched your bed, my love!'

How can a young man keep from embracing a woman who speaks to him like that while she's lying in his arms? He either has to refrain from sleeping with her... or not be twenty years old. And the kiss that unites mouth to mouth so far surpasses all other unions between lovers that only Teresa could at that point measure its strength against me.

Thus, sure of herself for the future and no longer worrying about seeing my door shut to her, she left my room.

◆

After several minutes that seemed more like several hours she returned as nude as she had left. I thought that she had gone into my adjoining room and I didn't find out until later that she had gone into her apartment.

She looked at me for a second and then, as if picking a question at random, said, 'Why do you like fucking so much?'

I replied teasingly, 'Because women that aren't crazy come best when they're fucking, and I like to make my partner come as well as myself.'

Pierre Louÿs

Teresa seemed to be in an excellent humour and she began to laugh instead of being peeved.

'So when, instead, you sleep with a phenomenon like me, the only woman in both hemispheres who can fuck through her asshole, and when you buttfuck this woman, and when you feel her discharge like a mare pissing...'

'Can't you express yourself a little more genteelly?'

'Certainly, my dear. And when you see that the more you stick your dick into her ass, the more jism gushes out of her pussy, you could at least have the good will not...'

'Not to want to fuck? All right, all right. I won't say anymore about it.'

She lay down on her stomach next to me.

'For a man that can never think of anything but screwing you do a wicked job of buttfucking. Where did you learn the motion?'

'I'm afraid I didn't learn very well. It happened first when I was fourteen. A young girl I was playing hide-and-seek with taught it to me at the bottom of her garden. Actually, she had never done it before and neither had I. However, after that there were a good dozen others... But I don't suppose you know why the sisters of our friends are so clumsy at it?'

'You suppose I don't know why,' cried Teresa. 'Do you think I've never seen your respectable young women buttfucked? First of all, there's no way of finding their assholes. They're always dressed. You have to take them in their pants and it's too easy to lose your path and slide into their cunts by mistake. Then too, there isn't one in four who has sense enough to grease up the hole a little bit to make it easier. They give you their holes and that's all there is to it. You can stick your dick into it or not. It's more exciting for them raw like that, but it hurts them like hell itself. They beat themselves off as fast as they can, but you're not allowed to move or it might hurt them too much. Often this results in them coming without you ever losing a drop. That way they can do the same thing again tomorrow with someone else. Am I right?'

'How do you know so much?'

'I'm pretty well informed in that department. And they're

stupid too, your young ladies, aren't they?'

'Charming, but pretty dumb, like you say. I remember an exception once, though, that had the habit and who let you do it softly and easily. She was patient, that one...'

'An angel!' cried Teresa gaily. 'You could clean her out from top to bottom and she didn't know how to give you a smack with her behind?. Is that it? What are you laughing for? I know your young things better than you do. And afterwards, let's see. After your virgins...?'

'What do you want me to tell you? Bawdy house stories? Those things aren't interesting.'

'I just want to know what you learned.'

'There was a little dancer who went for ten francs... She danced the belly dance in Montmartre...'

'Did she dance with her ass too?'

'Better than with her belly.'

'What was she, a brunette?'

'Naturally. I don't like blondes.'

'And her asshole?'

'Why are you so curious?'

Teresa, always supple, still nude, raised herself and lay over me on her elbows, only her breasts and stomach touching me.

'When you're not buttfucking me, I need you to tell me stories about other women being buttfucked.'

'Why?'

'Don't keep asking me why I've got a fire in my ass. It's your fault!'

I could have said that I hadn't done anything to cause that, but instead I decided to take the opportunity to end her questioning.

'Your turn,' I said. 'You began to tell me about your childhood before and you stopped at the age of seven.'

'This is on the subject of women being buttfucked?'

'Yes.'

♦

She was beginning to get excited and, as usual, her language strengthened proportionally.

'It's true that I've always been used to seeing women with pricks in their rears.

'The last thing I can remember of those days was a dinner where there were some men present, some friends. Afterwards, my mother and her three sisters started playing with them with their assholes. One of the men would stick his prick into one of them and the woman would have to guess whose it was. They laughed so much that I saw the men lose their hard-ons and have their pricks slip out. Nevertheless, those women had good-looking behinds!

'When I was still seven my mother sprained her shoulder and, since she could no longer perform, she quit the circus and her sisters and everything.

'It was then that she went to live with a little bitch at Marseilles that was a hundred times more of a whore than she and who was named Francine. A good looker, Francine, but whore enough to suck a dog for twenty francs. All three of us slept together. Francine kept up her business in the afternoons, but mother didn't do anything except pimp for her. Then they'd be at each other's asses all night long when my mother wasn't exciting me to beat myself off in order to develop my snatch.

'After a month of that life, mother started to take on customers with her ass too. She even learned to suck pretty well, and she finally charged Francine to undertake my training. I was just turning eight years old; it was time for me to take on a few pricks with my rear. Mother had first done it when she was eight, I too, of course, Charlotte also, and Lili six months earlier. The sooner you get started the sooner you get used to it.

'Francine taught me everything. In six weeks she did everything in front of me that you can think of with two friends of hers that used to come specially in the evenings just to help her teach me. I saw Francine get screwed and buttfucked in the forty positions, and suck and eat pussy and lick assholes and everything, I tell you! The first time I ever saw someone shit in a woman's mouth it was Francine that ate it. I was eight years old then. And all during my six weeks of training, any time anyone in that room came it was I that drank it. Francine even fished it out of the water in the bidet to put it on my tongue. And whenever my mother ate her out she took a spoon and collected the come from her pussy and gave it to me, the bitch.

'The day when I was eight, one twenty-fifth of April, at six o'clock, a man came and gave me a package that had in it a doll that said papa-mama and some red candy to suck. Then he stuck his prick into my behind after smearing it with more vaseline than you would have needed to buttfuck a mouse... Mother cried, Francine was as pale as the laundry, and they were both afraid that he'd kill me and that they would get a couple of years in prison... But he took the cherry from my rear so gently that a few minutes afterwards I didn't know which I was the happiest with, my doll, my candy, or the prick in my backside.'

◆

Teresa uttered these last words with all the spirit of a child! She had straightened up and was resting on her two hands, her back arched, her breasts tightened, laughing fit to burst.

'I feel like eating you,' she said at last, without the least transition. 'What's with you tonight, getting hard-ons like that?'

'You lie on me and you have to ask?'

'Tell me what it is that gives you a hard-on. My skin? My hair? My teats? My ass? My mouth? What?'

'Your skin.'

'But that thing gets just as hard in my mouth. You'll be sure to give me your come in my mouth, won't you? About twenty-six hours ago I promised you that I'd suck you and you haven't even made me keep my promise.'

'Ah! You think it's easy to choose when I sleep with you!'

'The thing is that I'm not as much a whore as you think. Go ahead! Go to a whorehouse. Get your negress on her back with all fours in the air and choose your hole. She'll tell you to go fuck yourself, your negress. But I, as long as I feel like coming, I'll know how I want it.'

'And now?'

'Well... I'll suck you later.'

'Cow that you are! I didn't ask you... You asked me, and now...'

I didn't have time to finish what I was saying. Teresa had just made me enter her body according to her taste, and in a voice trembling and warm she said, 'You'll have it my mouth, you'll have it soon enough. I want to suck your prick, lap it, have my mouth full of your come, but there are some things that you can't do until I tell you. When I say, "Piss your come into my mouth!" you'll do it. Ah! You don't think that I get as excited as Charlotte, but I do when you've got your dick in my ass! You thought she was crazy because she asked you to... But I'm not crazy am I? I'm hot but I know what I'm saying. Listen: I too want you to...'

'Shut up with that stuff!'

'I want it too. I swear to you on my mother's grave that you can do it to me. I know that you never do it, but I don't want it to disgust you. Oh! I'm going to come. I'm fingering myself, you're buttfucking me, I'll tell you everything... I just started to do it again with Charlotte.'

Started to do what again? I dared not try to understand. She continued, getting more and more excited with every word.

'An hour ago, just after you finished buttfucking me, I went back into my place, found Charlotte with her sisters, took her into another room and said, "Do you want his come? I've got some in my ass.'

'Shut up! Don't tell me!'

'Screw you! I'll say it anyway. I stuck my ass on her face and shit your come into her mouth and she drank it all! It's the same asshole that's got your prick in it now. There's muscle there, can you feel it? It's the same one where your Charlotte stuck her tongue trying to find the last drop of come that...'

'Teresa! If you don't shut up I'll strangle you! I've never wanted a woman as much as I want you, but you're saying things that will make you as disgusting to me as you are beautiful!'

'You're getting harder,' she said.

'And I'm ashamed of it! I could get harder yet with the negress in the whorehouse you just mentioned and I wouldn't be half as horrified at her as I am at you.'

At this she remained motionless and trembling on me, for

she was on top of me and the suppleness of her body enabled her to take me wherever she wanted to.

And then, holding up at the same time her coming as well as mine, she said triumphantly, 'At last! You've finally realized that I'm not your whore!'

'You're worse!'

'Worse! You said it! I'm worse, but I'm something else. A whore is someone who submits to the vices of men, but I give them mine. I teach them new ones, give them the tastes I have.'

'You'll never, never get me to like *that!*

'Ha! Ha! But look what you're doing! You never wanted to do anything but screw and look at you! You've buttfucked me four times because I wanted it. Does that make me your whore? Tell me! Am I your whore!'

'If you say another word...'

'Listen to me!' she said furiously. 'Revile me! Spit on me! Do anything you want, but I defy you to lose your hard-on!'

She held me with all her strength, menacing with her teeth what she couldn't with her hands, and I was still inside her, still held the same there as I was by her two hands.

I should have been able to... But how difficult it is to explain to others a scene so passionate as that, a scene they've never lived themselves! Men know everything else and yet don't even know the first thing about the science of love. I therefore split my readers into two groups: the ones who will have already criticized me for having beaten Teresa a dozen times on the shoulder... I struck a woman! Fie! Those persons have never really been loved who don't know how much pleasure a woman in love can find in being struck by her man, the pleasure they take in suffering from the same hand that caresses them, from the same arms that hold them. On the other hand, my other group of readers have not yet understood why, if I had already beaten this woman, I hesitated to throw her this time out of my bed. It's that... that it would have really done her some harm.

No, but don't you understand that a dozen blows to the shoulder actually give more pleasure than pain? But that if, when struggling with a loved one, you catch her in a position where you would be forced to take her by the skin of her flanks or the flesh of her breasts, the man who would have beaten her before would no longer attempt it?

Even so, however, I felt like killing that woman lying on my sex. And naturally that doesn't mean that I ever ceased to find her beautiful.

She shouted, but so close to my mouth that our lips almost touched, 'So, I'm the only one that doesn't have the right to any vices? You know, when I was eight years old I lost my cherry in my behind and everywhere else, and for twenty-eight years I have been passing my days and nights satisfying the vices of others. And now you want me to act like a Christian wife who screws every Saturday night in her dirty slip and prays to St. Joseph to give her a son and only washes her ass every eight days for fear that her come will drip away?

'So I've got some vices, so what? I even think I've got them all and that maybe I've invented a couple. It comes in handy when you're a whore.'

Since I made no protest at this last word, she assumed a ferocious expression. The whole thing was really quite remarkable since we were still united by our flesh, and not only could I not escape, as Teresa had defied me to do, I could not even fail her.

A sudden smile crossed her face and transformed the whole situation. That woman had her own way, there was no doubt about it. It pleased her to continue with a softer expression and a more tender voice:

'Is it a vice to be happy every time you buttfuck me?'

'Yes.'

'So much the better. I admitted to you that I've seen a lot of women buttfucked. It always seemed rather ordinary. Tell me that it's a horrible vice and it will excite me.'

'Slut!'

'Is it a vice for me to finger myself when I'm thirty-nine years old? Then write an article stigmatizing young girls for resorting to onanism and above all their mothers... a mother like me who lifts up her skirt between the dessert and the liqueur and says to her three daughters, "Shut your traps for a while. I want to beat myself off!"'

'As long as you don't call Charlotte to...'

'Wait. And is a mother vicious that lets her daughters finger themselves in front of her? When it is she herself who has fingered them the first time to take the stiffness out of their cunts when they were seven? When she has shown them with her own hand how a woman beats herself off like you take the hand of a schoolgirl to show her how to write?'

'If that were all you did!'

'Isn't that enough? Then is it a vice to have prostituted my three daughters, little confessor? Tell me while you're buttfucking me. [She was getting more and more excited.] My mother cried when I lost the cherry in my behind, but I beat myself off when I sold Charlotte, and I got more of a kick out of coming than out of receiving the money. Understand? I don't give a damn about money. It's enough of a vice for me to have given my daughters. I stuck all three of them on their first pricks and yet...'

She never finished her sentence, but she continued to speak and to hold me in her grip. I was going crazy. I have never been in such a position, and I kept saying to myself, 'Oh! Can't I even tell when I love and when I hate?' For the more relentlessly Teresa tried to vilify herself, the more beautiful she wanted to be, and was, with all her body.

She thrust her face closer to mine and let a smile once more light it up.

'Oh no you don't! You're not getting out of that ass yet! And you're not going to come either. I feel more like coming than that prick of yours does and I'm holding myself in. You can do the same thing until I've finished talking.'

'You're beautiful,' I said. 'There's nothing you can say, and the more you speak the more...'

'The more I speak the hotter I get,' she said. 'Look at my whore's knockers and see if the ends aren't stiff. You could stick them in a lesbian's behind!'

'Please!'

'You'll listen! I'm no lesbian like my mother and her sisters. I've gone to bed with hundreds and hundreds of lesbians: blondes, brunettes, redheads, brown-haired ones, even negresses. But I'm no lesbian. I prefer a prick. Even so, I still have a vice. Have I got the right to one vice? [Here her voice began to tremble.] It excites me to have my asshole licked out by my daughters. I'm very Catholic, almost devout, and a priest once told me that it was the greatest sin I could commit. Ever since then I've done it every day. Even when I'm fingering myself, one of them always comes to suck at my hairs. Even when you're buttfucking me it excites me to think about it. Charlotte's stupid, but when she has her tongue there I tell myself that that's my eldest daughter and it makes me come twice as much.'

She began to twist her body and I knew that she wouldn't be able to rest in her quivering immobility much longer.

'The imbeciles that buttfuck us one on top of another think that incest... Ha! Ha! Ha! And it's all for my pleasure!'

Then, working her long supple body back and forth with movements of her rear that finally began to appease my interminably frustrated desire, she chose this moment that she had so carefully and patiently worked up to, the moment when I could no longer either repulse and interrupt her; with me more ardent than I had yet been, though perhaps less bewildered, she began to speak slowly without raising her voice.

'My three daughters are my bordello. I strip them naked in my living room and I take my choice. I take the one that tempts me most at the time and that one, in front of her sisters, sucks the lips of my ass, licks the slit between my buttocks, sticks her tongue into my behind, then comes around to suck my snatch and swallow everything I discharge. And I have trained them so well that I can shit the come of men who have buttfucked me into their mouths. I told you a little while ago that I took Charlotte into another room? Well, it wasn't true. I awoke the others too! They saw everything! And Lili was jealous! She came to lick my asshole afterwards because she thought there might be a drop left!'

I heard no more. I was morally exhausted, and even my physical fatigue surpassed all measure, without a doubt as a result of the long wait I had just undergone. For two minutes I remained motionless on my bed without a thought in my mind.

Chapter Ten

When I opened my eyes again, Teresa had re-entered, still completely naked, bringing with her Lili; a Lili entirely new for me, a Lili in her nightgown with a braid of hair down her back; a Lili asleep on her feet.

She dropped the girl into an armchair like a rag doll and came over to whisper into my ear, carefully separating each word:

'Let me alone now. She's my daughter, and I can raise her how I want. If you insult me in front of her or try to keep her from doing what I ask, I'll never forgive you.'

She could have saved her breath, for I had not the least intention. I was completely dazed. I had no intentions, good or bad, towards either her or Lili.

Teresa made the girl get up from her chair, where she seemed to have fallen once more to sleep, and somehow awoke her completely with the words, 'Show us how you can wake up when you see a man. Ready? One! Two! Three! Are you still asleep?'

'No, mama.'

'Good. Now what does a little girl do when she is standing in front of a man and she is in her nightgown?'

And just as she would have recalled a rule of polite behaviour that all good children should know, Lili, with a funny little smile, raised her nightgown to her waist and spread her legs a little. Then she threw herself around my neck and, kindly but slightly scolding, said, 'You were buttfucking Charlotte! She told me all about it.'

'I'm not surprised! She told me quite a bit too.'

'About what?'

'I know how you eat your cookies.'

'My cookies? You mean when I stick them into her pussy before she fingers herself? And what else?'

I turned towards Teresa. 'Can I ask her how she was born?'

'Certainly. Tell him Lili.'

She hesitated, however. Then, seeing that I already knew, she began to laugh.

'Charlotte is my father. She knocked up mama with her asshole.'

She even (and since I'd never seen Lili crack a joke of this type, I think that this was maliciousness) quickly added something I had not asked for.

'In our family we always make the kids that way. Mama just made another one tonight with Charlotte, but it didn't take because it was in her mouth instead.'

Lili never laughed when she joked, and, seeing that I wasn't laughing either, Teresa quickly said, 'Are you keeping that nightshirt on so you'll look like an angel, my under-fucked little toad? Or is it something to catch the drops of come in?'

Scarcely touched by the blast, the little angel removed her gown and said to her mother, 'Do I have to undo my braid?'

'No. Come over here to me and tell us what you did with him yesterday.'

'I had his prick in me everywhere, mama. From the front, from behind, and in the mouth.'

'Is that all?'

'Yes, I only have three holes. It's too bad that you didn't give me fourteen.'

'Listen to her... And what else do you know how to do?'

'Anything you want.'

'Tell us what.'

Lili hesitated, sighed, then after glancing towards me, replied with all the discouragement of a young girl who has given up trying to bring her mother up properly:

'A lot of things that he doesn't like, mama. I saw that right away.'

'Oh? You saw that?'

'Yes. He's not the kind that likes to piss on little girls and make them do all kinds of stupid things. He doesn't like anything that's dirty and he likes everything that's good... And he isn't vicious either. He isn't the sort to use a whip. But I know something that he won't say no to.'

She whispered excitedly into her mother's ear.

'Repeat it out loud,' said Teresa. 'Don't be afraid. Say it just like you said it to me.'

Lili lowered her eyes and spoke in such a reluctant and embarrassed manner that she sighed deeply between each word.

'When he... When he...buttfucks you... mama... I'll put... I'll put my hand into your pussy and... and I'll... I'll...'

'Little imbecile!' cried Teresa. 'You'll take his prick through the skin of my cunt and beat him off into my ass. What are you making so much out of so little for? And if I suck him?'

'I'll lick his balls and his ass.'

'And if we fuck?'

'That would bowl me over!' said Lili seriously.

Teresa burst out laughing and howled until her loins and her stomach shook.

Up to that point, Lili had been a victim of stage-fright. So free with either myself or her mother, she let herself be intimidated by the sight of both of us together. For her the two of us formed a public and she had behaved accordingly. Now, her mother's laughter suddenly transformed her like an unexpected success sometimes transforms a young actress. From that moment on she wore an entirely different expression, and Teresa, quick to note any change in her daughters, said loudly, 'Miss Lili! On stage! What do you call that costume you're wearing?'

'This is a suit little girls wear when they're completely nude. My mama made it for me working with her...'

'And the thing that hides your sex, miss?'

'Oh! For all the sex I've got, madame, it's hardly worth the trouble bothering to hide it.'

Lili could be good when she had gained a little aplomb. I began to question her also.

'Do you want me to hire you, my dear? As dancer? Singer? Acrobat? What do you know how to do?'

'Suck off the director,' said Lili unhesitatingly.

She was doing well! And in the same tranquil voice, without ever looking for a word, she continued, 'As an acrobat I'm the spitting image of my grandmother. Would you like to see the snake-girl number, good sir? With the trick of finding a lesbian in your bed when you get in by yourself?'

'Yes.' said Teresa. 'Let's see it.'

'If my mama knew what I was doing,' began Lili. And from there on I thought that she was reciting a role she had learned by heart. I didn't know her well enough at that time to guess that she had made the whole thing up herself from scraps of sentences she had chanced to hear plus the natural gift of a child-comedienne.

She squatted at the foot of the bed, elbows on knees, feet beneath buttocks, and said in a melancholy voice:

'You see here before you the most unhappy girl in the world, the child-martyr the papers have been so full of lately. They didn't dare tell why she is a child-martyr, it's so terrible, but it's because I have a perverted mother, good sirs! God forgive her!'

'You listening?' asked Teresa.

'There are little girls who are beaten, whipped, chained up, martyred, that people stick tacks into and deprive of food, but my case is even worse! Do you know what is forbidden to me until my twenty-first birthday? Ah! Good sirs! No one could ever guess where my mother has inflicted her punishment on me! She forbade me to beat myself off!'

'You'd think it was true!' said Teresa again.

Lili never batted an eye. She continued in the same slow, resigned voice, a child naming her misfortunes without the least hope of consolation. There was almost a modesty in her manner as she related the rest of her tale:

'Sir, I ask you to be my witness. I used to beat myself off like this, like any good child would: one finger in the ass, one finger in the hole, and one finger on the clitoris. I didn't hurt myself, I assure you, but it was no use telling that to mama. Grown-ups never understand anything.'

'Poor thing!' I sympathized.

'And the things they shout at you!... Mama made me

swear that I would never again acquire the deadly vice of masturbation! Imagine a word like that right to my face! And me just a little girl!'

'They allow such things? And you never again took up this terrible habit?'

'No, what could I do?'

'And you didn't commit suicide?'

'No, because I say to hell with it like to hell with my three virginities. Since I can't beat myself off, I suck myself.'

Instinctively, Lili gave this, last answer without the least trace of an accent, keeping the same simple, soft voice. Ten years in the theatre does less for most actresses than fourteen years of existence had done for Lili. I couldn't help whispering to Teresa, 'She should be on the stage!'

'True!' replied Teresa. 'She offers to suck the director without even bothering to tell him what she can do. What else can you teach a girl like that?'

But Lili was finishing her monologue, modulating the grossness of her language with an angelic voice.

'So it's entirely my mother's fault if I no longer beat myself off under my nightdress like a model little girl. Instead of that, I spend an hour completely naked, rubbing my behind against my mouth, saying, "Lili, you're no dummy when you can still suck your own come!" Grown-ups, kind sir, never know what bad advice they give we children because, fortunately, we never listen to them; we only pretend to; but if, once in a while, we do listen, look what happens.'

'Oh, really, Lili!' cried Teresa, gaily scolding.

'You're not here, mama,' replied Lili, immediately taking up her role once again to finish by saying that she could tell no more since her exercise made it rather difficult to talk.

And then she proceeded to do what she had said. She rolled herself into a tiny ball, her shoulders on the bedsheet, her legs open behind her head, her arms crossed on her buttocks. Her mound was touching her chin... and this detail wasn't the only one I was most interested in.

I was amazed at her body, so small already, so slim, so short, so light, become twice as small, reduce itself to almost nothing, as if she were turning herself inside out by going back inside her own little shell.

Lili prolonged the position, and when I wanted to order, 'Rest!' Teresa gave a contradictory command.

'Better than that now. Enough for the snatch, stick your tongue into your cunt. Good. And is that all you can do? Can't you go any farther? Is that kid a real whore or not? What about that little rose bud I can see? Better than that, Lili! Your whole tongue into your ass...! Look how she's sticking it in! What a little whore...! That's fine, Lili! Not bad at all! Engaged for the season!'

Lili came up very red in the face and...

All educators will understand what I am going to say: either it should be forbidden to little girl-serpents to engage in Sapphism on themselves in front of their mothers' lovers, or, if it is permitted, they must be praised for their performances.

Therefore, I was just beginning to offer the young acrobat the compliments that were her due when Teresa interrupted us.

'Go into the bathroom, honey. Close the door, make yourself pretty, brush the hairs on your ass, and come back in when I call you.'

Lili obeyed with good grace. However, the ghost of a curious smile fitted across her face at the words, 'Brush the hairs on your ass!' It seemed to me that she was saying to herself, 'If I wanted to be bothered to answer that, I could be funnier than she!' But she knew another way to prove that she was not stupid: she said nothing at all.

♦

When the door closed there was a silence. Teresa said nothing, and although I knew that she loved Lili at least maternally if not more, I would have been really naïve if I thought she was waiting for me to compliment her on her daughter.

She looked into my eyes.

She let her hand creep across to my flank.

Her thigh to my thigh.

That was all. A minute had been all she had needed to obtain, without touching the desired article directly, the result she sought. More weary of mind than of body, I was slothful enough not to greet the instant success of her remote control magnetism with a ringing oration. I don't like to submit myself as subject for thaumaturgical scenes; and besides I was beginning to know Teresa: I saw that she wanted more to excite me than to satisfy me.

'I refuse to say another word to you unless you get an erection!' she said unpityingly.

'You see before you,' I smiled, 'the young-man martyr the papers have been so full of lately.'

'Get a hard-on and wait! Do like me. When Lili licks me you'll see if I hold in or not.'

'Is it because of your religion, Madame? Is this staunch resolution the result of a vow?'

With a little growl she quieted me. 'I'm getting a little tired of these jokes!' But it was only a threat, for she proceeded to tell me what she was now going to offer in the way of pleasures, what awaited my perseverance, and the role that Lili would play. I won't tell you now what they were, not in order to hide them, but because you will read them on the next page. Besides, Teresa gave me a resumé that was a little long for a production of only one act.

I would have liked to have explained to her at this point that I had not had the good fortune to receive at birth a miraculous organ that never wore out, but one susceptible to one of the proofs of human weakness. But she wasn't listening. She cried, 'Lili!'

'So!' said this one seeing me as yet relaxed. 'It hasn't begun yet. What are you going to do?'

'Three things. Come here to me. You can guess them by yourself.'

Teresa helped her a little, letting her, as if by accident, see the state of excitement she was in. Lili cried joyously, 'Oh! Is all that for me?'

'And then? What haven't you had today, little fart?'

'A prick in the ass... But I hardly dare ask for that.'

'I think we might lend it to you, if you return it. And after that; what will you do for us?'

Pierre Louÿs

'The hand inside!'

Nimbly and more serpent-like than ever, Lili slid across her mother's body and stuck her face between her thighs. Her little head disappeared in the long black hair where my hand had several times lost its way. Teresa, always so supple, twisted the top half of her body towards me, resting on one shoulder, and held me tight.

She wanted to talk and I had to listen. She said the following things, murmuring them ardently but evenly, punctuating them with little smiles:

'Sssst! Listen. I'm calm now; you can believe me. There's my vice, and my happiness. I went into my bordello, picked the little whore I wanted. You can call her whore, like Charlotte. I'm the only one you can't call whore.

'And what a whore! She's not even my lesbian. She hasn't made me come, she's just licking the come that I made for you. Yesterday it was the same thing but with a different whore. I discharged in Charlotte's mouth for your prick! Your prick ! Your prick! And you didn't even understand, you virgin!'

Very clever, that last word! She knew that I was not listening to her, that Lili had amused me and that I was still thinking of her; and with one word she caught once more at my straying attention, exasperating me for the third time with that word 'virgin.' That done, she closed my mouth for me, redoubled the violence of her language, and began to tremble slightly between murmurs.

'There was never a mother who gave so much milk to her daughters as I have given come to mine. This one is ten years old and she's still sucking me. But not my teats. You can have my teats to warm your hands or caress your balls, or hold your prick. If there was any milk in them you could have that too, but not her. Look at her sucking! Like a kitten under the mother cat's stomach! She's only fourteen years old. How many more years do you think I'll be able to have her tongue in my ass? Charlotte has been sucking my come for twenty-odd years now and she still hasn't been weaned.'

'Do you think there was ever a more infamous mother than you?' I whispered.

'Say that some more. That excites me. Makes me flow. The more you say that, the more Lili will have to drink.'

'Are you going to come, bitch?'

'No. She's licking what you left from before. I was flooded. She hasn't even finished yet! So, I'm so bad a mother as all that? Are you sure? There are so many others!'

'The others have at least the excuse of giving themselves to the vices of men; but the incestuous scenes that you've been showing me here...'

'I'm worse than a whore, I know.'

'A hundred times worse! You're frightening, you're so bad! You're worse than the whores, the lesbians, the procuresses, even the customers at the bordellos.'

Here, Lili raised her head and, without having heard anything of our whispers, said, 'What's going on up here, mama? The more I suck the more flows out.'

'That's enough!' said Teresa, pulling herself together with an effort. 'Do something else. Go rub some soap in your behind. Clean it out and come sit down underneath him.'

Heaven never gave me the temperament to be a spectator. Besides, Teresa had held me in a state of excitement for a long time and I was happy for that reason to be given a chance to work it off. I'll admit it even to those moralists whom I shall never hope to change and who will reproach me again for the following scene: I was happy to be given a chance to finish.

But, as she had once already, little miss Lili committed another outrage to all modesty when she came to 'sit down beneath him' as her mother had said, so I made her change her position. Besides, I was getting tired of lying down.

Without overworking my imagination, I stood the girl on a stool next to the bed with her body leaning forward. Unfortunately, in real stories like this one the positions are always more simple than in novels.

'Hold steady now!' said Teresa. 'You look like a little violet vendor standing on her basket so she can be buttfucked in the shithouse of a bistro.'

'And to look like a little princess, how do you have to be buttfucked?' asked Lili.

However, she behaved herself like a good child and became serious again at the proper time.

Turning her head to the side where her mother could not see her face, she looked at me over her shoulder with a kind expression in her eyes and a little barely pursed shape to her lips that seemed to say, 'I can't say anything to you because mama is here.' I returned a glance which replied that we understood each other; but I incorporated the same mystery into it, for the smaller the little girl, the greater are her secrets.

Our silent dialogue was interrupted as quickly as it takes to tell it by Teresa, who could no longer hide her excitement. She shot me a smile in which I thought I saw ferocity lurking just beneath the surface, a smile with the teeth rather more than with the lips. She said into my ear, 'You can prostitute my daughter of fourteen and it's nothing! What makes me hot is to take your prick out of her and... Listen! Listen!'

She lay down on the bed in the middle. 'Your tongue, Lili,' she cried. 'Lick my asshole. Make it good and wet. Spread the hair out. Now, take his prick, my child! Stick it in to me yourself. And tell me what you call a little girl who would help buttfuck her mother. Tell me.'

Lili found two answers. She whispered the first to me in a breath:

'It's the daughter of a whore.'

Then out loud to Teresa:

'It's easy to see that she would be a little girl that was made from an asshole!'

The first answer amused me so much that I forgot my role and missed my entrance despite the care with which Lili had prepared it.

I don't think Teresa heard either the first or the second. And since she had her back turned, she didn't see the smile that darted across my face. But she spoke in such a way that my desire to laugh soon vanished. She spewed and vomited her words. She became really terrible. In front of a little girl – 'a bit of a whore' undoubtedly, but with a sense of humour and a sense of propriety – in front of a girl too young to understand the delirium of the senses, it seemed to me that this flood of obscenities was utterly senseless. But Teresa wallowed in it. She was trying to surpass even what she had said in front of Charlotte, as if the frailty of the girlhood of her youngest daughter excited her even more.

Lili, attentive, not in the least intimidated, but silent nevertheless, then proceeded to her last task.

Her tiny hand was small enough to fit completely into the none too large sex of Teresa. Once inside, the adroit member opened it little by little, groped, seemed to flutter, and seized firmly across the membrane the penis that could not escape it.

I do not hesitate, at this point, to admit that until that hour I had never accepted the gratifications of a woman's hand. It seems to me ridiculous and undesirable, but the exercise that Lili performed was of the utmost finesse in conception and execution. I was speechless in admiration.

I wished that Teresa had been as silent as I! But she never once ceased crying, 'Ah! What a whore this girl is! What a come-pumper! Ah! Turn around, my child, so I can fondle your ass, my little bitch!' and a hundred other things of like nature. It dazed me so that I was frowning like a preacher. When an acrobat does his speciality the orchestra stops playing, and in the same way this supreme trick of Lili's merited a little silence. Incest itself was only another stimulus to Teresa's pleasure. I would have passed it up for just that reason.

However, to take a beautiful woman in the way that brings to the surface her greatest ardour, and to feel down at the bottom of her entrails a tiny hand, soft but firm, that takes you, that grips you, that feels you, that caresses you... Truly, if you have never had such an experience, believe me that it is superfluous to attempt to add a moral conception such as incest to so intense a physical sensation. It is sufficient in itself when one knows how to regulate one's desires, moderate one's passions, and live content with a little that is at the same time a great deal.

Chapter Eleven

By what renewed chance did I encounter Mauricette a second time on the stairway a few steps from my door? I don't know, but I must admit that I was scarcely surprised. Chance of this sort repeats itself, strangely enough, more often than it varies.

Silent and pouting, she turned her head away from me when I attempted to kiss her, but followed me freely into my room – in order to make a scene. I was waiting for it, and I deserved it: I had mounted her first of all; she gave herself to me; she had sent me her mother and her sisters out of a sense of family loyalty; but for two days now I had completely forgotten her – she to whom I owed so much.

I was remorseful at first; in a few minutes I was even more so, for Ricette suddenly seemed to me even prettier than she had before. And I must admit that our remorse usually mirrors the fluctuations of our attractions very faithfully.

What was she going to say? I quickly prepared several responses to reproaches that I anticipated. But if I anticipated a sentence it was always a sure thing that it was not the one that Ricette had on her lips.

'You're going to break my cherry,' she said calmly.

And since my face clearly showed that I was much more stupefied than impressed, Ricette did not wait for my reply.

'Ah! That's great! You're a nice one! The day before yesterday I showed you my cherry and today when I offer it to you you don't want it!'

I took her on my knees unprotestingly, but before I could say a word she continued:

'What a character! You always do the opposite of what

one wants. For three hours Charlotte pleaded with you to call her whore; it excites her when she's going to come; and you didn't want to; she told us that she never before met such a headache in all her life. But the next day you called mama whore ten times because she doesn't like it. You're a queer one!'

'Not queer at all.'

'Oh yeah? I'm not even finished. You know that mama and Charlotte like to be buttfucked. So what do you do? You tell them that the only thing you like is to screw. But when I have my virginity to sell, and I decide to give it to you...'

'You're a dear!'

'Go on! When Charlotte wants it from the rear, you want to give it to her from the front. And when I offer it to you from the front, you don't want it at all.'

I sighed deeply. To be obliged to give a long explanation, knowing in advance that it will not be understood, is a terrible situation. I therefore renounced my best arguments in favour of those which Ricette would understand most easily.

'Listen. You're fifteen and a half?'

'Yes, and I should be able to screw if I can be buttfucked.'

'Good. You can screw. But did you know that it will hurt you a lot worse from the front than it ever did from the rear?'

'That's okay,' she said tenderly.

'And did you know that it won't make me any happier than you?'

'I care even less about that,' she said gaily.

'And then what's going to happen in the evening? Since all four of you are lesbians your mother and sisters are going to see right away that something is missing. Teresa will be furious. We'll all get shot together when she gets wind of it. And what'll we have left after all that? The memory of half an hour in which we had a lot more pain and trouble than pleasure, and all the while I'll be regretting that you will be in the process of fucking others. Let's do the contrary. Let's have someone else take your cherry, and then we'll screw as much as you want.'

Mauricette remained thinking. I realized later that she undoubtedly wanted to ask me why it was worth two thousand francs if I didn't want to do it for nothing. But she remained silent. And while she was lost in thought, an idea came to me that ended by winning her over.

'Why don't you give me your other cherry instead?'

'Which one?' she said surprised.

She didn't get it. Since she was still on my lap I pressed her against me and said in a low voice, 'Let's see. I won't be lowering you in front of your sisters, but no one will hear us. Aren't you ashamed of yourself, at your age, not to know how to suck yet? Is that it?'

She certainly was! She blushed like a child whose confessor has reproached her for a mortal sin.

'How is it that you're almost sixteen and you still don't know that?'

'Ah! If I told you...'

'Yes, but that was childishness. We have to cure you of all that once and for all. Do you want to try? Would you like to try it once with me – all alone?'

She put her arms around my neck and, hiding her head between my cheek and shoulder, replied, 'Yes. I'd like to try it with you.'

Hardly had she accepted my proposition when I regretted having made it. How in the hell, I asked myself, could I refuse this kid's virginity because I didn't want to spatter myself with blood, even when it would have made her very happy, and then accept something that might leave her with just as bad a memory? I'm running the risk of bringing on a nasty case of nausea for her and getting myself drenched with vomit at the same time. That will be gay if it ends like that!

These depressing thoughts slowly disappeared before the more attractive one of giving a lesson in sex to one of Teresa's daughters. And then even the difficulty posed a challenge, a problem to resolve. I hoped that with me it might not be the same as it had been with the others; no one likes to think that he is one of the herd; and since she had to learn to do it some day anyway, why not make it myself who gave her the taste? Yes, I said the taste. I don't doubt anything any more.

Mauricette returned from the toilet nude, and her first

words plucked up my courage.

'I think it will be all right.'

Then she added, unfortunately:

'Where can I spit it?'

'Spit it out? But you don't spit it out! That's the principle of the thing! You mean to say you left a boarding school filled with young girls getting set to go into society and no one told you that you're supposed to swallow it?'

'Oh, yes! They told me, and God knows the things they swallowed! There were some there who could have taught things to Lili. But I'm not a society girl, so I'll do it like at a whorehouse. I'll spit.'

'You'll swallow, my dear girl, and right away too. There'll be none of this holding it in your mouth two or three minutes until you've gotten it all. Understand? You were certainly badly brought up in your family.'

Without replying, she threw herself on me and, with her lips against mine, said in a much warmer voice, 'You're really going to come in my mouth? Then give me your tongue first... And promise that you'll give it to me again afterwards... And I'll tell you something on my honour: I've never before drunk the come of a man, never! So if I fail you it will be because of that, see? And if I succeed, you don't need to think that I love you! I don't love you at all! Not at all! at all! at all! at all!'

Upon which she gave me the nicest, sweetest kiss I had yet received from that family of diverse personalities. I thought of a verse from Clément Marot, but I didn't have time to dream. Mauricette was already at work.

'Easy! Easy!' I said. 'You're taking it like you would a lesbian. We haven't reached the advanced studies yet. Just try to give me a little pleasure at first, and the only person you need worry about is you. I don't have a young nymph abandoning herself to nothing but lewdness before my eyes. Not that at all. I only have a delicious little Ricette who is as pretty and shy as a fawn and who is going to say, "Is that all there is to it?" when she has finished.'

'But you're stopping me from...'

'Quiet! When you are sucking you don't speak. First

principle: don't open your mouth to ask the man how his grandmother's health is. And you're not supposed to laugh either. This is serious.'

'But it's you that...'

'Quiet! Now continue. I'll warn you in time. Do you want me to hurry it? I can do that quite easily. You hurry too, but remember the rules: you swallow immediately, you say how good it is, and you ask for more. Ricette my darling! How good it is in your mouth!'

This last sentence, as I should have foreseen, gave her a great deal of pleasure and increased her zeal. The praise that we cherish the most is always that which is made on our weakest points. And besides, young girls who have never sucked before do it exactly as they make love; therefore they have to be brought to a certain pitch of passion.

I continued in the same vein, and in only a few words Ricette was worked up to the necessary point... I warned her... She shuddered, closed her eyes, paled as if she were accomplishing some great feat of prowess in the face of danger... and when she had finished she sat up on her heels, her mouth open, completely stupefied.

She looked at me out of dazed eyes. I opened my arms for her. She threw herself into them, at once proud, surprised, ashamed, tender, and above all so moved that I could feel her heart beating beneath her little left breast.

'I did it,' she said. 'It's not possible! I could never do it before and this time I swallowed everything, but everything! Just like you said.'

'And it's not so bad either, is it? There are a lot of girls who really like it.'

'I don't know if it was good or not,' she said dreamily, 'but it made me happy – because you came.'

And after I had kissed her for that, she took up the thread once more:

'And besides... and besides... do you think your come is like everyone else's?'

'Certainly.'

'No, it isn't.'

'Yes.'

'No.'

She was dreaming again and said, crossing her hands, 'Mama is the one who will be surprised! She'll never believe it!'

'What'll we do?'

'Do it again!' cried Ricette. 'We'll do it again in front of her!'

◆

The idea was worth a reward; we both thought of this at the same time, but Ricette spoke first and I was a thousand miles from guessing what she was going to ask me.

With her arms still around my neck, she said softly, 'I want something. Say yes.'

'All right. Yes. What is it?'

'You've been trapped. I know that you don't like it, but you said yes already, and I feel like it.'

'Feel like what?'

She took a few minutes like a young actress; then bent to my ear and said loudly, despite herself, and in a voice that trembled with laughter:

'I feel like beating myself off.'

'Little horror! And you think that I'm going to let you do it? Ask me for anything, but...'

'Nothing else. Later on I will. But now you said yes in advance, and besides, you know that I'm in the habit of doing it. I told you the last time I was here.'

'Then you're as bad as Charlotte? When you feel like the finger, you finger yourself? Even in front of a man?'

'Especially.'

'And can't I offer you anything in its place?'

'Later. It won't stop us from doing anything.'

It was really the family vice, all right, but I still couldn't get used to it and I felt a sort of jealousy at seeing the girl taking her pleasure by herself. She hardly touched herself and went very slowly, never jerking her finger. At first, seeing that I had given in, she was teasing.

'Look at my cherry! Look!' she said, opening her thighs. 'Will you finish?'

'I have to finger it since you refuse to take it.'

The joke made me furious, but her face remained so kind that I forced myself to joke too.

'My dear young lady, is flagellation one of your habits also?'

'Oh, yes sir. Just like my sister Charlotte.'

'Fine. Go get the whip. What you've just said is worth a good thirty lashes on the behind.'

'Oh! And when I'm all bloody, you'll buttfuck me won't you?' She was laughing. 'Do you think I take you for a man who would whip me?'

'You know that I can't take your cherry because I'd never see you again, so you stick it under my nose and beat it off as if I weren't capable of taking it? And you don't think this is worth the whip?'

Between the four women in that family I went from surprise to surprise. Mauricette this time became suddenly serious and said simply, 'Give it to me.'

Then she had a little crisis that reminded me in a lesser degree of those of Charlotte and Teresa. Trembling in my arms, she repeated, 'I want you to hurt me.'

'Who? My darling? The little fifteen-year-old girl who came all nude into my bed? But I'd be a monster!'

'You already did it without knowing. The day before yesterday I only moistened my ass with a little saliva when you buttfucked me. It was good. It was as if you skinned my behind and the more I suffered the more I beat off.'

'What? You're as vicious as all that?'

'No. But I like you to hurt me a little when I'm fingering myself,' she repeated, her eyes narrowing, her fine white teeth beginning to sink into her lower lip.

'And that's what you really want?'

'Take the ends of my breasts between your teeth and bite! And I'll give you my cherry from in front so that you can hurt me some more with your prick, so that you can rip it, so that I'll bleed. Now that I have drunk your come, I'm yours. Hold me tight, I'm going to come. Hold me with all your might. Crush me. Break me...'

Decidedly, I thought to myself, Lili is the only sane one in this mélange. The other three are crazy.

♦

However, I was beginning to understand why Charlotte had said, 'That kid will end up by disgusting all three of us.' Charlotte, though she was more than twenty years old, was still almost a child. Mauricette at fifteen was a woman. While the eldest sister had a slow mind and little spirit, the second girl was precocious both mentally and physically, had flesh that was prompt to respond, and a real instinct for vice.

It was too early to tell what Lili would become after adolescence, but that year, that day, it was Mauricette that reminded me most of her mother.

However, at that point I wanted to make Ricette talk, and I spoke a phrase to her that I'm as ashamed of as if it had been a crime. There are no prettier Latin verses than those in which Tibulus smiled at the white lies of love. But I can't smile at the one I told. This is a confession. I am being perfectly frank, telling everything; but I would have taken much more pleasure in inventing a story where I could give myself (so easily!) a sympathetic role.

Recall Mauricette's age, her precocity, her ardour... Imagine above this base the unlimited sentiment which she must have had for the sacrifice she wanted to make! And how much... But why say any more? I've already written enough to hang myself in the eyes of my readers. I loved Mauricette, but I didn't love her like you love a lover. So to make her speak, and with no other reason, I said to her, my lips against hers:

'I adore you.'

'I adore you too,' she whispered, without knowing that it was almost the same reply that Melisande had given. And as I had foreseen, she spoke; but immediately, without any transition. She spoke with the same brusque crescendos as Teresa.

'You don't believe me? Okay! You'll see! You'll lash my

behind with a whip yet and then buttfuck me in my flowing blood!'

'I'll do *that* to you?!'

'Yes, you'll do it if you love me. I've just done something for you that I had never done for anyone before. I swallowed your come... You never whipped a kid? So much the better! You have a horror of that sort of thing? Better yet! Then I can teach you something, too!'

I never for a second dreamed of consenting, but instead of replying to this effect, I questioned her some more.

'How come you have the taste for that sort of thing at your age?'

'Because I'm mama's daughter.'

'What do you mean? That your blood is the same? Or that...'

'Or that she trained me? Go ahead and say it! It's her own word. Yes, she trained me like a trick dog. And I like it. I'd like to be able to do as much as she.'

'How did she train you to...?'

'Oh, it wasn't hard or long! Since she has the same taste herself she saw right away that I too... It was just like in the circus. I had my exercises every day before... Oh, but you know how they train dogs; they do their tricks before they can eat; for me it was before coming. And little by little mama saw how far I could go...'

I raised my eyebrows. She hesitated and then, in that voluptuous voice that young girls can sometimes assume when they wish, said, 'You want me to say it? It excites me almost as much to think it when I'm next to you as to have you do it to me.'

'And I'd a hundred times rather listen to you than to beat you.'

'Beat me? If it was only that! I can see you still don't know mama!'

And in concise, definite sentences, she drew up the following summary of her family:

'I can't make Lili understand that mama isn't a whore. But you've seen her, haven't you? Charlotte is a good girl. Lili is a whore – she's the only one of us that is. Mama is a whoremonger. When she gives a performance in front of a customer it's she that gets really excited, that comes... And I'm like her! I'm a whoremonger too, and when I received your come in my mouth...'

'Is that right? And I suppose you'll give me a present as a token of your satisfaction?'

'Yes, and a brand-new one: my cherry.'

By the quickness and agility of her reply she quickly hoisted herself once more to the height from which my stupid wisecrack had attempted to hurl her. And, quickly, she re-undertook her narrative in the same light-hearted tone.

'You know how she handled it, mama, when she saw that I... that I liked that sort of thing. She simply said to me that we would see how far I could go in taking punishment without it keeping me from coming.'

'Nothing simpler!' I repeated. 'And was it she who did the beating?'

'Naturally,' said the girl innocently. 'And she made me do a lot more than the others ever did.'

'I don't follow you.'

'Didn't Charlotte tell you that there's no one who can finger or suck a girl like mama. So when it was her, she could really make me a martyr and I'd still come.'

'Make you a martyr?'

'And how! Even Charlotte was crying and had to leave the room. She couldn't stand to see it. But I never cried. I clamped my teeth together so I wouldn't cry out or... Ah! You don't know what you're going to hear! Look at my knockers. You see anything?'

'I hope so.'

'No, I mean any marks.'

'No.'

'That's because the needles were sterilized.'

'What needles?'

'When she used to finger me like she could, stopping every time just when I was on the verge of coming, she could stick thirty-two needles into my breasts! Thirty-two! Before I said

I couldn't take any more!'

'Your mother!'

'That's nothing. There aren't any marks on it either, are there? You think she doesn't know how to do things like this? Well, there where it's even more tender she tore out my pubic hairs in groups of four hairs each. That hurt me more even than the needles! But the thing that Charlotte couldn't stand was when mama would stop beating me off to chew me.'

'Chew your cunt?'

'Yes. The lips. Oh! That really hurt! The last few times, she chewed until she drew blood and then...'

Ricette threw her arms around my neck as if to excuse herself to me for all this, and after a short silence, said:

'Oh, well! You know mama! I told you: she's not a whore, she's a whoremonger. While she was sucking my blood I thought she'd go crazy. She had to have Charlotte come save her... then she beat herself off while she was grinding her teeth on my cunt-lips, and I was more afraid than hurt. I thought that when she came she would rip me away in pieces! Oh! But... I've said enough. You don't understand these things anyway.'

'Not enough, if you want me to understand. The way I get it, your mother taught you the art of coming while you were suffering. And now you have to suffer before you can come. Is that right?'

'That's it. Good. I'll tell you some more then. Do you know how I finger myself at the dinner table?'

'Can't say that I do.'

'As if you didn't know that we all beat ourselves off right after lunch! But I... You'll see if I like to suffer when I'm coming! I smear my snatch with mustard and then I finger myself all awkwardly so it rubs in. But pimento salad is the best. When I can get it I always use pimento salad.'

God! This one was the worst of the three! She was completely mad!

I asked one last question.

'And what do you let men do to you?'

'Oh! Not what mama does! Nothing but whips and rods with men.'

She started to smile, but lowered her eyes and said in a sad little voice, 'Poor Charlotte! If you could see us next to each other at times like that! I get all excited and stick out my behind. But she, from the first stroke of the whip, starts crying; and since I love her I can't hit her any more when she does that. They hardly ever take us together any more because of that. But they always want to take me with mama because, for that, mama and I are exactly the same. You know it as well as I do.'

'I know it as well as you do?' I asked uncomprehendingly. 'Oh!'

Mauricette's cry was so frankly indignant that you would have thought that I'd lied to her. She sat up quickly on her heels, her hands on her knees.

'I have to teach *that* to you too? The day before yesterday when mama came back from here she said that you grabbed her pubic hair and hurt her so much that she almost came.'

'If you think I did it for that, you're crazy!'

'And she told me this morning that she finally got you to hit her, but that it was so...'

'Oh, I socked her a couple of times on the shoulder, but that's got nothing to do with flagellation.'

'Maybe not for you! But for mama, yes! You mean to say that you have slept with her three times and you still don't know what she likes?'

'Her daughters.'

'You don't know how right you are! She has to have one of us under her when she's being whipped, and then you can do anything to her you want to! It's frightening. She cries, she comes, I've got blood in my hair and come in my face...!'

She was wild-eyed and excited, and she interrupted herself to shake her head and throw herself onto me.

'If you really love me, if it was the truth, I'll take her place. I'll get on top of her and you can buttfuck me in my blood while she sucks me off. Then it will be her turn to have my blood in her hair and my come on her face while your prick is in my behind!'

I had never seen Ricette in so excited and exalted a state, and I thought that she had reached her peak when her exaltation suddenly leaped even higher as she thought of a new infamy.

'No!' she cried. 'You can take my cherry dog-fashion while she catches the blood and come with her face from underneath!'

And what a tone of voice she said that in! At that instant I knew what it was to receive an order.

She spoke curtly and warmly as she continued.

'I know you'd rather screw me than buttfuck me. I'd rather have you buttfuck me and hurt me while I'm beating off, but since you like to fuck, we'll fuck. I know better than you do why you don't want to take my cherry. It's because you never try to buy them from girls and you think that mine is for sale, so you don't want to steal it. Well, it isn't for sale. I'm going to tell mama this evening that I'm giving it away and that she'll see who's getting it soon enough because she'll have her mouth underneath when it happens.'

Shaking her head and hair, she smiled, and then she had an explosion of sincerity that revealed to me something I had never suspected.

'You think that she will be angry? You think that she will say no? Ha! She'll be only too happy, the cow! When I tell her that you are going to fuck me on top of her, that she'll have her mouth full of blood and come, she'll be beating herself off for fourteen hours at the very thought... Did I tell you that I loved her? Yes, I love her tongue, her finger, her body, and she excites me. And I told you that she wasn't a whore, didn't I? Well, she isn't. She's a slut!'

♦

Mauricette's outburst surprised me much less than Charlotte's had before her. First of all it was a second changed viewpoint that I had unearthed. That is the trouble with memoirs: they get monotonous. In a novel, this kind of repetition can never be excused, but in life it has to be accepted. As M. Ingres once said, 'Bread and pencil are one and the same.' For a novelist, these words of a painter should be dogma. For those who write memoires they should not. In the latter case, the pencil should never change life to conform to the interests of dramatics.

Secondly... But you have to know the two girls. There was to be found in them a series of contrasts that you wouldn't have the patience to listen to if I had it to write them down. At the age of sixteen, Ricette pranced through every word she spoke, while Charlotte, at twenty-something, was languor itself. The precocity of the younger girl left less room for surprises than the tired, passive character of the sad Charlotte.

However, I don't think this is the place for me to keep a distraught silence in order to better deliver an exercise on the psychology of comparison and parallel.

I must get on with the story. I have digressed long enough already.

A young girl had come to offer me her virginity as if it had been gold or myrrh or incense.

Eternal misunderstanding. Young girls always overestimate the pleasure that we take in receiving much a gift; and young men rarely understand that if their virgins, through an error caused by innocence, think that their present is worth all the young men's love and that they are offering it to them with all theirs, then it is worth what they think it is and should be received accordingly.

I had proven to this girl that imprudence had separated us forever, and she had discovered a way to circumvent the difficulty. The method was as extravagant as a theorem in spatial geometry, but, at first sight, it was irrefutable. Irrefutable, that is, unless I brought into play the principles of chastity, something I could never again do except out of audacity, or rather out of ridicule. I therefore agreed with all the tender eagerness and thankfulness that one demonstrates through one's kisses in situations such as this.

The calm tone of the remarks I have made here are simply out of distraction (for this story excites me as little as if I were explaining to you how I finally learned Greek grammar)... In fact, I am becoming so distracted that I have now begun to start sentences without knowing how to finish them, something that never happened to me before. For the beauty of the example, I will not strike anything out.

To resume, you have probably forgotten by this time that we left Mauricette in a state bordering on delirium, a Mauricette changed into bacchante – dishevelled, purple, convulsive, spitting out insults and obscenities against her mother that she wouldn't have dreamed of an hour ago.

My 'yes' changed the current of her nervous system from one pole to another. Contrary to the ancient philosophy of which Renan speaks, and in which the sperm, once excited, mounts to the brain, Mauricette's desire now left her imagination and took possession of her flesh.

'I feel like fucking,' she murmured. 'I feel like fucking because you like to fuck and so that you can give me a taste for it. Did I really swallow your come? Is it true that I drank the come of a man for the first time and that it was yours? What's fucking after that? And don't be afraid of hurting me! When mama is fucking me I can't feel anything but her tongue unless I want to; but for you the more you hurt me and tear me the more I'll come.'

Suddenly, with her facility for metamorphosis, she raised her head and reminded me with a phrase of her real age.

'Do you want to come?'

'Sure; but not taking your virginity.'

'Yes. Why not take my virginity where I'm not a virgin!' She laughed.

'What a kid you are! And what a laugh you have! Who is this? Not the same Ricette that has just been telling me stories of blood, sperm, incest, Sapphism, sadism...'

'Oh! And what else! Where did you get all those two-dollar words?'

'You're fifteen and a half? No. There are times when you're at least thirty-nine and others when you're about seven.'

'Mama too.'

This reply left me speechless. It was one of the truest and most extraordinary remarks I had ever heard. It seemed to me that Ricette was thinking, *You're more of a kid than I am if you don't know that that's true of all women no matter how old they are.* She might have thought it, but she would never say it, for young girls never want to believe that they're smarter than their lovers. Every excellence they attribute to their man they use as an excuse: who could resist being seduced by a person of so many perfections?

And, sure of the adornments they have given us in their own eyes, they cover us with qualities to our faces solely out of generosity.

Mauricette returned to her original idea.

'You will have taken two cherries out of three, and I'd like to give you the third too, or rather the first... Anyway, the one I don't have any more... I mean the one I sold... The one in my behind... Do you understand?'

'You want to make it tight again with some alum water?'

'Oh, you dog!' she said laughing. 'Don't think now that my cherry in front has been re-done. Cherries that have been fixed up aren't given away. They cost an awful lot of money, you know.'

And she burst out laughing again at what she had just said. Then, rubbing her body against mine, she once again climbed to a point just between childishness and lasciviousness: two words that are practically synonyms.

'We'll play some more. Forget that you buttfucked me a couple of days ago. Forget it.'

'Can't remember a thing.'

'I'm just a kid again. Mama doesn't exist. I don't know anything, not even what a prick is. You're a satyr and you're going to rape me through the ass.'

'Rape you?'

'Don't you want to play? You just want to say no every time I try to do something with you? I use the word "no" because I'm a whore. If I were a society girl I'd say "shit".'

'Listen, my dear little Ricette,' I replied laughing. 'Don't go telling me now that you're a whore. I never understood better the young satyr that you are. You're as full of vice as an old magistrate. But, unfortunately, I'm incapable of raping a woman. Resistance freezes me instead of warming me up. To play at rape... if it's only a game, we'll do it... But if I fail you? I'd be despaired. I'll do it if you want...'

'But virgins who are being raped never resist! I'll just do like them. I'll cry into my arms and open my thighs.'

'But how will you know that I'm raping you?'

'How will I know it?' she repeated, gritting her teeth. 'I've never been buttfucked completely dry. You go ahead and do it and then ask me afterwards how I knew I was being raped. How do you think I could imagine I was really losing my cherry back there?'

'All right, I'll do it if you want. But tell me again that you really want me to, that you'll like it. Otherwise, I swear to you, I won't be able to.'

'I want it! I want it! I want it!' she said softly, her eyes wide. 'Rape me through the ass! And the more I cry that it hurts, the more I'll be saying that I love you!'

It's really more than painful for me to relate the following scene in detail. In fact, I cannot. It makes me ashamed of myself. I did not have the first instinct for the vice that Mauricette wanted me to satisfy. I've had to beat women that wanted to be beaten, but that's nothing, nothing at all after the memory of those terrible five minutes...

In short, when I 'raped' Mauricette, I felt through my flesh more than I had ever understood in my mind how much both pleasure and pain were necessary to delight her senses. I remembered the last of her secrets, or rather her temptations and, as I would have stroked a woman who loved to be caressed, I crushed the lips of that virginity that so loved to be bitten. I crushed them between my fingers, slowly, unceasingly, and probably more cruelly than Teresa had bitten them, for after a few moments of an equally extraordinary endurance and sexual excitement, Mauricette burst out sobbing. I will never forget that moment as long as I live.

And it was nothing but an instant. Immediately, her body bleeding, but nevertheless turning towards me to hold me, she said, she cried, her mouth against mine, between twenty kisses:

'Oh, I'm sorry! I'm sorry I cried! I'm... but will you shut up! I'm the one that's ashamed! Ah! You tortured me so well! It was good! I came as if I were dying! And then... I don't know why... but I started crying like a baby...! It's just that... It's just that...'

She sobbed and sucked in her breath until I thought that she was suffocating; then she burst out crying again, held me with

all her might and with admiration in her voice she found this
sentence to express her love:

'No-one ever hurt me as much as you did!'

Chapter Twelve

Thirty hours had passed since the preceding scene. Teresa and her girls had spent the night in a suburb at a relative's house, a woman who was also partially whore herself and who, for that reason, was the more impressed with them. However, I already knew that after a fairly long and heated discussion in which all four of them took part that Teresa had capitulated to Mauricette. I even knew the terms of the surrender.

As Mauricette had foreseen, Teresa had finally cried, 'I'd rather suck than sell your cherry, my child! I'd rather open my mouth beneath it than have to offer my hand at one side. And it won't prevent a thing, your adventure. I'll just glue it up again. You give the real one and later we'll sell the false. That way everyone will be happy.'

This sort of gift is the kind that generally proves expensive to the receiver. All moralists are in agreement on this point: when a young man lets a mother give him the cherry which she had hoped to sell, he owes a pretty good present to the girl, a gift of equal importance to the mother, and also thanks to God.

If the girl has two sisters it's even more amusing and even more expensive. Good luck, tripled like that, is enough to ruin a student inside of six weeks.

But, although many young men whose tiny fortunes have thus been dissipated retain the bitter feeling of having been duped, there are just as many who are quite willing to squander their largesse freely on those uncalculating courtesans who give everything, risk everything, seem to await nothing from us, but on the other hand upend on us some new tenderness every day. Ah! The tact with which they often receive that which they have not expected; the way in which they sometimes increase their gratitude as if to turn ours away; the manner in which they modify only their surprise in the face of our gifts; the supreme sensibility which I sometimes wonder if they really owe us.

♦

The appointment had been fixed, not at my place now, but at Teresa's, where the installation of her goods had just been completed. I crossed the stair landing to her door at ten o'clock in the evening.

Mother and daughters all received me completely nude, a fact which surprised me less than it embarrassed me.

Can you think of a more pitiful situation than that of a young man shut into a room with four women to each of whom he has said, 'I love you' and whom, therefore, he cannot greet with a respectful and distant deference for the very reason that by their nudity they have invited more personal attentions?

When I had kissed all four of them, adding on the side a few pats and caresses such as Christian morality disapproves of but of the type which nude women generally greet rather warmly, Teresa took Mauricette by the shoulders and before both the assemblage and any other question asked me, 'Did this kid really suck your prick without puking? Did you really come in her mouth? And she really swallowed it? She could never do it before, you must be a magician.'

'As a matter of fact, it was easier with her than with your highness, madame.'

Mauricette was thrilled by this response, and Teresa, hands on hips, still good-naturedly, spoke again.

'So! Is that the kind of answer *I* should get? I who have sucked three thousand men in my time?'

'But not that one,' said Lili. 'You're the only one in the family who doesn't know what his come tastes like. Even Ricette knows! Even she's sucked him before you have! That's terrific!'

'And you want to take this child's cherry!' continued Teresa.

'Some child!' said Lili. 'If I had as many hairs on my cunt

as she has between her buttocks...'

'Shut up! White of a bidet! Losing a cherry is a serious thing. Look at Charlotte. See if she feels like laughing.'

And Charlotte, who had been barely able to keep back her tears before, had thrown herself on the sofa and was crying her head off. I took the opportunity to rejoin her and say a few affectionate words. She was so pitiful... But Teresa interrupted me.

'Let her alone! You don't know Charlotte. When she has finished crying she'll feel like beating off, and when she's finished coming, she'll feel like crying again. It's like that around here from morning to night. I sometimes think she discharges tears and cries out come. But wait! Wait! There! What did I tell you?'

And, as a matter of fact, Charlotte was wiping her eyes dry with her left hand while her right was already busy between her legs. As her mother spoke she opened her eyes, saw ours fixed on her, and said, getting up, 'Oh! If you're all going to watch me...'

She slid her hand into a dresser drawer and took out two dildos which she then inserted, one after the other, into front and back. Then, lying once more on the sofa, but with her thighs spread far apart this time, she started the work of her finger again and said with a sad smile, 'Is it more interesting now?'

We left her alone. Teresa again took Mauricette by the shoulders and arranged and straightened her hair as if she were offering her to some rich customer. Then she repeated:

'You want to take this fifteen year-old's cherry!'

'Yes. We swore it between us, she and I. We have dispensation from the archbishop.'

'But what will you agree to swear to between you and I, if I give her to you?'

'I don't know, what?'

'You won't give this kid a kid, will you? She discharges like a dyke breaking, you know, and that always takes easily. So watch yourself. I'll have my face right between and if you give her so much as a drop of come, you'll get something else from me.'

'Don't do that. I'll be good.'

'So where will you wind up at?'

'Ah, decisions...'

'My mouth? It's a good time.'

'Ah!' cried Mauricette. 'I knew it! It's because your prick will be all red with my blood! That's what she wants! I told him you wouldn't want to lose a drop! That you'd stick your tongue in it! That you'd wind up with your mouth full of blood and come!'

'Huh? Do you think she's really old enough to lose her cherry?' said Teresa simply.

'Yes, yes, I'm old enough!' repeated the girl. 'Mama, let me say something to him just for him alone.'

To be sure that she was speaking in secret, Mauricette took me into another room and closed the door. You can guess whether or not we kissed.

'My wedding night?' she said prettily.

'Mine too.'

'You love me? I love you so much!'

'I love you with all my heart.'

'Are you going to hurt me?'

'Mauricette!'

'Tell me that you'll hurt me more than yesterday! More than yesterday! Rip away everything! Tear me! Make me bleed like a slit pig!'

She probably would have continued in the same vein had the door not opened. Teresa appeared and, as if she had heard Mauricette's first sentence, said, 'You're not getting all excited are you children? I'm not going to marry you until midnight.'

'Oh! Why?' cried Mauricette angrily.

'You two must both be nothing but a couple of big kids if you don't know why!'

Since my education meant less to her than did Ricette's, it was the latter that she now addressed.

'What? Think a minute. Don't you know that men can pull it out before they discharge better after they've had a piece already than they can the first time around? And do you think that taking your cherry will be like leaping through a paper hoop? Do you think that you'd still be a virgin after all the fingers that have been in you if I hadn't made you a leather cherry as well as a leather asshole?'

Pierre Louÿs

Ricette blushed, annoyed to have received a lesson in front of me; but Teresa hadn't yet finished.

'What will happen if I let you go at it alone? Either, after five minutes he'll come in your hair and it'll all be finished, or he'll be so shaken that he'll have forgotten to pull it out in time, and then...! Ah! Then! You'll have had it, girl! I'd cut off his balls, but it would be too late. You get me?'

It was the language of wisdom with a vocabulary which, though it was not that of a sermon, nevertheless had force and even a certain amount of eloquence. In crying out her 'and then...! Ah! Then!' Teresa had no doubt been unaware that she was introducing a prosopia into her discourse, but it isn't necessary to know the terms of rhetoric by their names in order to, like Bourdaloue, press them into the service of persuasion.

Was it the apostrophe, the hypothesis, the exhortation, or the prosopia that carried the argument? I don't know. However, Ricette lowered her head and asked only, 'Who will get the first shot if I can only have the second?'

'Come back in. We'll draw straws.'

That time rhetoric failed in its reply.

Mauricette was furious, and she sunk immediately into the worst excesses of the language.

'Ah! No! Now you're trying to screw me, all three of you! He's my lover! I found him! I'm the one who gave him a hard-on first! And then I was honest enough, stupid enough, to tell you about him, and for three days you've been wetting your pants under him, the lot of you, and even this evening when he's supposed to take my cherry I have to be satisfied with what's left!'

And when Teresa smiled unemotionally, without seeming surprised, Mauricette, crazy with rage, made a terrible scene. The words she used surpassed anything I had heard yet. I never thought that a girl, even one trained in the profession of vice, could use words like that when addressing her own mother. She raved at random in a low, trembling voice, spouting out every outrage she knew, but without order, without reason, simply in the joy of hurting, in the disorder and incoherence in which they came to her mind.

'Don't touch me! Shit on you! Shit on you! I'm getting out

of this dump tonight! I shit on you, you dirty bitch! Dirty beast! Dirty fairy! Dirty slut! Dirty fucker! Dirty whore! You don't like to be called that, do you? Good! Whore! Whore! Whore! Whore! Whore! Whore! Whore! Whore! Whore! Whore! Whore! Whore! Whore! Whore! Whore! Whore! Whore! Daughter of a whore! Mother of whores! Whore licker! Whore smeller! I'm no whore like you! I'm a virgin! You let your whore of a mother sell your cherry, but I'm not a strumpet like you! I'm not going to let my cherry be sold, I'm going to give it away! Look! Look there, dirty trollop! Look, my fine bitch! You wanted a hundred louis for it, didn't you? Well, you're not even going to get a hundred sous! The only thing you're going to get is blood and come in your filthy trap!'

Standing, her thighs spread, her head bent forward, she opened the lips of her sex with both hands. Then she closed them again and spoke once more in the same heavy, hateful voice:

'Yes! I've had enough of showing my knockers in your bordello of buttfuckers! In your bordello of cocksuckers and whores who'd do anything! I've had enough of sitting down to dinner at your table and seeing you pull out a thread of come with your toothpick and laugh because you don't even know who it belongs to! I've had enough of sleeping in sheets where there isn't even a dry spot because a whole bordello has been coming there, the whoremongers, the pimps, the fairies, and the whores! I've had enough of finding shit on my face towel every time one of your lovers wipes his prick on it. Pig! Garbage! Manure! Bitch! Daughter of a slut! Cocksucker! Shit-for-mouth! Hot-piss seller! Ass-licker! Shit-eater! Cunt-eater! Count on me! Count on me now, chippy feeler! Count on me to curl your cunt hairs and lipstick your asshole! I don't want any more of your tongue nor of your dirty teats rubbing against me! And I shit on you! I shit on you, mama!'

That last word, that 'mama', made me shiver. Mauricette started to come to me, but seeing the stunned way in which I had been listening to her, she stopped short and threw herself onto a bed, her face in the pillow.

All during that terrible scene I had watched only Mauricette. But now when I raised my eyes and my hands towards Teresa to prevent her from killing her daughter, as I

Pierre Louÿs

thought she was going to, I saw before me a woman as calm as if she had just been directing a stage rehearsal. She was tapping the ends of the fingers of one hand into the palm of her other, as if to simulate a little bravo without making a sound, and she looked at me, surprised at the paleness of my face, and said, 'Don't you understand what she wants?'

My God! What had I been thinking of? No, I hadn't gotten it, but her sentence was clear. I saw what she meant and I replied hurriedly, 'No! No! Never in front of me!'

'Fine. Go away and leave us alone.'

'Not this evening, please. Not this evening.'

Teresa sighed and, with a patience that was customary in her, said from within closed lips, 'Ah! Lovers! All right. Stay here. But don't do anything. Promise?'

And I stayed in the room along with Mauricette.

♦

There was a twenty minute intermission, then we returned and, not eagerly but not pouting either, daughter and mother embraced as if nothing had happened.

And, like a student at the Conservatory might make the leap suddenly from tragedy to comedy, Mauricette, as gay now as she had been furious, improvised a carnival pitch with an amazing facility of language.

'Ladies and Gentlemen, here you have the young savage announced outside our tent. We present her to you completely nude, after the custom of her country. This is the genuine article, nothing faked, nothing changed. Go ahead and touch her if you want. There is no padding in the thighs; the stomach is guaranteed, ladies, genuine virgin skin; there is a little horsehair between the buttocks but that is for ornamentation. You want to tap her teats, miss? Go ahead, it doesn't cost a sou. Pull her pubic hairs. You can see that at no point are they glued on, neither on her cunt nor under her arms. This is the real, the inimitable, the celebrated Mauricette whose name you have read on our posters.

'This young female savage, ladies and gentlemen, is a most extra-ordinary creature. She makes love through her asshole... You say you do not understand, miss? When she has a man on top of her with an erection, she does not fuck like you. Instead, she turns gracefully over, takes his prick delicately in her hand, and guides it skilfully into her ass like all the women of her family, a fact that does not prevent her from coming better than you, miss, with your hairless little pussy! What are you making faces about? Be careful! When you laugh in front of the savage girl she becomes enraged and eats little girls beneath their tummies.'

Lili was dying of laughter. Even Charlotte was laughing. But Teresa was the happiest of the three. Evidently, the preceding scene had held no importance whatsoever for her. Mauricette, flushed by her success, continued her monologue:

'The savage girl that you see before your very eyes, ladies and gentlemen, carries her cherry between her legs. You cannot see this cherry because her body is so bent over by her habit of presenting her rear to lovers, but for the slight supplement of fifty centimes per person, we will show you this phenomenon at close range... Has everyone paid? Yes? We now have the pleasure and the honour of presenting the savage girl's cherry.

Come closer, please. Don't be afraid. It's very red, but it isn't vicious. The young savage masturbates with all the ferocious refinements of young cannibal women; she puts mustard on the end of her finger when she's beating herself off and then... Oh! Madame! You think that her cherry is blushing out of shame? No, it is only onanism that makes it red like that. Please do not touch the cherry, miss. You will make it all hot. Look closely, ladies and gentlemen, but please do not touch. And now listen, everyone, as the programme of the evening will be announced.

'At the end of the show you will see the solemn taking of Mauricette's cherry before the honourable assemblage. The young savage will present herself dog fashion... That shocks you miss? Young ladies who like to be buttfucked think very highly of this position. She will therefore present herself dog fashion over her mother's face and between two excited sisters, who will, in their turn, sob, finger themselves, kiss, cry... And that is nothing, ladies and gentlemen. We will begin the programme with another complete number, a completely new performance that the celebrated Mauricette perfected only yesterday and that she will give before the public for the first time this evening!'

'She'll suck?' cried Lili, clapping her hands. 'Oh! For Ricette that's even more wonderful than losing her cherry!'

'Yes, ladies and gentlemen, our advertisement told the truth. For the first time publicly the young savage girl will suck a man. And what is more, instead of letting him come in mid-air, she will permit him to discharge in her mouth; and instead of spitting out the come like *you* do (a vicious habit, miss), the celebrated Mauricette will swallow everything while licking her lips with a gracious smile! We thank you for your attention.'

'*There* is a girl born into a circus family,' said Teresa proudly. No doubt. But she was also the only one of the three who had had enough formal education to be able to give to her pitch the proper amount of buffoonery.

Quickly, Ricette whispered something in my ear. I replied, 'Yes, if you wish.' Then, out loud, spontaneously, in front of her sisters and I, she made a sort of public apology.

'A few minutes ago I was nasty to you, mama. I ask your forgiveness and to show I mean it, I want him to fuck you the first.'

'Me?' said Teresa.

'Yes. You on top of me, as later we'll do it the other way around. And then he can finish in my mouth, so that I'll have both your come and his at the same time.'

'What a love, this kid of mine!' cried Teresa, clasping her in her arms. 'See!' she said to me. 'Don't I know her better than you?'

Chapter Thirteen

Lili couldn't believe her ears.

'What an evening! Ricette sucking! Mama fucking! And the taking of a cherry at the end of it! You couldn't do more to entertain the King of England!'

'And is that so rare? That "mama fucking"?' asked Teresa gaily.

'I guess so!' said the imp. 'You didn't even fuck to make me!'

The reply was true, prompt, and spoken in Lili's droll little voice, but the excess of laughter that greeted it was out of all proportion to its value. Charlotte, who had been weeping for over an hour, was racked by spasms of laughter interspersed with groans, as if she suffered more from her hilarity than from her melancholy. Teresa was gasping and clung onto her to keep from falling. 'Hold me up, Charlotte.' As for Ricette herself... Laughter is contagious, and Ricette burst out into shrieks last of all. Only Lili remained to laugh in moderation at her crack. And I began to think that one day she would be the most thoughtful and intelligent of the four.

Ricette, ex-schoolgirl for whom arithmetic held no more secrets, began to figure, and by the science of numbers brought us back once more to serious considerations.

'Mama gets buttfucked about three times a day on an average. That makes eleven hundred times a year.'

'And something over?' said Charlotte.

'And the dildos!' said Lili.

'And the nights like last Christmas when she did it eighteen times.'

'I said, on an average eleven hundred times a year. She began when she was eight; she's thirty-nine now. I figured it all out. That makes well over thirty thousand buttfuckings.'

'Thirty thousand!' they chorused.

'And she fucks about once a year, more or less.'

'Oh! I haven't fucked more than thirty times in my whole life!' declared Teresa. 'When was the last time that I did it, Charlotte? Was it last summer in June? Ah! Believe me,' said she turning towards me, 'I'm almost as virgin as Ricette! Charlotte is like me too. The only one who fucks around here is Lili.'

'Mama, mama, mama!' cried Ricette impatiently. 'When are we going to start?'

The consent that she obtained stopped neither her thoughts nor her words. She seemed concerned. She didn't lie down. Forgetting arithmetic to attack a curious problem of erotology, she looked seriously at her mother and said, 'Can we...? I don't mean that I think that my programme is impossible... It isn't easy to suck a woman who is being buttfucked; but under a woman who's being fucked... above all if she's losing her cherry... Your tongue will never touch my snatch.'

'I've never done it,' said Charlotte. 'But then we do so little screwing here...'

'I've done it!' said Lili.

'Oh, you! You're dislocated in more places than one!'

Teresa took her time, like a teacher searching for a formula easily accessible to the mind of an adolescent, and finally replied slowly, 'How many times have I told you that positions are the affair of women and not of men or lesbians. In the position that we're going to take up it will be up to the woman underneath to get in the right place. However, if the woman being taken will bother to hump her back a little bit there should be no trouble for the tongue underneath.'

'You can believe that I'll be all that I advertised when it comes to that!'

'Okay! Okay! But first watch how I do it and then you can imitate me when your turn comes.'

♦

The obscenity with which Teresa usually accompanied the opening of her rump dog-fashion was something with which I was already familiar. Dog-fashion is not quite enough to say here, I feel. Like a bear would be more descriptive. From the rear she was nothing but hair. However, since she had very well-formed buttocks and nicely shaped thighs, you couldn't really reproach her even mentally for being more heavily furred than other women and, such was the impudence of her position, you would rather have thought that she imposed her aesthetic on you.

Despite the fact that my sexual exercises are ordinarily as reserved and conservative as my language, my moral scruples do not go so far as to prevent me from fucking a mother on top of her daughter and then deflowering the same daughter on top of her mother. I have only done it once, but I would gladly take the opportunity should it be presented to me again. I am speaking now to the young women who are holding this book and I would like to say, in the words of Mauricette, 'I am not trying to shock you, miss. If your mother is thirty years old, if she is pretty, if you love her enough to do for her the things you would do for your little girlfriends, you will understand the following scene. And if you are not grateful for what she has always given you, if you have never used your tongue to send shivers of pleasure through the flesh that suffered so that you might come into this world, then blush at your own actions and not at those you are about to read of here.'

I therefore accepted Teresa on top of Mauricette and even under her. And the roles she played seemed to me neither superfluous nor disagreeable. However, two roles that I would have eliminated had I been writing this scene into a novel were those of Charlotte and Lili. They were of no use whatsoever; Charlotte only bothered me by her display of emotions, Lili by her giggles, and both of them by their gabbing, their curiosity, their advice, or simply their presence. I wished them to hell for a good fifteen minutes.

However, let us forget that for the moment and review the situation:

Ricette was lying on her back. Teresa was lying head to foot with Ricette, her cunt over the latter's face and open to me in the position I have so recently described.

Sapphism practised doubly and simultaneously is something that is not appreciated by all lesbians. Only a man can fuck and give pleasure at the same time he is receiving it without losing his head. A woman, at the approach of her orgasm, is entirely incapable of rationally directing the spasm that she wants to give in exchange. Thus, with two women who have placed themselves head-to-cunt to each other, only one will come, and, since the hearts of damned women are made of the same stuff as the souls of saints, the lesbian that makes the other come and doesn't herself is the happiest of the two.

Another night, in the same position, Teresa's tongue had put Ricette out of action inside of a minute. This time, however, there was no hurry, and Teresa did nothing but give her a few kisses, leaving the girl in full possession of her faculties.

I waited...

Mauricette parted her mother's hair and lips with her two hands, raised her head to the cunt, and began working feverishly with her tongue to hasten the moment when she could say:

'Now. Stick it in.'

The great drops of rain that announced the beginning of the storm began to patter onto Ricette's cheeks, and when I advanced my member Lili couldn't hold back an, 'Oh! Mama fucking!'

I entered easily, fearing only one thing: that Teresa's motion would be too much for me. However, Teresa never forgot for a moment that she wasn't there for her own pleasure and that another of her duties was to explain to her daughter the art of the position.

Thus, she took the first step towards explaining the pedagogy of the *divertimento*.

'Watch, Ricette! Watch now how I give it to you. Have you got my snatch? You have it? You see that his balls aren't in your way and that you can easily get at me with your tongue... Later when you do it imitate me; and when you get in front of my tongue you don't move, you hear? If I weren't holding myself in now, I'd be waving my ass all over the place and I'd lose your tongue. I feel like coming so much that I think my ass is going to fall apart, and that bitch of a prick that's tearing up my cunt... that's fucking me... But wait... You'll see if I can't come without moving.'

And she was, in fact, lying practically motionless, though shuddering. Mauricette was being flooded, and I too, but I couldn't pull it out without losing what was necessary to the second part of the act.

It was rather strange, that second part, for it seemed to interest the women much more than it did me, and they all got worked up into a state of excitement that I couldn't attain, although I was probably the best placed of any of them.

Charlotte and Lili were crowding around trying to see and becoming even greater nuisances than before.

Mauricette, red and excited, wiped her face, which Teresa had been deluging consistently with something other than tears. She was doubly excited, first by the act which she was attempting to bring to a successful close, and secondly by the spectacle which she was giving.

'I've got stage fright and I feel like coming,' she wailed. 'I'm afraid I'm going to botch it up.'

'Not at all,' said Teresa. 'The more you feel like coming the better you will do. To look at you, I don't think I should suck you, but do you want me to finger you a little?'

'Yes, mama.'

'And if you don't believe what I have just told you, my little savage, I'll show you I meant it. I'll heat up your come with a little mustard on your asshole.'

'Oh!' cried Ricette, raising her eyes towards the ceiling, 'I'll go crazy! Then... don't finger me. Just touch me. Above all, don't make me come before him! Then you can finger me when I give you the sign.'

While her mother left the room to get the mustard, she threw herself tenderly into the arms of her oldest sister with an, 'Oh! Charlotte! Charlotte!' that seemed to ask all her indulgence and encouragement. All that and more Charlotte would have given for nothing, but Ricette wanted to earn it, and after a tongue-to-tongue kiss she said, 'My Charlotte! Give me a little of your come too!'

And throwing her sister onto the divan, she thrust her head between her legs.

'That's something!' cried Lili. 'When you wind up with all those different comes in your mouth you'll find yourself with a kid.'

This time I was the only one to laugh. Teresa, who had just come back, and the two girls were much too excited to change expression.

Ricette jumped up and prepared to take the mustard. She stood up, leaning slightly forward with her buttocks out, opened the cheeks of her ass herself, and let her mother do to her what the trainers do to the bulls before a bullfight. I don't know what kind of hot mustard Teresa used, but when it was in place Ricette jumped violently and, touching the spot with her finger, cried, 'What did you do that for? Now I want him to buttfuck me!'

'Not in the mustard,' laughed Teresa.

'Then you, or Charlotte...! A dildo at least. Ah! Damn! I'm afraid I'm going to come!'

'Then suck him right away. What are you waiting for?'

Mauricette leaped over to me and, just as she was on the point of beginning, said in her most ardent voice. 'You'll buttfuck me tonight even so, won't you? Before you deflower me? I'll take the mustard out and you won't feel anything... Ah! But she stuck fire into my asshole, I know it! God, I feel like having a prick back there! What are you doing back there now? Oh, it's you...'

Her mother had run a dildo into her ass and was working it with her hand. Ricette started up. I couldn't tell whether the dildo was relieving her excitement or irritating it even more, but she cried, 'I don't need that to love your come! I didn't have anything in my ass yesterday when you came in my mouth, did I? Tell that to mama! And give me some more to drink! Quick! I'm thirsty! I want it!'

She took me so voraciously that I could feel her teeth more than her lips. I did not want to say anything in front of Lili because she would have made fun of Ricette's inexperience, but I hurried my orgasm and warned her just before it came.

Mauricette was a brilliant success with her new little trick in its first performance before her family, the new trick that was for her as Lili said, 'More wonderful than losing her virginity!' Unfortunately, she gave a second proof of her inexperience by wanting to prolong the climax further than my nerves could support it. But, by that time, the poor thing no longer knew what she was doing. Teresa, who still had her finger in Ricette's cunt, had worked the girl up to a peak, held her in, then released the spasm in her flesh immediately after mine. And the little beginner, blinded in all her senses, almost swooning, was hardly aware of the success she had with her mother and sisters.

♦

Lili, so nude, so thin, so smooth, crossed her arms and stood in front of Teresa, whose body was so heavily furred, who wore her dark breasts like oriental jewels. For me, this contrast of nudities was without precedent in art or literature.

With a comically resigned air, she sighed, 'We're a couple of nuts, huh, mama? She's just sucked off our lover under our noses and didn't even leave us a drop.'

'Wait! I'll get some the second time around!'

'You will? Congratulations. And I can sit by and rub my cunt to see if I can make the hairs grow, huh?'

Lili's metaphors were often very personal, but they were worth even more like that because of the ease with which she delivered them.

Teresa possessed her daughters body and soul, as a romantic once said, and guessing their thoughts as well as their desires, she sensed that Lili was beginning to get under Ricette's skin and that at her age she couldn't understand the state that her sister was in.

Here again, the highest philosophical authorities resolve the question without debate and almost in the same terms, for theorists divulge between themselves not only their ideas, but their modes of expression as well. *'A young courtesan in a state of impuberty who indulges in anal coition can be excused from misunderstanding the double physical and moral disorder that a nubile adolescent experiences the night that she first opens her thighs to offer her virginity.'* Thus runs the ancient formula of

Erasmus, copied so many times and to be found in all manuals and textbooks.

Teresa had only two means to shut Lili up and close the incident. She gave the child her choice.

'Do you want to go to your bed, insect! Do you know what time it is?'

Here, Lili made a small gesture... A gesture that I do not advise my young readers to use on their parents. She turned her back, stuck out her behind, and opened her hand as if to thumb her nose, but replaced the latter with her asshole.

Teresa gave her two good smacks in the same place with her hand, then took her easily into her arms, caressed her against her breasts, made her laugh, and said, 'You don't want to go to bed? You want to watch Ricette lose her cherry? All right! You'll have to perform during the intermission. Go get into your costume. We'll wait for you.'

Whore though she was, Lili was too naïve to understand that Teresa only wanted to get rid of her, and with a joyous little hop, she tore out of the room.

Teresa smiled at Ricette and I, then turned to Charlotte. And the scene that followed was even more painful to me than the one that still rang in my ears between Ricette and Teresa. What was wrong with her at that point? I don't pretend to know. Was she guilty then of a sentiment more human than maternal, driving her to return to one of her daughters the injuries that another had heaped on her head? Or had the 'programme' of she, Mauricette, and I unnerved her even more than it had us? She burst out with a torrent of insults from the first word.

'The bitch! She's fingering herself again!'

'Oh! Mama!' cried Charlotte. 'You've been fucking, you've come, Ricette learned how to suck, you made her come, you stuck mustard and a dildo into her ass, I saw all that and didn't have anyone, and you don't want me to come after you?'

'After us? But you did it before! Ricette had a dildo in the rear? All right, but you had two! One in each hole! If you had fifty holes you'd want fifty dildos stuffed in them every fifteen minutes, dirty little bitch!'

Charlotte stopped. She didn't cry, but she put her elbow

on her knee and her chin in her band: dejection personified.

I was suffering more than she was from what I had heard, when, in a single phrase, I understood what was going on. For as I started to get up Ricette held me back and said in my ear, 'Be quiet now, this sort of thing excites her.'

However, I was up despite Mauricette and halted the scene with my movement and the look on my face.

Teresa stopped me from saying anything in her turn, but the scene didn't follow the same course it had begun to trace after that.

'Tell him then. Tell him yourself, in front of your virgin sister. Tell him what you are.'

'A poor prostitute.'

'Why are you as naked as a girl in a bordello? Aren't you lower than any of them?'

'Oh, yes! They won't do the things that I'll do!'

'Okay, then. Go with Lili. Put on your whore's costume and come back. We'll have some words with you.'

'Me too!' cried Mauricette.

I no longer understood. But while Charlotte left the room slowly and sadly as usual, Ricette dragged me with all her might to the far corner of the room and said in a low voice, 'Ha! You know what mama stuck up my ass? Fire! I'm going mad. I'll go put on my costume, but when I come back you'll buttfuck me! You will! You will! You will! You will! You can have my cherry later. I'll come back with Charlotte and we'll do a scene, but be sure to play your role. Call her whore and take me, you know. Understand?'

A strange declaration! The more I knew this woman and her three daughters the less I understood them.

Alone with me, Teresa began to speak. I thought that she was going to explain my role, but she had other things to talk about.

'Lili was right,' she said. 'Coming in Mauricette's mouth is much more sensational than taking her cherry. What kind of come do you have that she swallows it so well?'

With her body and her lips Teresa was becoming even more pressing than with the words she had just spoken, and, since she was, in any case, far from being a woman to chill me, I replied while kissing her, 'Ask your daughters. All three of them have drunk it.'

'Which mouth do you like best?'

'Yours.'

And I wasn't lying. I preferred it before the act as if I had already tried it. Teresa, however, started at this reply. I was afraid that the door would open at any moment and, above all, that I would not be able to continue with her in this tone. I spoke quickly therefore, trying to find out, in addition, what was going on.

'What's up, anyway? What are they doing in there?'

'Screw that,' said Teresa, pressing her lips against mine.

I cut the kiss off with difficulty and brought her back to the subject in a suppliant voice. After a minute of silence during which time I feared the arrival of one of those crescendos that I have already described, she kept her voice under control and replied to me with her face so close to mine that her hair brushed against my cheeks, 'How long have you been like that? It's nothing but a game. It makes her happy. You know as well as I do that she likes the role.'

'Who?'

'My Charlotte,' she said tenderly. 'I don't get to see what those two are up to together, but I know. Charlotte dresses up like a woman of the streets, and Mauricette is something else. Neither one of them is anything but a kid. They even put on little comedies when they're by themselves, so play with them this time, huh?'

Then getting up, she added, 'I've had them fucking away stark naked in your bed for long enough now. If you don't know what they're like by this time...'

But all three of them came back in at that moment, each dressed in the most unlikely outfits.

Chapter Fourteen

The first one I saw was Mauricette wearing a clown costume, the same one, no doubt, that Charlotte had had when she was the same age and of which she had spoken to me at such length in connection with her famous bet.

Charlotte, following her, struck me first of all by the expression on her face. She seemed excited to be able to 'play a role' in both senses of the expression for, even more than me perhaps, she had sensed how useless and even importunate her presence had been before. Still driven by the mania she had for debasing herself, she had put on a black dress, a large apron, a red ribbon around her throat, and her hair was arranged, or perhaps disarranged, in such a fashion that you would have thought that you could have given her twenty sous for her virtue under the Notre Dame bridge and been generous at that.

The last was Lili, dressed like a schoolgirl: black apron and pigtails. I was a little young myself to play the role of satyr in front of her.

The first thought that came to my mind was that we could never evolve a plot between three so dissimilar characters and the one young leading man. Either that or the whole thing would be ridiculously absurd. How I wish that all this were not true! And how I would choose the costumes they were to wear if it were not! However, back to the story. Have you guessed yet what happened? Young whores and young girls who are not so openly whores never draw back before the manifest absurdities of the little comedies they concoct. In fact, the more extravagant they are the better they like them. Their youth overrides all else.

Once more, Ricette took me aside and said laughing, 'Play

this role fast! I'm in a hurry! I've got a fire like the fires of hell in my behind!'

At that, she laughed so hard that she could not utter another word for several moments. However, she got hold of herself again and said, 'And I'm out of luck because I'm the last one. After me, naturally, there will be an intermission.'

Charlotte interrupted us, but with an expression of joy on her face that I had not seen before that evening.

'You know what we're going to do?'

'Me? Haven't the least idea. In fact, I'm curious to know how you're going to be able to construct anything at all out of a whore, a clown, and a schoolgirl. You three must have good imaginations!'

'We're not so clever. We just do scenes like in a revue, one after the other.'

That was more like it. Not for you, I suppose, but for me. When you're getting ready to deflower a young virgin it's better not to wear out your faculties in advance. I therefore let the three girls split up their roles and even dole one out to their mother, although she had no costume. But Ricette, who could not hold herself in, and was hopping from one foot to another like a young girl who needs to take a piss, insisted that her act be the curtain raiser. This upset the whole order of things but did not seem to shock anyone. Ah! How easy it is to run a theatre!

'Sir,' she said to me, 'I've come to dine privately with you, but only on the condition that you behave yourself.'

'Why do you want me to behave myself?'

'Because I'm a little drunk.'

'But not enough.'

'And because I'm a virgin.'

'Too much. Show it to me. God! What an unfortunate infirmity! How long have you been like this?'

'Ah! Good sir! Ever since birth.'

'Do you suffer?'

'Horribly. It burns me constantly.'

'Are you taking any treatment for it?'

'Oh, yes! Massages. With the end of my finger.'

Despite the laughter from her sisters, Ricette remained

sober-faced and serious. She added softly:

'Four times a day.'

'And nothing else?'

'Oh, yes. But I can't tell you. It's a secret we girls keep to ourselves.'

'I won't tell a soul.'

'Cross your heart?'

'I swear to you on the perfection of your patron saint Saint Mauricette.'

'That's not worth anything. She's not on the calendar. I was given a Christian education, sir. I know the three theological virtues and history up to Moses. But Saint Mauricette, since she doesn't exist, has nothing to do with the thing I sit on! And it's not she who will punish me if you give away my secret... Oh! How my head reels! Wonder what I drank to cause that? Can you tell that I'm drunk, sir?'

'No, no. But what is your secret?'

'Mama told me... that to calm down their cherries... without losing them, young girls should... Whew! It's hot in here!... should massage themselves from behind at the same time that they massage themselves from the front.'

'From behind? But where?'

She showed her teeth ferociously but good-naturedly, a look that seemed to say, 'Ah? You don't get it?' Then, with her natural facility for improvisation, she took up once more her role of innocent and continued:

'Mama made me a clown costume with an inch-long buttonhole right between my thighs so that I have room for my finger and a little removable panel in the back. You see?'

'But what good does that do?'

'She told me when I was getting dressed, "Remember to be good now, show that you've been brought up properly, don't say any bad words, but when you see that he's getting a hard-on, you take his prick, you stick some butter into your asshole, and you open your buttocks saying to him that it's the first time you've ever done it. Then you say that it's shameful to do things like that, that you don't even dare confess it at church, and that you'd throw yourself in the river if your mother ever found out about it."

Pierre Louÿs

You understand?'

'Is that all she said?'

'No. When she was kissing me good-bye at the door, she said, "Be sure to finger yourself when he's buttfucking you and don't ask him where in the bordello you can shit out the come. But wash yourself out, my child, from your ass to your mouth, discharge into your slip, puke into the piano, piss into the carafe, earn your fifty francs with your asshole, and above all don't say any bad words." Don't you understand yet?'

'Less and less. It's your modest nature, miss. You seem to have some difficulty in explaining these things clearly...'

I was becoming twice as malicious and three times as odious, for Mauricette had been playing her role extremely well. And as happy and gay as was her heart and soul, I saw that she was on the brink of flying into a rage. I barely had time enough to say to her while touching her forehead lightly, 'Ah! Now I understand!'

'Miracle of Saint Mauricette!' she sighed patiently.

'This little flap of cloth... can I lift it?'

'You still trying to be funny?'

'And see what's underneath, like the little girls at La Rochelle do?'

But we had finished. With my lips on hers I prevented her from replying. My wisecracks were less funny than her act, and I had only prolonged them so that I might draw her out to greater length. I was afraid that at the first contact of our bodies she would put an end to her act, but the love of the stage in young girls is almost as strong as their love of sensual pleasure. For several minutes more, therefore, Ricette kept up her role of beginner alone with a man in a private dining room.

'You see, sir,' she said, 'the difference there is between vice and virtue. The shameless women who dance nude wear nothing but a small cloth in front over their sex. While the virgins who give themselves to be buttfucked have a little panel that lifts up from the rear and are otherwise completely dressed.' She began laughing uproariously.

'I don't know the secrets that young girls keep too well and I'm afraid that I won't...'

'No, no, kind sir. Let me do it. Mama taught me one thing if nothing else: "If your customer is a shit, let him buttfuck you!"'

She laughed even more this time, but I was fed up. I don't like that kind of joke and she only objected in vain to me that a virgin has the right to be indulged in a few eccentricities while she is being sodomised. Ricette received, for the principle of the thing, two or three little slaps that she well merited. And then... (I forgot to mention one small detail: the room was enormous. Teresa, Charlotte and Lili were grouped together at the far end of the divan, and we were playing a good distance from them, as in a real theatre. So that Mauricette could speak to me in a low voice without being heard by the others.) ...she stopped laughing, turned her head, and said to me ardently but in a low voice, 'Is that what you call a slap? Your dick hurts me more than your hand did. Do it again.'

'Certainly not!'

'Yes. Listen to what I'm going to say. I'm going to speak in a very low voice. Remember what you did to Mama without wanting to? Grab me by the hairs, they won't see anything. They'll just think you're beating me off... No, not those hairs there... lower... around the lips... yes, there... pull... pull them... pull them, damn it!... What the hell are you waiting for? Pull! I'm going to come...'

And she grabbed my hand to make me pull out the hair like a handful of weeds.

◆

The intermission only lasted a minute. To give us a little time to rest up, Lili in her schoolgirl outfit went up to Charlotte dressed like a whore and said with a suspicious air 'You're already sick? I *thought* your brother's prick had a funny taste this morning.'

When Charlotte's emotions rose to the surface she could retain neither hilarity nor tears. Surprised by this unexpected opening sentence, she laughed behind her hand before replying. Then the scene began, but on a completely different level than Mauricette's. Between she and her two sisters stretched out the long distance from college to the boarding school. Occasionally,

Pierre Louÿs

Lili could leap the gap, carried by her natural instinct for fantasy; however, Charlotte spoke only the language of obscene and sentimental realism. The role that she had accepted, had in fact demanded, hardly resembled those famous types of Bruant. It was, on the other hand, that of the weary, faint-hearted girl who is used to submitting to all manner of humilities and injuries and (almost a saint without realising it) who accuses herself first of all as the cause of her troubles.

She therefore assumed an unhappy air and when Lili repeated 'A very funny taste,' she spoke with the same manner.

'It's not enough that he should go around sticking his tail into little snipes only fourteen years old,' said Charlotte sadly, 'but then the kid comes and starts complaining to me about the taste. Those things never happen to anyone but me!'

'Little snipes fourteen years old? Even if she is only fourteen, she's less of a fathead than you! She's beaten off the secretary of the chief of police and when she decides to suck him, she'll get you sent off to the pokey.'

'Ah! That's all I need now. That's the one thing that hasn't happened to me yet. But what have I ever done to you?'

'You emptied your brother's balls before I got there and then you wiped his cock off with your cunt.'

This new expression of Lili's ravished Mauricette, who raised herself up on one elbow to follow the scene.

'The lock-up!' shuddered Charlotte. 'Probably Saint-Lazare! No, my pretty little thing, have pity on me. I'll do anything you want... for nothing.'

'Too expensive,' said Lili unperturbed.

'Do you want to see my hairs? My knockers? Do you want me to eat you out?'

'I've got my lesbians already.'

The detached voice the schoolgirl assumed here was so comic and so disdainful that everyone started laughing, even Charlotte Lili continued, however, without ever changing expression after having pulled a piece of bread out of her basket.

'Make me a nice come sandwich. Then go and get some honey to sweeten it. Bring it back to me and have one ready every day so I can take it to school for lunch. And no foolishness!

If you try to screw me up, I'll have you clapped into the can so quick it'll make your head swim! Is that understood?'

'Ah! I could even make you *two* with the come that I get from earning my forty-five sous. There, under the bridge, there's a puddle every evening... And every time I go there I stick my mouth into it to have some... Is that all you want?'

'I want to watch you doing it too. Look! There's a passer-by for you! Go ahead! I'll hide!'

This last sentence, 'I'll hide!' was really a fourteen-year-old's; however, I hardly had time to appreciate the merits of her acting for I suddenly realized that the passer-by was supposed to be me. Charlotte quickly said, 'You know what you're supposed to do? You stick it in my mouth, but nothing happens. You don't get a hard-on.'

This conception of dramatic art was so simple that it reminded me rather more of Aeschylus than of the modern theatre. The scene to follow should therefore have three sections. And the third would be so easy to act in the state in which Mauricette left me that I decided to go along with the second as naturally as possible to try to satisfy poor Charlotte's mania. The second part also was as disagreeable for me as the one preceding, and I only followed it as in a dream. All of this was probably caused by the fact that I played my role very poorly. I had not been in the least ashamed to have held up my end with less distinction than Mauricette, but I was rather put off to find that even the simple Charlotte knew better than I how to carry out this role and expand her characterization.

She came to me, her head raised, her hips weaving, and took me by the sleeve.

'Want to have some fun, dearie?'

'No.'

'Come on. I haven't had it yet this evening and I just washed my pussy not fifteen minutes ago. Come on under the bridge. I'll lift up my skirt and you can screw me. Come on.'

'Me screw *you?*'

'I'm all right. I'm clean. I just went for a check-up today. And even if you don't want that we can do something else. I'm a good kid. Listen...'

'Fuck off, lady.'

'No, listen! I've needed to take a piss for two hours. You want me to piss in your hands? You can wipe it on me afterwards.'

'You disgust me. Don't touch my sleeve with those hands.'

'Let me tell you at least... I'm a real pig! All you got to do is ask and I'll do whatever you want. Come on and I'll suck your dick. You can come in my mouth.'

'I don't need a whore for that! I can get a girl to do the same thing.'

'Do you think they can do the breathing fish like me? You know what that is? Listen and I'll tell you...'

'No! Hit the road! First of all I've only got ten sous and it'll take me four to catch a streetcar home,' I added, rather ashamed of these imbecilities.

'All right. Give me six sous, that's all. You'll be more generous the next time. Give me the six sous and I'll do the breathing fish for you. That's when I suck you and I blow the come out through my nose.'

Charlotte was making me nauseous. I still had a vague smile plastered across my face, but to hasten the end of the scene I said violently, 'Will you get out of here or do I have to buttfuck you!'

This is a formula that is often very efficacious for getting rid of street-walkers; however, occasionally, it backfires and makes it even harder to shake them off.

Charlotte, who was playing her part up to the hilt, replied in a low, indifferent voice, as if I had asked her to do her breathing fish through either the right or left nostril, 'Go ahead and buttfuck me. I don't care. You don't think that I'll do it for six sous? I have to live. And then you can screw me if you want. Stick it in good and far. Don't be afraid of getting your clothes dirty. I'll wipe them off with the inside of my skirt.'

'Charlotte, you're filthy!' I whispered into one of her ears.

'This is a role I can really feel,' she replied sadly.

Despite the disagreeable sentiments with which the scene filled me, and which I hardly need to explain here, it was finally terminated by an accident which the young ladies who read this may not understand but at which the young men will be less surprised.

One thing that a young girl should learn before her first date is that there is no relation between love and the erection. On the contrary, to fail a woman is often to prove that you love her to the point where your senses are blinded. However, to unexpectedly find oneself with an erection before a woman that one does not in the least love is to treat her like a whore, gallantly but categorically.

And that's what happened to me in Charlotte's mouth. 'In her mouth?' you say. 'Some miracle. An octogenarian could have done as much.' Even so, neither I nor anyone else expected it. First of all, I was supposed to remain cold, and nothing had seemed to me easier to do, for Charlotte's comedy had not in the least excited me. Then too I had just left Mauricette's arms. However, therein lies the explanation. That had been a half an hour before. Using her mouth had not been too wise.

My accident threw everyone into a turmoil. Understandably, it flattered Charlotte, but Teresa laughed until the tears rolled down her cheeks. I blushed for I didn't find anything funny in it. Neither did Mauricette, although I motioned to her not to be worried.

Fortunately, Charlotte's sketch was constructed so loosely that even this unexpected development changed neither the intrigue nor the characters. It even added more force to the final scene.

Charlotte, still in her role as street-walker, intoned dully, 'I told you that I was a real bitch, that you'd get a hard-on in my mouth. And a very pretty one it is, too dearie. Listen! My brother has been fooling around with a kid and she's listening now... Listen! I don't want your sous. Just buttfuck me good and deep, let me finger myself, and if you make me come you don't have to give me anything. There! Look, there's my ass! Put it in there! Quick!'

She stood up, leaned forward, raised her black skirt up over her buttocks in an attitude which she assumed naturally and which represented the extreme of servility in prostitution. And then she asked in a sad voice, 'Where is it?'

'You'll have to find another.'

'Oh! I make you hard, I suck you like I should, I tell you to buttfuck me, that it won't cost you anything, and you don't lose your erection, but you fail me all the same. Do I disgust you? Doesn't it please you to buttfuck a whore? What do I have to do now to get my six sous? Do you want to piss on my face while I close my eyes and open my mouth?'

'Listen, Charlotte. You're exaggerating!' I said, trying to stop her.

Then, stepping out of her role and speaking for me alone with an expression that I'll never forget, she murmured:

'No.'

Chapter Fifteen

Mauricette leaped up and ran to me, overjoyed that I had cut short the scene even at the expense of the drama inherent in it. She neither wished that Charlotte should be the cause of the state I was in, nor that I should fall into an indifferent lassitude for lack of solicitude.

And immediately she thought of another scene, then came out with one of those sentences that seemed to be so natural to Teresa's daughters and which always left me completely stupefied.

'Lili,' she cried. 'Stick your tongue into my ass and see if there's any mustard left!'

And while Lili was lifting the panel in her clown costume, she said, 'It's terrible how my asshole gets me! But no! Mama did it on purpose to get me hot and I like it. You'll have to buttfuck me a dozen times tonight before you deflower me! Well, Lili?'

'Well,' began Lili, 'it smells of come, garlic, cocoa, whores, marshmallow, pricks, pussy juice, Spanish fly, dildo rubber, suppositories, the bottom of a bidet, lipstick, towels, vaseline, starch, musk, bordello shit-houses, and bitcheries I don't even dare mention.'

'That you don't dare mention!' repeated Ricette. 'Oh, thanks! Come here and let me give you a slap in the head.'

'Instead of that, how about giving me what I just gave you?' said Lili, approaching without the least fear.

'Look!' said Ricette to me. 'Look at her! See if she doesn't know I won't hit her! Clever for her age, isn't she? And the only whore in the family, I tell you! She just gave me one of her famous digs in the ass, and I can still feel it.'

'Sure I did,' said Lili, 'but if I were really a whore it would have been worth six sous, as Charlotte said.'

'One, two, three, four, five, six! And paid!' said Ricette, giving her six kisses. 'And...'

She struck a wonderful pose: a skinflint of a miser suddenly trying to be generous. 'And, in honour of the occasion, a special prize, entirely free of charge. What I am holding in my hand is mine for the night, but mama had it once in the cunt and Charlotte once in the mouth, while Lili sighed and said she was going to rub her mound to see if she could make more hairs grow.'

'And they're not growing!'

'Therefore, we have the special privilege to present, with the permission of the gentleman here, a little three-part scene in which our special guest, the schoolgirl, will have my lover for a period of time not to exceed one minute and on the condition that she return him intact at the end of that period.'

'Be careful,' said Lili with a straight face. 'If he got a hard-on in front of Charlotte without wanting to, with so beautiful a woman as me he'll play hell trying to keep from coming!'

♦

And the game that followed presented to me a frankly negative and therefore rather rare and interesting phenomenon. A thing that proved fascinating because it was entirely foreign to any previous known conception of mine. In other words, these short erotic scenes had as little connection with dramaturgy as with love.

And I describe it here without fear of being repetitious. Please be kind enough not to think that I am making up these childish programmes. If you can accept my style as not being that of a primer, have the grace also not to think that these dialogues are the fruit of my imagination. I have noted them down because I felt that they were more 'schoolgirlish' than 'whorish' despite their subject matter and vocabulary: a contrast I found amusing. However, like the drawings of a child, they would lose all their character under the editing pen of another.

Before plunging into it, I warned Ricette that I was once

more in a physical state less marked by ostentation and therefore less willing to be opened to ridicule. So they gave me a little respite in this direction. But not for long.

The scene began with a fortissimo, like a classical symphony.

Without the slightest preparation:

'You're just leaving school, little girl?' asked Ricette. 'That can't be true. It's seven o'clock. Your mother's going to give you a good scolding.'

'Yes. She already gave me a clap in the chops because I came home with a dildo stuck in my rear. And one that I didn't even know about.'

Lili's beginnings were always unexpected, but always prepared. Lili always directed the scenes she was in, and, of all the strange things that I saw in that family, the things she did surprised me the least. Ricette, however, was definitely surprised and had to laugh behind her hand before she could continue.

'It's still there? Whose is it?'

'How should I know? There are so many bitches that buttfuck me... And since I turn my back to them, I can never recognize them. My mother was squawking all the time I was home: "What? Not another whore of a whore who forgot her prick in your ass!" Was it you, miss?'

'Me? Me the bitch who buttfucked you? Me the whore of a whore who...'

'Oh, don't get all in a lather. I said to her, "It was on the stairway, mama." And she said, "Good! Go see that lump across the hall and ask if it's hers." So here I am. I'm being very kind to come to you with it like that.'

'And I'll stick it back inside you! I've never seen such a thing, a kid coming to pay a formal visit with a dildo in her ass. Anyway, don't you even lick people from the front? I suppose not!'

'No! I haven't met all the different kinds of lesbians yet. Just those who buttfuck you from behind and those who wash your face in their come... You fuck more with them than you do with men...'

'What? You mean you've already lost your cherry? At your

Pierre Louÿs

age?'

'Oh, Christ! What a snob! Do I have to be a virgin to lick your ass? Why did the good God give me two holes if I wasn't supposed to use them?'

'I only use one.'

'That's nothing to brag about.'

Lili never had to look for a reply, and Mauricette, whose glibness had amused us so much before, sensed that she would fare better to quit dialogue for monologue where she shone to greater advantage.

'And if, instead of a dildo, I give you a living prick?'

'Much better than a dead one,' said Lili calmly. 'I try to stick to living ones when possible.'

'Then pay attention! If you want one, you'll have to thank me ahead of time by giving me a jolly little working over while my friend is asleep in the room next door. First of all, kisses on the face, your tongue around my ear, and your teeth in my neck. That's the beginning. Then you suck first my right nipple and then my left nipple until I say enough. After that you let your tongue wander lightly and without wetting anything around my cunt; you chew the lips of my pussy, your tongue then passes underneath and just touches my ass lightly, as if it scarcely dare do anything there, then plunges deeply inside. When it returns, it works over my cherry, seeking out all the little unknown corners, and finally it attacks the snatch itself. And when I've finished coming, I'll give you a nice, handsome prick, all warm and hard, to play with.'

'Oh, miss!' said Lili unenthusiastically. 'That's worth more than a prick, all that. That's worth fifty francs.'

This reply that sent Teresa off into such gales of laughter proved to me that Ricette was right when she said that Lili had the instinct for her trade. But now it was my turn to play, and I almost missed my entrance.

From her first words, Lili brought us once again back to the subject.

'Good day, sir. Your lady told me that she is really too ugly for you and that for a long time now you would have chucked her out except that she has given you other women as a distraction. Now she's obliged to dress herself up like a clown and send you schoolgirls. You're a little nutty, is that right? Oh, I don't care, mind you! I'm used to it.'

That wasn't in time original script! 'The little beast!' muttered Mauricette between her teeth, but Lili continued:

'Older women like that don't know how to do anything, you know. They've got cherries all over the place and you have to turn them over and over like a pig on a spit before you can find an entry. And when they finally do learn how to do something like sucking a dick, it's so sensational that they invite their whole family to applaud as if they were swallowing a sword!'

'You'd better shut your trap, you little monster!' said Ricette, unnerved by her mother's laughter.

'Oh! Miss!' said Lili calmly. 'You won't have to beat me to give your lover a hard-on. I can do that alone. Besides, I don't like torture scenes like you do. So go take a leak, why don't you. Come back in five minutes, give me the money, and I'll return the gentleman to you in good condition. Go on.'

Lili's authority was overwhelming. Even Mauricette, after looking first at her mother and then at me, had to laugh too and leave the room 'to take a leak' as she had been invited.

I was looking forward to the rest of the scene with apprehension, for I did not know exactly what would be expected of me in the role of a man presented with a schoolgirl by his mistress dressed in a clown costume. I was therefore happy to see Lili once again re-set the stage, speaking with a new intimacy that surprised me.

'Ah! That's a vicious little chicken you've got there! She knows that you've slept with me. She gave me a good half-hour lesson in lesbianism and now she's gone to the toilet to finger herself and she wants you to screw me when she comes back. Even the president of the court of appeals didn't ask that much before he stripped.'

I would be relating this story very poorly indeed if I didn't note the howls of laughter that kept me from replying to this last sentence. Only Lili kept a straight face. In fact, she even seemed in a hurry, for she raised her short skirts to her waist and said, 'Hurry! This is serious! If you laugh, you're going to fail me in the clutch!'

I knew it as well as she, but Lili inspired in me more hilarity than lust, and Teresa's overflowing laughter made it even harder for me to get serious. I found it almost impossible to get hold of myself properly, and only the fact that Mauricette unexpectedly prolonged her absence by several minutes permitted Lili to continue the scene according to her wishes and gave her the assistance from me that was so necessary.

When her sister finally did return, Lili once again took up her role.

'Is it true, miss, that you've been working on the gentleman here ever since the day before yesterday without ever getting anywhere?'

'You think so, eh little toad? At ten-thirty I sucked him, at eleven he buttfucked me...'

'That's what *you* say! When I saw him in front of you he was limp as a rag and now look how I'm returning him to you! That'll be twenty francs, please. Do you want a receipt?'

Mauricette made a gesture of reprisal with her hand, but remained in a good humour and with no lack of imagination once again took up her own role in the comedy so as to keep her promise.

'I don't have any money, but that thing in your hand is worth more. You take it first, but don't empty it. Then return it to me and we'll be quits.'

Lili, at that point, had the most comic expression of any of us: a mixture of disillusion, politeness, and indifference, and taking her hand away from me, said to her sister, 'That'll be twenty francs more.'

Obviously, Mauricette was only waiting for a pretext to show what a good sport she was, an opening that wouldn't be a wisecrack aimed in her direction. Laughing, she embraced Lili, then grabbed her around the waist, lifted her skirts, and said to me, 'Now! Take her whichever way you want!'

Another daughter would have found it amusing to cry, 'Mama! I'm being raped!' But Lili wasn't making any more jokes and besides she had something much more important to say.

'Wait! Wait! I'm just a schoolgirl, remember! I've got my

vaseline jar in my little basket!'

'Oh, what do you need that stuff for?' cried Mauricette. 'Here, I'll spit on it. Hold still!'

Lili took up a position as if she were going to play leapfrog and Ricette climbed on top of her, but back to front, with her behind on Lili's neck. From there she leaned down her sister's back and ran her tongue everywhere it could possibly enter. Then, holding onto her waist with her thighs, she said to me, 'Mama has two cunts because she has as much hair behind as she does in front. But when Lili opens her checks it looks like she has two assholes.'

'That's even better,' said Lili from somewhere beneath Ricette.

However, the thing I proceeded to take was still a vagina, and do I have to mention the precautions necessary? Yes, I think so. It would even be useful if I insisted on them to emphasize the moral character of my narrative. Listen carefully then, young reader, and take heed. Note that the day you try to fuck a youngster dog-fashion, if you are not very careful, you will tear her to pieces and she will survive neither your clumsiness nor your excuses. Nothing is more dangerous than to try to take a slender girl in a posture like that. I am not saying this for the schoolboys who secretly buttfuck their sisters, but rather for those who fuck them and who risk hurting them seriously if they have not read this page.

One of the most widespread of popular errors is that which concerns the deflowering of a young maid. Many men seem to think that the only way to do it is to thrust their penis up the vulva so hard that it comes out the mouth. Or, on the other hand, to run it down the larynx so that it pops out between the legs. Myself, I've never tried this *tour de force*; however the anatomists with whom I have spoken on the subject have advised me against it. I in turn advise you the same. You can no longer say that my book isn't it to be read by some.

God, how virtue often goes unrewarded. My prudence and my scruples will receive little recompense for this wisdom dispensed.

However, joking aside, to play in one woman while

embracing another is not at all my idea of a ravishingly good time. I am so little used to deception in love that even adultery is repugnant to me and I would ten times rather relate this story of a family of whores to you than to set down the methods by which I fooled a man one hundred times in order to make free with his wife.

Under Mauricette and I, little Lili seemed to me to be playing a completely useless role, for the least interested of the two was definitely not the one I was embracing. And this unlikely combination, this reversal of realities under the guise of illusion, bothered me so much that I made a hurried sign to Mauricette.

She asked me in a low voice that no one else could hear, 'My turn now?'

'More than you know. And let's have no more of this crap about the mustard. That's finished. You're going to lose your cherry right now.'

Her face flamed with desire, she stuck out her breasts and opened her lips to cry, 'Yes!' then suddenly shut them again without uttering a sound. With a sudden shift in that fantastic will of hers, she murmured, 'Quick! I want to say something to you behind the door!'

Gently, with a kind little gesture, she kissed Lili, tickled her ribs, made her laugh, and pushed her into her mother's arms to keep her busy while she quickly followed me out of the room.

'Which of us feels like it the most?' she whispered, grabbing me and holding on tightly.

'Me.'

'That's what you think, but... Thanks anyway for saying it, and so much the better if you really believe it... Only, how about waiting for an hour first?'

My face paled and she saw immediately what my sentiments were before I uttered a word.

'Then I'll have to tell you everything,' she said, holding me even tighter. 'Didn't you hear what mama said? I've got a cherry made out of leather like Charlotte used to have... It'll be a butchery!'

Ah! She had found just the word it took to tempt me the least.

'And that's all right with me,' she continued. 'The more you hurt me, the happier I'll be; but when we've finished I'll be roughly half dead... At first I wanted you right away, but now... we're having fun... I'm enjoying myself... I don't always enjoy myself around here.'

As she finished her sentence, she lowered her head and her voice sounded almost like Charlotte's. I felt so sorry that I had made her feel sad that I promised to do anything she wanted and secretly resolved to have as much fun as she in the meantime. Since I rarely resolve to do something in this manner, I like to do it, when the occasion does occur, with temerity.

Chapter Sixteen

Charlotte smiled when we came back in. She had only had to fix her hair, wipe off her rouge, take off her apron, and replace her ribbon with a prim little collar... And now, in her black dress and soft, sad air, she was an orphan girl given a position as governess in a family.

She sat down in front of a small table with her little charge and said without the least hope of obtaining a correct reply, 'What are the provinces of Outer Mongolia?'

'If you only knew how little I really give a damn!' said Lili.

'You haven't learned your lessons?'

'Oh, yes. I learned one of them. I'll tell it to you, but first let's see the hair under your skirt.'

'Oh my God, what a brat! I suppose that because I made the mistake of letting you do that once you're now going to want me to do it every day.'

'I wouldn't be surprised.'

'I'm your governess and you're supposed to obey me. But not only don't you do that, you now want me to bend to all your caprices.'

'That's about right.'

'And afterwards you'll recite the one lesson you did study?'

'Yes.'

'Really! I don't know! I'm much too indulgent for a child as spoiled as you.'

'Oh! Quit flapping your trap!' said the little one in an outrageous voice. 'That'll be enough! Don't try to give me any more shit! Shut your mouth, open your legs, show me what

---

you've got there and swallow the rest of that claptrap. When I ask to see a cunt I'm talking about part of you, not all of you.'

And Charlotte fell silent. Her laugh was as quick to come as her tears and, clapping a hand over her mouth to suppress it, she lifted her skirts and let Lili wander off into her own fantasies of improvisation.

'Good! Good! I got a good look at it this time and I know what it's like to the last detail. Now, if you don't do what I want you to, I'll tell everyone that you were trying to pervert me and that you showed it to me then.'

'What do you want from me, then, you little devil?' asked Charlotte in her sad voice.

'I'm the one who stole that packet of letters you've been receiving from your girlfriend, and I know all about it now. Nothing but filth in any of them, is there? You two have really been up to some pretty little tricks!'

'Oh, I'm lost...'

'Screw that! But no! Go ahead and say it as much as you want. It won't dirty your tongue half as much as licking my behind like you're going to do, will.'

'Me?'

'Who else? And if you don't, I'll run and tell mama that you wanted to!'

Of all Lili's lines, this last one was that which surprised me the least. I have always thought that the wife of Potiphar must have been about fifteen and not forty as certain painters have imagined her. I appeal first of all to those who have lived in the Orient and second of all to you, if you know anything about adolescent psychology, for support.

The little student obtained what she wanted from her governess without much trouble, an act which governesses and charges perform more often than parents realize.

Lili remained silent while Charlotte, on her knees before her, always ready to stoop to a new humiliation, prolonged the scene. But Lili never left her role, and if she took a good deal of time before making her next crack, it was only to set it in greater relief. What the indifferent little voice finally came out with was:

'I much prefer this, my dear governess, to reciting the

Pierre Louÿs

provinces of Outer Mongolia.'

Then she added in a kindly voice:

'Now show me from in front.'

Charlotte sat down and lifted her skirt with her two hands. Lili knelt in front of her, but stopped, staring at the state her sister was in.

'Oh! You're flowing too much for me, Miss Charlotte! That's too much for a girl my age. That's the adult dosage, not the schoolgirl's... But wait... What's going on here? She's beating herself off! Hey! That's enough! No floods please!'

She took Charlotte's finger away and glued her mouth to the same spot... and the scene had hardly begun when it was interrupted by an unforeseen development in the plot.

Teresa in a dressing-gown suddenly crossed the room with great strides in the role of Lili's mother and Charlotte's employer crying, 'Ah! So that's the kind of lesson you give my daughter, eh?'

'Madame!'

'I put a child of fourteen into your charge for you to teach her history, geography, mathematics, and foreign tongues and that's the sort of tongue you show her how to use? Get into your room, Lili! And you, miss, come into mine!'

Then, out of the blue, Teresa turned to Mauricette who was sitting on my knees and said, 'I don't feel like acting, I feel like coming. Also it doesn't take so long.'

Then taking Charlotte by the arm, she said in a softer voice, 'A little while ago I found the packet of letters in my little girl's dresser drawer that she stole from you. Your friend treats you like a lesbian, a whore... it's terrible! She can't seem to stop talking about your tongue... She's always asking how many times you beat yourself off thinking about her.'

'Ah! Madame! Should I kill myself?'

'Don't bother.'

'Oh, I'm nothing but a poor miserable creature.'

'Confess everything to me and I'll pardon you.'

'But I have practically every known vice.'

'Me too.'

And Teresa shot us a glance to show how easily she could

---

change the drama to suit her own purposes. The conclusion of the piece was easily foreseen, and the only interesting aspect of it for me came from the fact that Lili had enough tact not to bother her mother out of revenge for the dirty trick she had played on her.

She waited patiently until Teresa and Charlotte were finished, then, her imagination still working overtime, ran to them and spoke in a low voice to tell them their roles in the next sequence. She turned, at this point, and announced to us:

'Second act! Eight days later!'

At the beginning of the first act, the governess and the schoolgirl sat down in front of the little table.

'You know your lessons much better now than you did a week ago,' said Charlotte. 'But what's so funny? Be a little more respectful, please!'

'It's one of the hairs from your ass stuck between my teeth. It's tickling my tongue... No, maybe it's one of mama's hairs. Anyway, that's what I'm laughing at. Certainly not because you have a moronic expression on your face.'

'Lili! Come on now! Recite those two pages that you learned yesterday. What is a little girl?'

Mauricette, as soon as she heard that, squirmed around on my knees and said, 'Listen to this! It's that catechism that was written for Charlotte when she was small. Lili knows it by heart!'

Charlotte repeated the question after the interruption, and Lili replied in a monotone, as if she understood nothing of what she was saying.

'What is a young girl?'

'It's a little bitch that doesn't think of anything but handling pricks and cunts, that fingers itself from morning to night, that pisses everywhere, and that is always lifting its dress to show its ass so it can see the asses of others in exchange.'

'What is a young girl good for?'

'No-one knows.'

'What miracle has God wrought out of the goodness of his heart to make young girls happy?'

'That miracle is the gift that nearly all young girls have of making men get hard-ons like they would in front of fully-matured women.'

'Explain yourself.'

'It's a mystery.'

'And what else has the goodness of the Creator done for them?'

'The Creator poked two holes in them and gave them one mouth in addition so that they should not be humiliated to find that they had given any man a hard-on for nothing and so that, miraculously, they can be of some use to them.'

'And in exchange for these divine gifts, what is the duty of a young girl?'

'Every young girl that gives a man an erection must make him discharge also.'

'Is it up to her to choose the hole that she prefers?'

'She has no choice in the matter. She has only to give the hole that is asked of her.'

'Should she wait for one to be asked of her?'

'No. The young girl that finds herself alone with a man should raise her dress as high as possible, excuse herself for having sparse hair, and say politely: "Would you like to fuck me? Would you like to buttfuck me? Or would you rather I suck you?"'

'And if the man should reply, "Go beat yourself off somewhere else, I only screw women," what should the girl do?'

'In this case, the girl should go away, but she can abstain from any form of masturbation without being considered lax in her religious duty.'

At this point, Lili left her role in the middle of the act, something she rarely did, and said to me:

'You don't think they taught me some real idiocies?'

And Charlotte immediately added, 'This is nothing for her. But me! I had to learn this at the same time that I was learning my catechism! When we got to the church I got all screwed up and I just missed reciting the wrong things to the priest about twenty times!'

Then, at a sign from Lili, they returned to their roles.

'Very good. Is that all you know for today?'

'Oh, no. I know something else. I know that the worst little bitches that walk the earth aren't young girls. They're governesses.'

'Ah! Something like that was bound to happen sooner or later! I'm only getting what I deserve. I've been saying to myself: "What must this child think of me?"'

'Would you like to know?'

Ricette whispered into my ear, 'If she tells her, Charlotte will start fingering herself.' But Lili knew it as well as she and, like the famous captain who followed his men wherever they wanted to go because he was their leader, she ordered what she was unable to prevent.

'Don't waste any more time! Give me the lesson in masturbation I'm supposed to have and I'll tell you before you finish.'

'Where have I failed?' wailed Charlotte, raising her skirts. 'Did I pass all my exams in order to give lessons in masturbation?'

'Which exams? Your whore's exams? And you didn't cheat to do it?'

'You dare to speak to me like that? You would treat your governess like a whore?'

'Look at the beard! I'm waiting, miss. I'm awaiting my lesson. Discharge first, you can rave at me afterwards.'

There was the same ease to be found in the tone of voice in which Lili delivered her remarks as in the choice of expressions she employed. But these are things that are impossible to describe.

'I'm ashamed of myself for two reasons,' began Charlotte. 'First of all I have to teach you horrors like this, and secondly, I can't teach them as they should be taught.'

'That's easy to see. I know you're pretty stupid, but go ahead anyway. I understand everything.'

'Beginning with the elementary course... That's the one I know the best,' said Charlotte laughing. 'It isn't hard. First you wet your middle finger like this... Then you stick it in here, and you move it back and forth like this... there, see?'

'And serve it hot, eh?' asked Lili. 'Hey! Stop! Look who's fingering herself while I haven't learned a damn thing! What a dolt this governess is! She's as stupid as she is whore! Will you please continue with my lesson?' she said, grabbing her sister's hand.

Pierre Louÿs

'To repeat,' said Charlotte, patiently, looking for more technical terms. 'This here is called my vulva.'

'You would have thought it was a cunt,' observed Lili.

'You stick your finger here, in the vagina, and you wet it with the... the... what do you call a woman's come?'

'You can tell me tomorrow. Continue.'

'Then if you can wait, you tickle yourself inside here with two fingers or pull these little lips here on the outside. If you're in a hurry, you touch the clitoris right away; you push against it, you rub it from left to right or else you go around...'

'And look who's doing it again! And at top speed this time!'

'I can't anymore...!' murmured Charlotte.

'What an education!' sighed Lili turning toward us. 'Disgusting to have a mistress like that! Instead of teaching me how to write, she teaches me how to finger myself! Me, a little girl who doesn't even know the provinces of Outer Mongolia!'

'Neither do I.'

'She drips juice all over all the furniture, she whacks away at mama's pussy, mama who is such a saintly woman, she smells come like I do orange blossoms, and when you look in her work table, what do you find?' And here Lili pulled a dildo from her pocket.

'Oh! In that child's hands...!'

'You really disgust me, miss!'

'I disgust myself even more.'

'And now you're going to see how much I respect you. But first finish beating yourself off... That's enough!' Lili pulled Charlotte's arm so her hand should leave its occupation.

'Oh! Lili! Lili! I was just going to come! I'll have an attack!'

However, Lili got a moment from her. She donned the dildo by fastening the over-large belt attached to it with a pin and, fixing her dress so that the instrument protruded like the enormous phallus of a grotesque epicene god, she said:

'A whore of a governess can at least be as polite as a little girl, right? Remember what you just made me recite?'

'What?' groaned Charlotte, almost deranged.

'Even more bitch than whore!' said Lili compassionately.

'Look here, my good woman. Look at me. You'll get it in good time. Look. I'm a man and you have must given me an erection. That's obvious isn't it? So, what do you show me now? Well? Raise your skirts, damn it! Oh! Oh! I'm as hot as a firecracker!'

'I don't even know what she's saying,' murmured Charlotte, lifting her clothes as if in a dream.

'And when a filthy beast like you shows her two holes to a man, what does she say?'

'Will you... screw me... buttfuck me... or should I... suck you...'

'On your knees! Give me your buttocks! No, but look how she opens them! And how I drive in there! What a calamity to have a governess who shows her ass all the way through a lesson and then lets her little charge stick a dildo into it at the end... What disgusts me the most, miss, is not that you are a whore, but that you're stupid enough to let me buttfuck you.'

And then...

♦

Then what happened? The saddest, most unfortunate incident of this whole story.

Had Charlotte over-estimated the capacity of her morbid taste for humiliation? Lili, like all youngsters, didn't know where to stop in farce of this kind; had she gone too far in her role?

No. The explanation that I read from what had preceded is entirely different, and all the more difficult to explain since I am writing this book in the first person. But, faced with Charlotte's love, 'there is nothing to brag about' as Lili said. It is certainly not this story that I would have chosen from among my experiences if I had wished to impress on anyone the brilliance of my attractions or the effect of my seductions. And I hope that you will not be moved to any such condemnations, young ladies, if I say that during that evening when I scarcely left Mauricette's side for a moment, Charlotte, who grew more and more nervous from minute to minute, seemed to me much more unfortunate. My presence was responsible for her state.

It was Mauricette that finally unleashed the crisis. She

laughed. I do not know why. Lili's last line had been one of the least funny she had spoken in an hour or so, but it had been injurious and Mauricette had laughed. Immediately, Charlotte had burst out sobbing.

And what sobs! I thought I knew Charlotte's sobs, but I was wrenched heart and soul by what I heard.

She lay on the floor like a dying beast, holding her skirt in one lifeless hand while Lili, unnerved, continued to ram her from the rear. And all the time she sobbed out great wailing cries. Not tears, but racking, choking, rending cries that shook her body unceasingly.

Teresa said quickly as she paused by me, 'They kept her from coming. It's the kid's fault. She should never have tried to keep her from coming when she was ready. That's what always happens.'

Even so, the crisis was so strong this time that it frightened even her sisters as much as it did me. With Teresa, they picked her up and stretched her out on the divan, taking her in their arms. But the storm didn't cease as quickly as it had burst, and it was only some time before Charlotte could overcome her sobs enough to gasp out these few despairing sentences:

'You're right, my Lili... I'm as stupid as... as a whore... I'm nothing but a bitch and a moron... Everyone mocks me... And no one will ever love me.

Epilogue

Fortunately for my health but unfortunately for my pleasure, this ideal existence was interrupted several days later.

One evening my concierge handed me an enigmatic but decipherable note that said:

> *'They were bothering us back there because of number three. This time I will take them a long way away; however, we shall return to this country some time and we will see each other then. We have been very kind to you, but you to us also. Love from all the girls and from me.'*

Do I have to say that until that moment I had not really understood what an adventure like that had had to offer of the unusual, the complex, the pleasurable? The hopelessness that I felt upon reading those few lines was a hundred times stronger than would have been my pleasure had the note said, *'Come over this evening.'*

It brought to mind the Spanish proverb: *Ayer putas, hoy comadres* (Whores yesterday, friends today). This saying, originally coined for women, was truer for me than for any gossip of Zaragora or Avila. But, with a sentimental awkwardness typical of my twenty years, I only loved those four whores an hour after their departure.

It was absurd and yet, as a priest once told me, even this absurdity is a mark of God's grace. It would have been even more absurd should I have fallen in love with them after they had been at my door for fourteen years.

It is a pity that God does not exist, because what he does

he does very well.

After re-reading Teresa's note through tear-filmed eyes, I finally uncovered the meaning in it: 'I had a lot of trouble at Marseilles because of Lili, who is a little young. And apparently the affair is not yet closed. There has been trouble even here. I am therefore leaving for [Chile? Brazil?]... We will see you later.'

♦

And later, when my grief permitted me to think about it a little, the problem that had been my obsession and my mystery from the first day that I had known that quartet, returned to haunt me.

Why, immediately after my adventure with Ricette, had I fallen also into the arms of her mother, her younger sister, and her elder sister?

The problem, giving it a little thought, seemed to me more easily resolved than I had thought.

Ricette. That was easy.

Teresa. I frankly did not understand.

Charlotte. Soft, docile, would do whatever asked.

Lili. A virgin who wanted the same lover her sisters had.

And, as a matter of fact, nothing is more common than to see three sisters follow each other into the same bed and take, one by one, the same man for a lover. This practice may be strictly and unanimously condemned by all the old masters of moral theology, but mothers practically never put the book into their daughters' hands where is printed the sentence:

'If you sleep with the same man as your sister, you are committing incest.' The girls, therefore, may be excused.

THE EROTIC ADVENTURES OF TOINON

[Translator's note: All speech in italics appears in English in Louÿs' original manuscript, and is reproduced verbatim.]

I

On the stroke of nine o'clock, all eighteen boarders lined up at the foot of the staircase which led to our dormitories. At a signal from the headmistress, we climbed the stairs two by two in silence. I had been told to follow Jeanne Larive, so with her and four other girls, I entered one of the three dormitories. Well, dormitory makes it sound grander than it was. The room was not big. Four double beds, hung with white curtains, occupied its four corners. There was one door and one window, with a wash-basin at the third wall, and at the fourth a huge old-fashioned night commode and a bath-tub.

New though I was in the house, I quickly realised that two of us were to sleep in each of the first three beds, while the fourth bed, which was raised above the floor, was reserved for the mistress, a young American lady. "Isn't Miss coming up with us?" I asked my neighbour, Jeanne. "She's playing cards with the head," said Jeanne. "She's never around when we go to bed."

My five new friends were already rushing to get undressed. I was a little embarrassed by their silence, a little surprised too, and I was looking in puzzlement at Jeanne Larive – Jeanne was my new sleeping-partner, a sixteen year-old brunette with beautiful hair – when to my great surprise, I heard the eldest among us loudly declare, as she threw herself on her bed: "I can't stand it any longer, I'm itching to have a wank." As she spoke, she unbuttoned her white pants and shoved her right hand in between her open legs.

"Oh! Roberte!" said a shocked Jeanne. "Have you no shame in front of a new girl!"

"Oh, go on with you!" said another girl, teasingly, a petite brunette with a depraved look in her dark-rimmed eyes. "Just listen to Jeanne Larive playing the prude! And we know why! You want to teach the new girl everything yourself. You're afraid we'll steal her from you. Well, you needn't worry, we'll let you keep your baby. Your breasts are big enough for her to suck on." And with that, she pulled her shirt up to her waist and sat on the commode to pee.

I was startled by what I heard, and yet I was curious enough to look at Jeanne, whose slender body was indeed endowed with breasts extraordinarily well developed for her age. "Bad little bitch," she said angrily. "It's not very nice to do dirty things in front of a thirteen year-old girl..."

"Well, *I'm* fourteen!" interrupted the little brunette. "There's hardly any difference!"

"Yes, but you've been a boarder for six years now. You've had time to learn a thing or two, Fifi. Remember that she's only just arrived, that we don't even know her name. What is she going to think of us if she sees us this evening doing what we usually do?" Jeanne couldn't help smiling as she said this.

"Come on," said Fifi, "I'm going to finish Roberte off. You're talking nonsense." And she ran her little hand along her friend's hand and into her squirming pants between her open legs. At the same time, the other two girls, who hadn't said a word, stood at the foot of their bed, in a tight embrace, their mouths glued together.

Perhaps to hide all this from me, Jeanne suddenly sat me down on her knees with my back turned to the other two couples who fascinated me so, and pressing me against the warm skin of her big breasts, she said, "What's your name?"

"Antoinette. Toinon, I mean. Mummy calls me Toinon."

"Mummy calls me Toinon! What a mummy's girl! Well, I'm going to be your mummy now. I'll love you as much as she does, more than she does, if that's possible. What about it?"

"Oh, yes, please!"

"And I'm going to feed you just like your mummy did when you were little." So saying, she undid her swollen shirt and, nestling me in her left arm, offered me her breast. With a mixture of intimidation and delight, I took it into my mouth. I had no memory of my wet-nurse and so, as far as I could recall, this was the first time that I held a teat between my lips. This one was hard, very large and burning hot. I sucked hard on this long, rough piece of flesh. "You haven't any milk!" I said to her,

Pierre Louÿs

emboldened.

"Yes, I have!" Jeanne protested. "But you don't get it from there. We'll leave that lesson till another day. Keep going."

So I started sucking again, and as I did, her face grew redder and redder (or so it seemed to me). And gradually, her hand, which she had at first rested in her lap, moved upwards. It slid into the narrow gap between my clenched thighs and tried to push them apart. I looked at her in astonishment, but she gazed down at me so affectionately that I slowly opened my legs. She felt my smooth, bulging little slit with her fingers... Then, suddenly, we heard Roberte say: "Nine thirty. Lights out!" We immediately got up again and Jeanne helped me to finish undressing. Then she took off her underwear and put on a long white nightdress. As she did so, I caught sight of her brown back and rather fleshy bottom. We blew out the candles, got into bed together, and she embraced me with unusual abandon.

II

At the same moment, the door opened and a young woman's voice said very loudly: *"What! The light's out?"*

"Half past nine," chorused several voices. It was the young American mistress coming home. *"Well! I want a tongue,"* she went on. *"Fifi, lend me yours."*

Someone jumped effortlessly out of bed – it was probably Fifi doing as she was told. (In fact, though I know a few words of English, I didn't understand this exchange very well. Jeanne held me tightly against her and did not move.) Miss continued a little less loudly: *"That damned old bitch of a directrice is always ready to spend and feels tired when people want their turn. I think I'd like to drink a full glass of her thick, slimy stuff. Fye 'pon it!"* She paused and then added with a laugh: *"Fifi, dear, I know my belly is wonderfully hairy. However it is not quite impossible to reach the tickler. You're licking the curls, you dear little chit. In such a manner, I'll not come before tomorrow morning."* Then, after a brief silence: *"Well, tongue my arsehole. Perhaps it is more easy, though I've got hairs also around it. I'll frig myself in front.... Oh! you little whore, how you know it! You begin by the buttocks! I'm sure women in brothels don't move their tongue better than you... And now I feel it softly tickling my warm, tight hole. My whole bum is burning with heat. Push it in, Fifi dear! I'm nearly mad, O do push it in! Oh! Thanks for you, my love! That's too dreadfully exciting! It's like a prick in my bowels... Here! here your hand, dear little thing, feel how... I'm ... spending!... I think my whole life and blood are rushing out of my cunt!..."*

I did not hear any more, for at that moment, I was invaded by a delicious sensation. This is what had taken place in our bed. For the whole of the preceding scene, which lasted nearly half an hour, Jeanne at first kept perfectly still, unsure what to do (she admitted this to me later), not knowing whether to cover my ears or to give in to her urge to initiate me earlier than planned. She had to do one thing or the other, because, although

I wasn't familiar with English words like arse, tickler, frig, bum or cunt, Miss's long monologue threatened to give me a rapid lesson on everything I didn't know about life, and Jeanne did not intend me to be taught by any hand but her own.

Suddenly, she made up her mind, and just as Miss said *"I know my belly is wonderfully hairy,"* I felt my bed-partner quickly pull her long nightshirt up to her breasts. In feverish haste, she took my hand, directed it towards her groin, where, to my amazement, I felt a sort of thick fur, made of wiry little curls like astrakhan, and her hot breath whispered in my ear: "Touch me there! Learn what a woman feels like!"

[Note: Two pages appear to be missing from the manuscript at this point.]

III

Exhausted and shaken by this new and intense experience, I could not keep my eyelids open. I fell into a deep sleep.

I only know what happened next because Jeanne confided in me a little later. The idea of having made me come for the first time in my life had excited her so much that she frigged herself, she said, four times in the space of a few hours, while caressing my crack with her other hand. She could not sleep, and as each time her spasms were more acute and her emissions hotter, she was less and less able to resist the temptation to excite herself in this way. Never had she been in such a state before.

At about two o'clock in the morning, unable to bear it any longer, she woke me up, and I remember what occurred from this point on.

"Toinon, Toinon my love," she said in a low voice. "Have you slept enough? Are you rested? Will you make love to me again? Will you, darling?"

In answer to her question, I turned over on my side to face her and curled up in her embrace. This time, she was completely naked and so soaked in sweat from head to foot that the smell of her brown skin permeated the damp sheets and made my senses reel.

"Oh! I love you so much!" I said to her. "If you only knew!" I had said these words with such sincerity that even her body was moved to respond.

"Don't say that, darling. You'll make me come all on my own," she moaned softly. As she had done the first time, she raised her thigh slightly and guided my hand. My fingers plunged into a lake. She had, indeed, already orgasmed. As she had done, I took off my nightshirt and pressed myself even more tightly against her musky, wet body. She was perspiring so abundantly that, from time to time, thin trickles of her sweat ran down my breasts and legs. With the tip of my tongue, I licked a delicious

Pierre Louÿs

light dew from the soft pulp of her breasts. From there my tongue moved down to her armpits. Surprised once again to discover new, hidden tufts of hair which seemed to be the source of Jeanne's wild animal smell, I felt the armpit nearest to my face with curiosity and rolled the curls around my finger. Not only did she let me do this, but she lifted her arm to open up her cup of perfumes, which bristled with long wet hairs. Squeezing me tightly against her, she even began to tease me, tempting my nostrils with her intoxicating odour, holding me so close that I felt her damp curls slide over my lips, and then stop. And then, in a voice which was scarcely a breath, she said one little word: "Suck."

I hesitated a little; but the silence and darkness emboldened me. First, I gave a little flick with my tongue to taste. It was very strong. It was even piquant, as if this bodily fluid was seasoned with salt, vinegar and spices; and yet, the lascivious odour of flesh dominated all others and drew my mouth to it. I slowly sucked and licked as many of the curls as my mouth could hold. My tongue searched out every tasty, intoxicating little drop and swallowed it.

Jeanne, however, already had other plans. Having initially felt some concern for my childish lack of experience, my enthusiasm had reassured her, and she was in a hurry to take all the virginities of my pre-pubescent little body one by one. Her hand slid over my back like a caress, followed the gentle contours of my bottom, squeezed it softly, pulled the cheeks apart and pushed one finger into the little hole. It resisted. In order to hide my shame, I sucked her armpit even more greedily, nibbling the hairs like a little goat.

Jeanne took her finger away, wet it between her thighs and pushed again at the frail little opening, this time so successfully that half of her finger went right in.

"Your mouth," she said to me with sudden ardour, "Take my tongue, Toinon, my darling. Oh!..."

Our lips glued together, and as her delicious tongue probed deeper into my still bitter-tasting mouth, I felt her finger move just as deeply into my burning bowels. Now and then, she would stiffen it, making me shudder with pleasure...

"I'm not hurting you?" she said on my lips.

"Oh, no! Don't stop! You're a dirty, dirty girl, my big, bad darling, but I love it!"

"Do you love me!"

"I love you as much as you love me. I love you more than anything."

"In that case," she declared in a more serious tone of voice, "I'm going to marry you. You'll be my darling little wife, my sweetheart, my mistress. I'm going to do to you, my love, exactly what married people do."

She embraced me with such passion that I thought I was going to suffocate; then, without withdrawing her finger, but wriggling it a little in its narrow little sheath, she turned me over onto my back, and kneeling to the right of me, just next to my shoulder, lightly stroked my tummy with the tip of her large, full, firm breasts, and opened my little crack by pushing my legs apart. Suddenly, her stiff, quivering tongue pounced upon the most sensitive spot in my entire body.

In a frenzy of delight, I waved my arms around in the darkness, blindly trying grab hold of Jeanne to embrace her. Her left thigh was raised and pressed against me, so I stroked it frantically with one hand, and with the other, I caught hold of the balloon-like breast that I felt slapping against my tummy. I wanted to give her the same pleasure that she gave me, but I didn't know how, and anyway, I was too distraught to do anything else on the bed but pant and writhe.

"Oh! Jeanne, Jeanne!" I almost shouted to her. "It's starting again! I can feel it... I can feel it again... just like yesterday... oh! my darling!"

Her tonguing grew more rapid, now pressing really hard, and cautiously, she pushed and pulled her finger in and out of my behind.

"Yes, yes... oh, again... oh! I'm dying, that's it, I can't take any more... Jeanne... you've made me come so much."

She knew she had all too well, licking up the frothy cream that welled out of my virginity with a couple of flicks of the tongue... I fell back exhausted, my mouth half open and my arms spreadeagled on the bed.

Pierre Louÿs

Then, in an almost frightening state of excitement, she lay full on top of me. Her finger, which was now beginning to cause me a stinging pain, kept on probing my tender little rump. She slid her other hand underneath my bottom, and lifting with both at the same time, she pressed her groin hard against my sensitive, swollen flesh.

"Jeanne... you're killing me," I sighed.

But she couldn't hear me now. She was rubbing herself against me as if she would never stop. Instinctively, I lifted my open thighs to meet her, my knees up and my feet waving in the air. Suddenly, her come flooded all over me.

How long did it all take? I don't know. Probably more than an hour. She didn't stop until she'd climaxed twice in a row, when, poor little girl that I was, I had just fainted for the third time.

"Toinon," she said to me with a smile, "open your eyes, pumpkin. Look, it's light already."

I replied in a very weak voice, "So it is. Oh, I've never seen daybreak before! What time can it be? We've stayed awake much too long! We'll be ill."

"It's not late, sweetheart, it's early. It's four o'clock. Another two and a half hours till it's time to get up; two and a half hours for us to put to good use."

A pale blue sheet of daylight filtered through the crack between the closed curtains. Jeanne was squatting next to me, naked, her feet tucked underneath her and her hands on my shoulders. I could finally make her out.

"Let me look at you," I said to her. "Don't move. Oh, how beautiful you are, my darling!"

"What do you want to look at, pumpkin? Whisper to me."

"You know very well, you naughty thing! You want to make me say it, but I don't know the words."

"How sweet! Listen, I'll teach you what to say. This is called a pussy. It's called a cunt, too, but that's not a nice word. Don't say that."

"Well, show me your pussy, I want to see what it's like."

"Here you are, then, darling, it's all yours."

Sitting astride my face, and grinning widely, she pulled her lips apart with her hands.

The lips were blackish and inside, purple in colour, but the whole thing glistened with a thick, smooth liquid which covered even the lustrous locks of her black fur.

Just as she had done the night before, when I was sniffing her armpits, she slowly lowered this musky, salivating mouth down to my mouth and, again just as she had done then, she whispered this one little word: "Suck."

In fact, this invitation to dessert was already superfluous, since a big, fat globule had run down from the corner of her pussy as soon as she had opened her lips, had hung for a moment on the end of a dribbling slaver, and I had just received a tea-spoonful of this lovely hot cream on my tongue.

I told her to lower herself more. Her thick fleece covered my eyes and forehead.

"Rub yourself up and down like before," I said to her.

"Oh, pussycat, do you really want me to?"

"Yes." I stuck out my tongue and thrust my lips forward, so that I could kiss, lick, suck and drink her flesh as much as I possibly could, and she rubbed her sex against me with unbelievable sensuality.

To say that she climaxed would be an understatement. She writhed as if she was giving birth, but this time a more liquid saliva poured out of her exhausted body, a sort of fever sweat, boiling hot and acrid tasting. The poor girl had no strength left.

"Oh!... oh!... I can't take any more..." she stammered, letting her beautiful, brown body fall back onto the bed like a log. "Oh! that really hurt!... it burned me... just moving makes me want to scream."

Then, she caught sight of my reddening face, streaming with her come. "Oh, darling, what a state you're in! Give me your mouth quickly... and your tongue, too."

Our tongues met in a passionate embrace.

The clock chimed half past four. The sun was now well up. I gazed at my girlfriend's body lying next to me, her deep brown skin standing out against the white sheets.

Pierre Louÿs

"You're only sixteen!" I said to her. "Will I be like you at your age?"

"Oh, no, my darling. I know girls of twenty who haven't got figures like mine. My mother is Spanish, that's why I've grown so quickly. I was already hairy everywhere when I made my first communion, I was the only one in my year."

"You dirty girl! How do you know?"

"Because I was out in the country with fifteen little peasant-girls, who knew everything that you don't, pussycat, and they passed it all on to me."

"Oh, tell me what they said!"

"I'm too tired this morning, Toinon. I'll tell you everything another day."

She fell silent. I leaned my head on her bosom and I tried to push my hand between her thighs. At first, she let me do it, and she even slipped her tongue back into my mouth, but as soon as I found her swollen little button, she gave a violent start and seized my wrist.

"No, don't! I can't take any more, you'd make me ill. I'm sore all over, darling, and I'm tired out. Remember that I've come nine times tonight... What about you?"

I raised three fingers.

"You see," she went on. "It's much too much for the first time, but just imagine how you would feel if you did it another six times. I feel so drained that I can't see straight any more."

I whispered into her ear: "Well, then, at least let me do it to you... the way you did it to me... you know... here."

And I felt between the cheeks of her bottom.

"Bunnyrabbit, that would be even worse!" she said to me affectionately. "That doesn't always make you come, but it works you up more than anything!"

"Oh, please, I beg you!"

"Don't beg me, my darling. Tell me that you want to and I'll let you."

"Alright, then, I want to."

"Well do it straight away. Here I am. I'll let you do whatever you like, do you hear? I won't refuse you anything. I swear! But I expect lots of love in return."

As she said these words, which I would remind her of so often in the future, she knelt down on the bed, with her head on her arms and her bottom sticking out.

It was only then (as I was getting ready to indulge my whim) that it occurred to me that we were not alone in the bedroom and that if one of our companions woke up early, she might open the bed-curtains and surprise us. But this idea just excited me all the more. I really would have liked the others to watch, and having seen what we did, to accept me as one of the older girls.

Jeanne had a thin waist, but her bottom was as big as her bosom. I placed both arms round this huge, brown thing, and covered it all over with kisses.

I remember that what I found most interesting was the sight of the two lips fringed with thick, black hairs, jutting out between the two cheeks, much easier to see from behind than from the front, the lips of the pussy that I had just brought off nine times, the pussy that had filled my mouth with streams of red-hot come. I began by slipping my tongue inside it, cupping her hairy mound with my hand.

"Toinon, you're cheating! That's not why I turned over. Go a bit higher, will you?"

Higher up, the cleft of her bottom followed a deep, dark line, bordered with hairs on either side, and these hairs were so long that they certainly must have looked like a sort of curious, thin plume, even when she was standing up, with her buttocks clenched. They finally curled round a deeply wrinkled anus, whose thick folds radiated outwards like the petals of a flower.

I scratched it with the edge of my nail, and had just begun to push, when Jeanne said: "Be a sweetheart and wet your finger a little. It's very tight, you know."

I inserted not one but three fingers into her still moist slit, and before she could protest, all three had gently yet swiftly penetrated her muscular anus. She stifled a cry:

"Ouch! you're tearing me apart, Toinon! Toinon!"

"Am I hurting you, my darling? Do you want me to take them out?"

She was panting, her mouth pressed against her arm. "I

screamed but I shouldn't have... I really like it, oh yes!... push them in a bit more, more... that's it... oh!... more, if you can... and stroke me with your finger-tips... yes, God, I'm really sensitive this morning... what's wrong with me!?" And she slipped her right hand underneath her.

"No, darling," I said to her, "that's enough. You said so yourself just now. Don't do it again, you'll make yourself ill."

"But pumpkin, I'm so excited, you don't understand... my cunt's on fire... your fingers are driving me mad."

"Listen," I said to distract her, "do you know what I can feel with my fingers?"

"You're the one that wanted to do it!" she replied with a laugh.

"How soft and warm it is in there, especially this!"

"When I think that you called me a dirty slut not half an hour ago! There's nothing left to teach you, you know. You've really made progress for your first night."

"I had a good teacher."

"Darling, listen, be an angel. Let me do it to myself just once, just one little time, I can't bear it any longer... I want to so much that I could bite myself..."

"Not now, in a minute. You've only just done it and you're too tired. We've still plenty of time."

I took my fingers out, and saw that they had changed colour somewhat.

"Oh, you naughty girl! I'll have to punish you!" cried Jeanne with more tenderness than anger, and taking hold of my three fingers, she thrust them under my nose.

"There you are, mademoiselle, that's what you've done, that's where you've been. It smells good, doesn't it, you dirty little bugger!"

With a malicious smile, I began to lick them with the tip of my tongue.

"Alright, then, alright, if that's the way things are," said Jeanne, her face almost blushing, "I won't say another word. Give me a hug, you darling child! I've been a boarder now for six months and that's something I still haven't done. You show promise, my little sweetheart. I have no idea what will become of you in future, but your husband will have no cause for complaint!"

Then, holding me tightly in her arms, she whispered in my ear: "Do it to me first."

"What?"

"This." (She wiggled her tongue). "Will you?"

"Yes, but you haven't told me where."

"Listen and I'll tell you, my wicked little darling. I want you to put your little tongue into my bottom, into my arsehole. Is that plain enough? You like naughty words, don't you? Well, I'll teach you lots of them, my little honeypot, my little red button!"

I was overjoyed. In a trice, she was back on all fours, and while I tongued her bottom as hard as I could, the dirty girl "pushed" to open herself wider, so that I was able to lick far up inside her.

When I grew tired, she did the same to me, with a skillfulness that put my own efforts to shame. At last, our tongues said thank you with a long, wet kiss of love.

I just could not stop admiring her. "Jeanne," I said, "what beautiful hair you've got! How far does it go?"

"Right down to my knees."

"Will you let it down for me?"

She let her hair down from the back with both hands, then piled it up in front into a wavy, black heap. I took hold of it, kissed it, and stroked my cheeks with it.

"I bet it covers your pussy, doesn't it?"

"Oh, yes, the whole thing. Look."

And she held six inches of her hair between her thighs.

"It's exactly the same colour as your pubes."

"Yes, but not as curly... Listen, Toinon, you know what you do when your hair's as long as mine, don't you?"

"No."

She twisted the ends of her hair into a brush shape, ensuring that all the strands were the same length, then, holding it tightly between her thumb and forefingers, she opened her thighs, pulled her lips apart with her other hand, and, looking straight into my eyes, tickled her swollen clitoris.

"Oh, that's nice!" I cried.

"Do you want me to keep going?"

"Oh, yes!"

Her eyes began to water. "And while I do this, will you suck one of my nipples?"

"Oh, yes!"

"And tickle the other one? Lie down like this so that I can see your little slit and think of you as I come."

"I'll make you come so much, my darling. I'll suck you as hard as I can, I'll lick you, and I'll bite you with all my heart."

And so Jeanne discharged for the tenth time that night.

When she'd finally stopped coming (her spasm was almost painfully slow), I sucked the little clump of soaking wet hair and then pressed my mouth onto my poor darling's sore lips.

The clock struck six o'clock.

"Oh, already!" she groaned. "It'll be time to get up in half an hour. To have to part so soon, my darling Toinon."

She squeezed me tight in her arms. "But you haven't yet met your room-mates. Come and let me introduce you to them while they're still asleep."

We got up, still completely naked, but as soon as we were upright, we almost fell over, we were so exhausted.

"It's not like this every night, you know, Toinon."

She led me to the first bed and half-opened the curtains.

"Look, that big ugly girl on the end is Roberte de Fesmes. Don't make an enemy of her. She's in charge of the dormitory when Miss isn't here. The little girl sleeping next to her is Fanny Michon, otherwise known as Fifi or Little Broom. She's a disgusting little slut who sleeps with everyone and will do anything you like if you give her a few pennies. When you speak to her, treat her like a kitchen-maid."

She moved on to another bed.

"This is Miss Maud Symons, an American from the deep South. She's our mistress. She's a good sort, she's very fond of us and lets us do practically whatever we like. Even if she scolds you, you mustn't answer her back."

She went on to the third bed.

"And finally, here we have Marie and Madeleine Gervais, two sisters. Fifteen and sixteen years old, but the sixteen year old isn't quite as grown-up as me. Those two little darlings love each other. And they're very sweet. Do you want me to wake them?"

I nodded. She touched each of them on the shoulder and sat on the bed.

"Here we are, girls, this is my wife."

"Have you already done it?" said Marie.

"You bet."

I beamed. But suddenly, Madeleine said: "My goodness, Jeanne, you look really awful!"

"Her too!" replied Marie, pointing at me. "I didn't see them properly at first, I was still half asleep. You're dead on your feet, children! What can the two of you have been doing!"

"I haven't slept a wink," Jeanne replied. "And do you know how many times we came?"

"How many?"

"She came three times and me ten. I can't stay upright any longer, my breasts feel like they've been beaten, I've got back-ache like an old soldier, and my pussy's in such a state that I don't even know if I'm going to be able to wash it. That's how we spent our wedding-night. What about you two?"

"Us? Oh, we've been together since we were born and we had our wedding-night a long time ago. We rubbed each other once, then we put the candle out and said good night."

"Well, do it again just for us. We've another quarter of an hour before it's time to get up, you've just got time and I'm sure my little Toinon would like you to."

"Oh, yes!" I insisted. "Will you, mademoiselle?"

"I don't mind."

"Me neither"

"You've excited us, you know, with your 'ten times'," Marie added. "One shouldn't come waking up innocent young girls at six o'clock in the morning to tell them such things. I'm sure you've made me wet." She put her hand underneath her nightshirt.

"Look!" she said, showing us her wet finger. "That's your fault!"

And she was smiling so sweetly as she spoke that I wanted to kiss her. But her sister had already stretched out on top of her, and, hoisting up both their shirts, began to rub her pussy against hers.

"Not like that!" said Jeanne. "With nothing on!"

But they didn't listen, locking their hot thighs together in a passionate clinch under their long nightshirts.

"Give us your handkerchiefs," said Marie when it was over.

She wiped her sister clean with Jeanne's, and herself with mine, then handed them back to us, saying: "There you are. So that you think of us until this evening."

Then, as the half hour struck, we kissed them on the mouth and ran back to our bed.

IV

Almost immediately after the half hour struck, the wake-up bell rang.

"Don't put your nightshirt back on," Jeanne said to me. "We do our toilet completely naked so that Miss can make sure we're properly clean. It's the rule."

Indeed, our four dormitory-mates were already up and walking around without anything on except light mules on their feet.

Perhaps it was a shameful thing to do, but I couldn't help looking at their pubic hair straight away, a feature that was so new and interesting to me. Marie's and Madeleine's pubic hair was hazel, almost chestnut in colour. They looked almost identical, except that Marie's, her being the elder, was thicker and bushier – but it was just a tuft of grass compared with Jeanne's dense shrubbery.

Roberte's pubes seemed ugly to me. A narrow wisp that didn't extend to her groin formed a kind of powder-puff under her belly-button that looked like a big piece of dried-up hemp, and her lips were so bare that you could see the whole of her crack between her long thighs.

In the end, it was Fifi's pubes that I found most tempting, in spite of Jeanne's warnings. They were little more than a shadow, but one that was already quite large, and the place that they would eventually cover was so flabby, so wide-open and so slackened by vice that such precociousness made me quite dreamy...

Miss, too, got up, but she had put a dressing-gown on over her nightshirt and all I could see of her were her beautiful, brown face, and profusion of long black hair. Jeanne was certainly brown, but Miss even more so. *"Good morning, Roberte and Fifi. How was the frigging?"*

"Rather lewd," said Roberte.

"Nothing from the tongue?"

"A long kiss. Nothing else."

"You knew Fifi's tongue was just getting out from my bumhole?"

"I relished it, because 'twas your smell."

"O you flattering girl! Kiss me for the answer."

She went up to Marie and Magdalen who were washing each other in the tub.

"Mary and Magdalen, tell me what you did? A 'belly on belly' as usual?"

"We did it twice."

"Oh! that's a little too much. Once is quite sufficient, even between lovers like you. I allow the second spending, however. Nights become so hot since last Sunday, perhaps you could not sleep unsatisfied."

She finally took a couple steps in our direction, but stopped in her tracks: "Good heavens! Jane! What happened! Are you ill, both of you?"

"We feel quite well, thank you," replied Jeanne in a slightly ironic tone.

"It's no use lying, you're worn out. Your eyelids look as dark as if you had been broken in by a hundred soldiers. What did you do with that poor little artless kind?"

"I couldn't say there's anything we forgot to do, Miss. Perhaps she was artless yesterday. I've brought her up."

"What a shame!"

"I thought 'twas better to teach her the whole of it at once. Besides, I'm not accustomed to sleep by featherless little slits like hers. I felt so very hot. I couldn't help asking her to frig me in every way. 'Twas our wedding night. You ought to forget us, Miss; we're so happy!"

"Jane, you know I admit everything except madness. Lean back 'pon your bed, I'll see what is the matter with your cunny, after such a stupid behaviour."

Jeanne obeyed, and Miss was able to observe for herself, with as much sensuality as solicitude, the redness and distension of her thick, juicy lips. I had to submit to the same examination.

"Well, if I let you go on, you'll be sick tomorrow morning.

That can't do. You must be severely punished. You know what I mean, Jane."

And she left us to dress ourselves.

V

"Well," I said quietly to Jeanne, "Miss is quite strict, isn't she? I'm to be punished on my first day! And you said she was so nice!"

"You don't understand, Toinon. She means that she expects us to spend the whole afternoon in her bedroom. It's Thursday today, and so there are no classes after lunch. Far from punishing us, she's rewarding us."

"Are you sure?"

"She winked at me and said: *'You know what I mean'.* We'll go and say we're sorry and she'll invite us into her bed. We won't be bored with her, you'll see."

At one o'clock, we knocked on the door of Miss's private bedroom.

"Come in!"

We went in. She was wearing a dressing-gown, sitting in front of her mirror, perfuming her long, dishevelled hair.

"Shameless girls!" she said in a tone of affectionate scolding. *"What do you want me to do? Something filthy, I'm sure."*

"We're begging your pardon, Miss," said Jeanne.

"Yes, but how shall you deserve it?"

"By all means. Especially by the worse."

"I don't understand. Speak plain."

Jeanne and I exchanged a glance, then, with a calmness that I found astonishing, she said to Miss:

"We intend to strip you stark naked, to throw you down 'pon the carpet and to make you spend like a bride, frigging and sucking you over, till you cry for mercy. You've been too naughty for us today. You must pay for it, Maud. Here, in your own room, by your own bed, we're but three shameless girls as you called us, and you were no less right to guess we wanted you to do filthy tricks. Off with your night-dress! Let us compare your nasty hairiness with my curled fur and Tony's smooth cunny. Off with

your night-dress, I say, you dear lustful hairy woman!"

With a laugh, Miss unfastened her dressing-gown, beneath which she was totally naked, and let it fall to her feet, then she hurriedly undressed us.

[Editor's note: A page is probably missing at this point]

"...You won't do that."

"Of course I will," Miss insisted, taking me in her arms.

"Well, I'll frig myself with the handle of your hair-brush and deluge it with such a slimy emission that you'll be unable to dress your hair today."

"So much the better," replied Miss with a laugh. *"Spendings in the hair make it grow brilliant. I'll spare my Macassar Oil, that is so dear nowadays. Much obliged to you, indeed!"*

She pulled me onto the bed with her and pressed me against her large body. Her big bushy pubic hair tickled my tummy delightfully, but what impressed me straight away, and almost as much, was the burning heat and firmness of her skin. Though not as big as Jeanne's, her breasts were much firmer, and her buttocks, which were also smaller, felt like two round, wooden globes under my hands.

She had immediately slipped her long tongue into my mouth, and I could already feel her hot breath on my lips as she gently rubbed her groin against mine.

"Sweet little thing!" she murmured. *"I'm in love with you, do you believe me? Do let your spittle glide into my mouth. How exquisite! No girl here has got spittle like yours... Open your thighs, darling. What a nice smooth little slit! Do you mind me to kiss it? No? Even if I tongue it just as I do your other lips? That's a dear girl."*

And in no time her mouth left mine and she dived between my legs, spilling all her black hair onto my thighs, but I was too exhausted by the previous night for even her quivering tongue to make me come again. However, I wanted to thank her, and so I said to her: "Miss, let me do it to you for a little."

With a shudder of desire, she turned onto her back,

Pierre Louÿs

slowly and carefully pulled her long, thick hairs apart, and when she had finished clearing the way, I caught sight of a big, bright red clitoris nestling between two folds of dark skin.

Her voice was trembling:

"Darling, if you do lick it, if you make me spend at once, I'll never punish you, I swear it... you're too exciting, I'm mad with you. Go at, or I'll swoon out of desire. My cunt is all in glow. I can't wait any longer. For pity's sake..."

I pressed the tip of my tongue onto the fleshy protrusion that she thrust at me. I didn't do a very good job of it, partly because I was a novice, but also because a revolting stench, a horrible fetid smell had just issued from the open cesspool of her cunt and was suffocating me. I realised then why she had begged me so much to do it. But I was so keen to know everything, to do everything and to learn about everything that, in spite of the nausea that filled my throat, I did not take my tongue away...

Fortunately, Miss Maud's rut was at its highest pitch and she suddenly discharged before my eyes, her whole body shaking violently.

Then, after an exhausted silence, she hugged me madly, calling me her mistress, her wife, her only love, with such wild and trembling passion that she scared me.

At the same instant, the sound of sobbing made me turn round. It was Jeanne bursting into tears, with her head against the wall, in a corner of the room.

"Jeanne," I cried. "What is the matter? Why are you crying? Are you jealous?"

She turned round, and said to Miss with sudden hatred: *"Oh! you filthy bitch! What a shame! You know you've got a quim that nobody can tongue, except that foul whore of Fifi; a cunt that's stinking just as a closet's pipe, and you must soil that poor kind's mouth with your miry juices! I would rather have seen you shitting 'pon those dear virgin lips, than giving to them such filth to drink. Perhaps your turd is less disgusting than the unutterable rottenness of your sticky flesh. Faugh!"*

I listened to all this in bewilderment and thought that poor Jeanne was certain to be severely punished. But Miss was decidedly a very sweet girl, for her only response was to jump up, grab hold of the struggling Jeanne, throw her over a chaise longue and rape her with her tongue.

At first, Jeanne resisted and kept cursing and swearing, then the flesh defeated her and she gave in, her thighs open and covering her eyes with her hands.

Then I got up and, not daring to kiss her, after all she had said, I just sucked one of her nipples. She felt me do it, put her arms around me and we mingled our saliva passionately, as she released her sweet-tasting come onto Maud's greedy lips.

"Well, are you still angry?" said Maud.

"Oh! don't speak any more about that, I'm really angry. Must I frig you, or suck your bubbies, or fuck either your cunt or your bum with the dildoe, I'm always ready, you know it. But you ought to understand that your cunt is unlickable."

"That's funny. Who's asking you to do so? Your friend proposed to lick my tickler. Of course I didn't refuse. Now, kiss me, and don't be sulky with your Maud. We've got a wonderful new girl since yesterday, but there's no reason to fight. Let us have a glorious dildoe-fuck before her. I hope she'll be interested with it."

"Yes, I'll fuck your arse, you wicked woman, and make you howl out of pain."

"If you make me howl, it will be out of pleasure, dear thing, especially if you enter me by that luscious way," declared Maud, giving Jeanne a kiss full of saliva. This time, Jeanne returned it with her mouth wide open.

Then, getting up, Jeanne strapped on a dildoe – an instrument that filled me with amazement – around her hips and on her mound. She wet two fingers inside her vagina, and then moistened the tip, crying: *"Lean forward and swell your rump. I'm ready, Are you?"*

"O dear, what a splendid idea you had to loosen my bottom-hole! There's nearly a week I had not even a pencil thrust into it. What a pity to neglect such a rapture."

As she spoke, with the tips of her fingers, she stroked the dark, wrinkly hole that Jeanne had in her sights. She even suddenly pushed two fingers inside, as if to give herself a foretaste of the game they were about to play, and finally, leaning herself on the bed, she stuck out her hairy rump.

"Quick, give me a kiss," Jeanne said to me before starting. "Are you having fun? Are you happy?"

Then, whispering in Miss's ear, she said to her: *"What do you want me to do?"*

"I want you to enter me from..."

"O you blushing maid! Don't you venture to say it flatly?"

"I want to be buggered by a loving lass who is as skilled as the best brothel's whores in the art of maddening arseholes."

"Yes, you'll be buggered, Miss Maud Symons, and in a most filthy manner. I'll burst open your fundament, I'll fill up your bowels, I'll soil my false prick with your very turd. Swell your rump, I say, and frig yourself beneath. That's a lecherous posture."

Jeanne leaned over, and with a fiery glint in her eyes, she stroked Maud's buttocks with her huge, supple, voluptuous breasts. Then, as if to beg forgiveness for her past anger, she curled her thick lips around the hole she was about to penetrate, placed a very affectionate kiss on it, and finally flicked her tongue into it, making Maud tremble so much that her legs began to give way beneath her – I noticed, however, that her tongue did not stray into the nearby slit.

It was time to finish her off. Jeanne, standing with her hands on her buttocks, aimed her instrument at the hole that she had just licked, then suddenly thrust her thighs forward, ramming it in up to the hilt. Maud, mad with desire, had raised herself on one hand: *"I'm coming!"* she screamed. *"Ha!... ha... wait a bit... I'm already spending..."*

But Jeanne was not listening to her. Grabbing hold of the thick tufts of hair that sprouted from the American girl's armpits, she kept pushing the long dildoe further and further into her anus. Finally, her abdomen touched the girl's bottom and she began a furious movement in and out of her bowels, discharging in her turn, shaken from head to toe by spasms of orgasm.

"Oh! don't!..." Maud sobbed, rent by the violence of the assault, *"Stop, my love!... I can't bear it...! You're hurting me...! That's so awfully hard! That's so awfully hard... I'm sure I'm bleeding..."*

"Well," replied Jeanne at the height of arousal, *"bleed on,*

that's all right: what would your arse spend, if not bloody drops? Swell your buttocks, I say, or I'll pluck off the hairs of your armpits."

"Ah... r ... r ... r ... e! You're too cruel...! It's like a stick digging my bowels... Don't work the dildoe in such a brutal manner... Ah! I didn't think I could suffer so dreadfully... Ah!... Have mercy, my love..."

I was terrified. Jeanne, my darling Jeanne, that had been so gentle with me, was foaming at the mouth and from her groin.

"Oh! please, stop!" I shouted at her. "Can't you see that she's crying! Poor Miss, you're hurting her! Stop it!"

"You want me to stop, do you?" she said to me briskly. "Alright. I will."

And yet, she did not withdraw the dildoe, but simply stopped moving it about, and sliding one hand between Maud's legs, she began to masturbate her frantically.

In an instant, Maud's expression changed.

"Heavens!" she said, *"What a bliss! Oh! dearest, dearest Jane!... Oh! do make me spend again... Oh! yes, go on trailing your bubbies 'pon my back as you do... Now the dildoe delights me... Work it slowly, smoothly up and down."*

"Do you wish it in your cunt, Maud?"

"No! It's far better in the arse, of course! Push it on, but no so madly as before... Oh! how lusciously I'm buggered and frigged!... Why! I'm coming... Oh! your lips and tongue! let us kiss!... I'm... pissing sperm... 'pon your finger... Feel it... Ha!... Ha!... Work the dildoe!... Work it harder! harder again! Fill my arse!..."

The two young women rolled around on the bed, with total abandon. Incapable of containing myself any longer, I threw myself in their midst, in an inconceivable melée of arms and legs, and breasts and hair. One of Jeanne's enormous breasts swelled between my thighs. My face was hidden in Maud's armpit, which streamed with bitter-tasting sweat, and my hand, thrust between my bed-companion's legs, was soaking wet with her come, which spurted out all the more.

Suddenly, I felt my clitoris devoured by a probing tongue, whilst a finger thrust into my bottom. I was so aroused that I

Pierre Louÿs

came immediately. Then, suddenly, I was gripped by an unmentionable desire – to sniff and perhaps to lick Miss Maud's fetid flesh...

She had got onto all fours again, with her legs wide open, so that her sturdy buttocks were fully accessible to the indefatigable Jeanne... I thrust my face into her pubic hair, found her lips and pushed them apart with my tongue: her vile odour settled on me like a cloud. Nevertheless, I thrust my tongue inside... then, as if astonished that I hadn't yet fainted with the smell, I licked hard, passionately sucking on her disgusting flesh. I devoured all of her with my tongue and lips, taking her clitoris, her bush, her dark, red and pink labia into my little mouth, drinking in all of the warm, sticky come that had collected deep in her vagina, after an hour's masturbation. It seemed to me that it wasn't until that moment, that I discovered, for the first time in my life, what real love is...

At last, Jeanne withdrew the terrible instrument of pleasure from Maud's anus, and I saw with some alarm that its foul coating was also red with blood.

VI

In the evening of that same day, Jeanne and I went to bed completely naked, just like the previous evening, and I tensed with pleasure when she pulled me tight against her with her arms and thighs.

"You're a naughty baby," she said to me, "to lick Maud's horrible cunt! Give me your tongue quickly, so that I can wash it in my mouth."

My tongue bathed in her warm saliva, and, as she sucked, she undulated her groin on mine voluptuously.

"What a bad little girl you are!" she continued. "So strong smells excite you, do they? But I smell strong as well, you know, Toinon, much stronger than blondes..."

"I love your smell too, my darling Jeanne. You have a good, strong smell. Don't tell me off, Maud does disgust me a little. I was almost sick into her pubes. I sucked her, because I was totally crazy. Tonight, all I can bear is the smell of your armpits. Let me go to sleep with my face under your arm. I'm exhausted. I can't keep awake."

She let me do as I asked, and I fell asleep, licking her bitter, warm sweat, intoxicated by her body's perfumes.

The next day, at break, Jeanne taught me all that was left for me to know about love, that is, about the relations between women and men, but she told me that that was a dangerous game, offering mediocre pleasures. I promised her that I would not think about that sort of thing. But I said to her: "Is it true that you have known a man?"

"Yes, my love, if I'm honest."

"And where did he put his thing?"

"Everywhere – in my pussy, in my bottom, in my mouth. He came in my hands, under my arms, between my breasts. There are many ways of making a man come. He taught me them all."

"Does Your mother know?"

"Don't be silly! You don't think I told her that, do you? It was my brother-in-law who became my lover. My sister and I were very much in love with each other and we had promised each other that we would be deflowered by the same man. As soon as she was married, she gave me to her husband."

"So all three of you went to bed together?"

"Sixty-seven nights in a row. Right through the holidays."

"And were you... completely naked in bed?"

"Of course. My sister is like me. She's wet as soon as she has her arms around someone. Neither of us can bear wearing a nightdress."

"Does your sister look like you?"

"Not at all. She has golden brown hair and blue eyes. I'm not my father's daughter, I'm the daughter of a Spaniard who took Mummy, as his mistress during a rainy season. That's why I have such brown skin, such a full bosom, and..."

"And such a big bottom?"

"Yes, you dirty little bitch. My sister's isn't half as big as mine. Which is why her husband always takes her from in front... whereas with me..."

"He turns you over?"

"Nine times out of ten. But I'm like Miss. I love it... Oh, darling, you can't imagine what it's like to be taken from behind, while a woman's tongue licks your thighs. I've fainted with pleasure more than once, coming like that."

"Men have some uses then, it seems?"

"Oh, we can do without them all right, as you saw for yourself yesterday. While I was poking it up Maud's bottom, you were doing to her yourself what I was just talking about, you were sucking her, you adorable little beast, and you must have felt her come, because she drenched your cheeks with it."

"You're not angry with me any more, are you?"

"No, my love!"

We had arrived at a little grove at the end of the garden, where we were quite alone. The shade there was very dark, because the place was tiny and covered with thick leaves. We sat down on a bench, and I went on: "Well, then, if you're not angry with me any more, lift me onto your knees like you did on that first evening and put one of your breasts into my mouth. I remember how good that was..."

"Darling! You like them, then, do you?"

"Do I like them? What bit of you *don't* I like?"

She unbuttoned her swollen blouse, took hold of her left breast with both hands, and slipped the nipple into my wet mouth. Then, like a mother, she cradled me with her left arm, and at the same time, like a lover, she put her hand up my skirt and frigged me gently.

"You mustn't tell Miss," she whispered, kissing me on the forehead. "You're going to come nicely, and not make any noise, aren't you? Don't squeeze your legs together like that, I can't find your button... There, now I've found it... You crazy little thing, will you stop it! How she wriggles!... No, I don't want you to come straight away... Toinon, my Toinon, hold yourself back, will you... Oh, she's coming, she's coming!... What a temperament!... I'm going to have to finish you off, now, you're dripping with juice."

"Oh, keep going!" I said, almost swooning. "Make me come again, again... I want to do it again. You've set me alight with your stories... Tell me about the things that you've done... when you went to bed with your sister, and with her naked husband. You've already excited me, excite me some more, my darling... It's so good to be aroused...!"

"But you're hard like a real woman, you little horror! If you think that you're not exciting me as well, with your stiff little button hidden underneath your hairless baby mound... Oh, don't lick my nipple like that, because, you know, I'm quite near the edge myself, and if you want me to tell you stories, you mustn't make me lose my head... You can keep it in your mouth, provided you don't tongue it... She's sucking me!... Darling pussycat!"

At this, she stopped stroking me for a moment, slipped a hand under her skirts, moistened one of her fingers in her own hole and smeared her teat with it, saying: "There you are, a little sauce to make it taste better."

"How sweet of you! Your smell is driving me mad! And your finger!..."

Pierre Louÿs

Her hand was back between my thighs, and she was frigging me so slowly and so gently with her fingertip that she kept me excited without sending me over the edge. A nervous trembling shook me imperceptibly. I continued suckling with my eyes closed.